Heaven had never been this kind to Cinderella, Julia thought.

She closed her eyes and leaned against the firmness of Alex's broad, steely chest as they danced. She could feel and hear the firm thump-thump of his heart beating. His grip tightened, his step on the stone terrace sure. Julia heard the last notes fade away, and drew her head away from the warmth of her boss's chest.

"I should go in, and you should say goodbye to your guests," Julia said.

"A waste of good moonlight." Alex appeared wistful as some guests approached him to say goodnight.

Recognizing the end of the moment, Julia gave him a wry smile. There would be no glass slipper magic for this pretending princess. But for the moment, still in her Prince Charming's arms, she could imagine her fantasy as reality. Julia Brown...Mrs. Prince Charming...

Dear Reader,

Have we got a month of great reading for you! Four very different stories by four talented authors—with, of course, all of the romantic exhilaration you've come to expect from a Harlequin American Romance.

National bestselling author Anne Stuart is back and her fabulous book, *Wild Thing*, will get your heart racing. This is a hero you won't soon forget. This month also continues our HAPPILY WEDDED AFTER promotion with *Special Order Groom*, a delightful reunion story by reader favorite, Tina Leonard.

And let us welcome two new authors to the Harlequin American Romance family. Leanna Wilson, a Harlequin Temptation and Silhouette Romance author, brings us a tender surprise pregnancy book with *Open in Nine Months*. And brand-new author Michele Dunaway makes her sparkling debut with *A Little Office Romance*—get ready to have this bachelor boss hero steal your heart.

Next month we have a whole new look in store for our readers—you'll notice our new covers as well as fantastic promotions such as RETURN TO TYLER and brand-new installments in Muriel Jensen's WHO'S THE DADDY? series. Watch for your favorite authors such as Jule McBride, Judy Christenberry and Cathy Gillen Thacker, all of whom will be back with new books in the coming months.

Wishing you happy reading,

Melissa Jeglinski
Associate Senior Editor
Harlequin American Romance

A Little Office Romance

MICHELE DUNAWAY

HARLEQUIN®

TORONTO • NEW YORK • LONDON
AMSTERDAM • PARIS • SYDNEY • HAMBURG
STOCKHOLM • ATHENS • TOKYO • MILAN • MADRID
PRAGUE • WARSAW • BUDAPEST • AUCKLAND

To all of my students,
Push through the shadow to where dreams come true

ISBN 0-373-16848-9

A LITTLE OFFICE ROMANCE

Copyright © 2000 by Michele Dunaway.

Visit us at www.eHarlequin.com

Printed in U.S.A.

ABOUT THE AUTHOR

In first grade Michele Dunaway knew she wanted to be a teacher when she grew up, and by second grade she wanted to be an author. By third grade she was determined to be both. Born, raised and currently living in St. Louis, Missouri, she's traveled extensively, with the cities and places she visits often becoming settings for her stories. After meeting her husband on a rained-out float trip in the Missouri Ozarks, they were engaged two weeks later.

Michele currently teaches eighth grade English and journalism, raises her two young daughters and describes herself as a woman who does too much but doesn't want to stop.

Michele loves to hear from readers and you can write to her at: P.O. Box 53, Valley Park, MO 63088.

Books by Michele Dunaway

HARLEQUIN AMERICAN ROMANCE

Dear Reader,

Wow! is all I can say. You hold in your hand my lifelong dream, my first novel. I've always loved romance, and I've always wanted to be a Harlequin author. As the mother of two young girls, I've watched the movie "Cinderella" dozens of times. Cinderella believes that dreams are the wishes your heart makes, and she's right. Belief that dreams can come true, and sometimes do in the strangest ways, is at the heart of my life. My husband swears he knew I was the one when he first saw me; he just had to convince me. That took two weeks (hey, he was still in college), and we were married in a romantic ceremony six months later on the day after New Year's.

I hope you enjoy *A Little Office Romance*. I had a great time writing it, and setting it in two cities I adore. I love romantic comedies, and Alex and Julia's romance is certainly that. For Julia has known Alex is "the one" ever since she first saw his picture. He's tall, handsome, sophisticated and powerful, yet he has a heart of gold. She's zany and unpredictable, but just naive enough. Sparks definitely fly when they're together. Now she only needs to convince him that she's the one. Of course, she's got a few problems to solve first: she only has three weeks, there's this little matter of a disguise, a few white lies and…well, read on and enjoy!

Best wishes!

Michele Dunaway

Chapter One

Alexander Ravenwood ran a hand through his thick dark hair, destroying the short feathery layer that swooped over his left eyebrow. So, it had finally come to this. Rita was leaving him to go to Europe with another man.

Okay, only for three weeks. Perhaps that made it slightly more bearable. But these next few weeks would be the longest of his life, of that he was certain. How in the world would he survive without her? They were a team. They had a system. There was simply no way he could do without his sixty-year-old secretary.

Even though he had been top dog at Ravenwood Investments for more than a year since his father's retirement, Alex wasn't stupid. He knew a man was only as good as his secretary. And his was fifty minutes from deserting him for her fortieth anniversary and a European tour.

Damn the infernal luck. The timing couldn't be worse. Not with the yearlong embezzlement investigation at the Florida branch finally reaching its culmination. There was nothing Alex hated more than to have to deal with dishonest, untrustworthy employees, or the aftermath. And he would be doing it without either of his most trusted assistants—his sister or his secretary.

Aware of footsteps, Alex looked up from where he was seated behind the huge mahogany desk that had once been his father's. Rita strolled in and smiled.

"I can't believe you're leaving me," Alex protested, shooting her a longing look, the one Rita swore made him look like a young Robert Redford with dark hair. For fourteen years it had never failed to get Alex what he wanted. Except this time.

Rita's double chin bobbed as she choked back a mischievous laugh. "Don't bat those baby-blue eyes at me, Alex. I'm immune to your charms. Besides, you'll survive. Your sister hired a temp."

"A temp. What's a temp going to do?" Alex objected, waving well-manicured fingers over the stacks of paper already burying his desk. He hated a disorganized desk. "We're partners. How is a temp going to figure this out?"

"Oh, now we're partners?" Rita raised an eyebrow, her classic dubious look. "Good try, Alex, but not good enough. You'll be fine without me, and Chelsea said the temp's efficient."

"Sure she is." Alex let loose a resigned groan, disbelief evident. "Rita, you know my sister tortures me when she hires temps. Some people's sisters are pathological liars. Mine's a practical joker. You remember the last temp. She looked like Miss America and was too afraid of breaking a nail to type or answer the phone."

"And how long did you date her?"

"One date, after you returned." Alex sighed. Trust Rita to catch his ruse. As one of the few women he could relax around, she knew him too well. "But, this is a crucial time, Rita. You and Chelsea will both be gone. Despite my sister's flippant side, you two are the only ones who really understand the mess we have in Florida. We could lose credibility, and even worse our ability to issue bonds. You're the only ones I trust. I need you.''

Rita smiled benevolently as she tried to pacify her boss. ''I'm sure Chelsea understands that, Alex. I doubt she'll try anything this time. She wasn't too happy with you dating Miss America. I'm sure she's learned.''

''You don't know my sister,'' Alex said, trying the sympathy tactic. Rita raised a gray eyebrow at him, and Alex groaned at her refusal to respond to his dejected puppy look.

''Twenty thousand if you stay,'' Alex said, making a futile last-ditch attempt to lure his secretary away from her dream vacation.

Rita deftly shot down the man whose business savvy had brought his firm to the top. Located in the outskirts of Washington, D.C., Ravenwood was the second largest investment firm outside New York City.

''That's so sweet of you, Alex, to offer me money, but Europe awaits. London, Paris, the Scottish Highlands. Besides, you know how honest I am. No amount of money sways me. So, on that note, how about I bring your temp in as soon as she arrives? I'll give her an overview before I leave and guarantee not to have her running for the door.'' Rita chuckled and couldn't resist a wicked grin.

''Stop laughing!'' Alex ordered, sitting up straighter in his chair. He gave Rita the evil eye. ''Maybe I'll just hire her permanently!''

Rita laughed at Alex's threat.

''Especially if she looks like the last one and has

brains, too, right Alex?'' Rita smiled and Alex knew he was done for. "You know, Alex, I've been with the company for almost thirty-eight years now. I will retire someday so it's good to see you're planning ahead."

"Out!" Alex pointed at the set of heavy wooden doors. "Take your sorry self to Europe, you traitor." He gave her a wry smile. "Be sure to have fun."

"Yes, Alex. I'll even be sure to send you a dozen postcards telling you all about it. You can share them with the temp. Will there be anything else before I go?"

Alex slouched his six-foot frame into his deep leather chair and frowned. His deep voice sounded almost like a growl as he realized he was stuck. "What's the temp's name?"

Rita smiled and Alex resigned himself to the inevitable.

"Her name is Julia Brown, and you're going to love her. Wait and see. These three weeks might turn out better than you think."

RACHEL JULIA GRAYSON, for the next three weeks performing as Julia Brown, adjusted the stringy black wig and skeptically took in her appearance one last time. Resigned to her "new" look, she turned away from the mirror to endure Chelsea Ravenwood Meier's military-like inspection. Julia felt Chelsea's narrowed gaze roving over her from top to bottom, and knew that again her best friend was making sure the disguise was perfect.

Impatiently Julia stomped the heavy combat boot on the floor. Despite the boot's battle-worn appearance, the plush carpet of Chelsea's bathroom silenced the noise. A heavy stillness cloaked the room, and finally Julia couldn't take it anymore. Throwing up her hands, she demanded, "Well?"

"Perfect!" Chelsea proclaimed, circling once more around Julia. "Absolutely perfect. I wouldn't recognize you if I passed you on the street. Julia, you've done a fantastic job!"

Julia felt the tidal wave of relief wash over her. Concealing her normal appearance had taken over an hour, but Chelsea had insisted on it as part of the job.

"I can't believe you talked me into doing this." Julia was still skeptical of the ruse. "We must be pretty good friends."

"The best." Chelsea smiled and rested her hands on her protruding abdomen.

Julia pushed a stray strand of shoulder-length blond hair back up beneath the itchy wig. She had found the wig and her clothes at a charitable clothing store. "I'm not sure getting a degree in fashion design prepared me for this."

"Oh, but it does! Look at yourself. You've created the perfect disguise."

Julia looked at her reflection. She had to admit it; she had done a good job. Three years of designing costumes and dressing professional actors for a St. Louis theater had come in handy. If she didn't know it was her own reflection, she wouldn't recognize herself. Julia caught Chelsea's gaze in the floor-length mirror.

"You're the only one I can trust, Julia," Chelsea implored, her eyes pleading. "I'm desperate. I've thought of nothing else for weeks. After today I'm not going to be around to run interference. I can't let Lydia win. She's not the right woman for Alex, no matter how much she may think she is. He'll marry her out of obligation, not love."

"I understand," Julia said simply. Comforted that she was doing the right thing, Julia glanced away to again stare at her reflection.

Although the luminous brown eyes looking back at her were the same ones she saw every day, she had altered everything else about her appearance. The long wig she wore was a hideous jet-black, and between the wig and the makeup she was wearing, her healthy skin now appeared chalky. Her full lips were stained blood-red, and her classic cheekbones appeared abnormally high and gaunt. She definitely looked older than her twenty-six years.

"Chelsea, he's going to think you hired a vampire."

"Good. I don't want him to know it's you. Besides, it's better you sucking on him than Lydia Olson." Chelsea shook her shoulders in disgust.

"But this disguise?" Julia protested changing her identity one last time.

"Julia, we've been over this before. If Alex knew it was you, he would treat you with kid gloves and Lydia would immediately be on guard. I want you to be above suspicion. Just trust me on this." Chelsea suddenly put a hand to her mouth. "I'm sorry, Julia. I know how hard it is for you to trust people, especially after what Kyle did to you. But I've never let you down, before, right?" Chelsea's voice trailed off.

"No, you haven't. And I know you're right." Julia wrestled with her emotions for a moment. Except for maybe her immediate family, Chelsea had been one of the few people who had never let her down. "I've just worked so hard to be pretty that to conceal it seems a waste."

"Julia." Chelsea's voice was gentle. "You were

never an ugly duckling. You just blossomed late, that's all.''

"For all the good it did me," Julia said bitterly. "I really thought Kyle loved me. But still he left with that, that—"

"A fresh start, Julia," Chelsea interrupted. She placed her hand on Julia's shoulder. The movement comforted Julia. "In three weeks you'll be free to go to New York, only with money in the bank."

"You're right." Julia lifted her chin up and looked determined. "Kyle's history and my new life starts with Operation Free Alex."

Chelsea glanced at her watch. "Five minutes left to back out and let me spot you the money."

"Let's not go through that again." Julia held up her right hand in protest. She knew that if she accepted Chelsea's offer, Chelsea would refuse to let Julia repay the money.

"No handouts," Julia insisted. "I've still got my pride even though it may be tattered. I've scraped together enough money for a deposit on an apartment that's in a good area of Manhattan, and with this job, well, let's just say I'm going to make it on my own."

"Of course you'll make it, Julia." Chelsea appeared totally confident in Julia's chances. "You're a survivor. That's what impresses me most about you. People listen to you. If Alex had listened to me, Lydia would already be history." Chelsea frowned, her distress evident. For a moment Julia wondered if Chelsea was having a labor pain.

As Chelsea's face relaxed a little, Julia dug the blood-red lipstick out of her purse and began touching up her lips. "Well, I know you tried."

"Of course I tried. But Alex is so stubborn. He's a

mule, like that one we saw in the zoo. Remember that? The more the zookeeper pulled the more the mule dug in. Well, that's Alex. The more you push the more he pulls. He doesn't see beyond the surface, except in business.''

"For your sake, I hope this scheme works." Julia dusted a piece of lint off the black blazer that topped her rather eclectic outfit.

"Of course it will! He thinks you go by your first name, like on the formal wedding program my mother-in-law insisted on. Besides, he's only met you once, or was it twice, so it's foolproof." Chelsea's infectious reply didn't make Julia feel better. Experience had taught Julia to distrust Chelsea's zeal; it was often misguided. "Besides, the timing for Lydia's removal couldn't be more perfect. What else do you have to do?"

"Enough!" Julia said grimly. After Kyle's command performance with her life, keeping her pride meant resigning her costume-designing job. Now in between jobs and homes, Chelsea's bizarre job offer was a godsend.

She adjusted the frumpy skirt that added two sizes to her perfect size-eight figure and glanced at her reflection one last time. Absolutely certain there was no way Alex would recognize her, she smiled wistfully and wondered what her college instructors would say if they saw their top student now. Gone was the slim blond girl who had sewed most of her designer wardrobe from *Vogue* patterns, and in her place was a pale woman with zero fashion sense.

Uneasily Julia wondered if she should have put in the cosmetic contact lenses that changed her brown eye color to purple. Well, it was too late for that now. Instead she slid a pair of black glasses with plain, non-prescription lenses onto her face. Despite the butterflies dancing in her stomach, she turned to face Chelsea. "Let's go."

As CHELSEA OUTLINED Julia's contract, Alex's first thought was that pregnancy had sent his sister out of her mind. This must be some temp.

"What are you trying to do, Chelsea, help her afford an apartment in Watergate?" Alex gave his sister an odd look that revealed his skepticism. "I don't even give Rita bonuses except at Christmas. That's six months away. It's July."

"Of course I know it's July. I've been waiting thirty-nine weeks for July. Give me a break, Alex. Don't meddle, just listen. I can do my job."

"Sorry. This situation in Florida has got me tense, and the last temp you hired couldn't type." Unusually agitated, Alex pushed his hair away from forehead. "I just don't know why this one needs a signing bonus of a thousand dollars."

"For a man who hates e-mail you really need to keep up with the times, Alex," Chelsea chided. Alex recognized the sarcasm in her voice. "I do know my job, even if you think Dad gave it to me just to be kind. I put the clause in there so you won't fire her when you see her."

"Fire her? Why would I do that? She can type, can't she?" Alex gazed at his only sibling. Despite a ten-year age difference, Alex and Chelsea had grown into close friends over the past four years they had worked together.

"Of course she can type." Alex missed his sister crossing her fingers behind her back. "Look Alex, I just know your temper. She's not Rita, and she's a little unique. Her personality is a bit quirky, and she's coming into this blind and…''

Alex impatiently cut his sister off and stretched his neck muscles. He had long ago shed the custom-tailored suit jacket. "This isn't a date, Chelsea, so why don't you just bring her in? I promise I won't bite or fire her on the spot. Will that satisfy you?"

"Okay." Alex watched Chelsea stand up. Pregnancy suited her, even if the doctor predicted the baby was going to be late. Alex had worried about his sister when she left Washington, D.C., for St. Louis, but she had thrived during college.

Of course, having the same roommate for four years probably helped. Alex's brow furrowed as he tried to remember the name of the girl.

A movement at the double doors caught his attention.

"Alex, this is your temp, Julia Brown."

Alex simply stared. No wonder Chelsea had been so worried about his reaction to her choice of temps. He didn't have to worry about his temp being the next Miss America. Far from it.

In fact, Julia had to be one of the strangest women he had ever laid eyes on.

And now that his eyes were on her, he was unable to pull his gaze away as, aghast, he stared at the apparition that stood before him.

Unlike his sister, who looked gorgeous in black, Julia looked frumpy, pale and shrunken under the oversize clothes she wore. Her black hair had to be dyed, Alex thought, because no woman's hair could naturally be the color of black shoe polish.

And her face. Even Rita's wrinkles didn't hide the fact she had once been pretty. Julia's face didn't have a hint of pinkish color to her skin, and for a moment Alex wondered if she ever got any sun. Rita had told him Julia was either on her way to or from New York City. He couldn't remember which, but rumor held that New York City supposedly had an entire group of people who lived underground in the subway tunnels. Maybe she was one of them. He shot Chelsea a furtive glance, but his sister was picking at her fingernail polish and refusing to look at him.

"Mr. Ravenwood." Julia greeted him timidly.

At least her voice was normal, Alex thought with startled surprise as he jolted out of his dazed inspection. He frowned. Such a pleasant and light voice didn't fit the oddly dressed figure in front of him. As if an afterthought, Alex remembered his manners.

"Julia. Come in. Why don't you sit down?" Alex walked the short distance toward her. Julia stood six inches shorter than he did. Courtesy dictated he shake her hand. This'll be quick, he thought. He reached out his hand, and Julia stared at him for a moment before she slowly put her hand in his.

Alex felt the jolt of electricity from the moment he touched the inside of her palm.

Astounded, Alex dropped her hand. Only once before had he felt an instant, chemical reaction like this. Alex flexed his fingers but the burning sensation of latent energy still lingered. Not only had the physical stirring from just touching Julia seared his hands, but it had traveled all the way to the tips of his toes, toes still tingling inside Bruno Magali loafers.

Alex struggled to regain his composure as he examined the effect she had had on him. Maybe she was a witch as well as a vampire. Belatedly he remembered the rest of what business etiquette dictated.

"Welcome to Ravenwood. Sit down and let's get acquainted. We'll be working as a team for the next three weeks."

Alex gestured to the sofa area, and despite the many vamp layers of black skirt that swished around black combat boots, Julia trod across the gray carpet easily. She sat on the middle cushion of the burgundy leather sofa and waited while Alex walked his sister to the door.

"That's a suit?" Alex hissed and discreetly pointed at the bizarre array of clothing Julia wore. The blazer had ridden up and threatened to swallow Julia's chin. "Her wardrobe has to go, Chelsea, and she needs a complete makeover. I can't have her greeting clients like that. This firm has a reputation to maintain. I have a reputation to maintain." Alex glared at his sister.

"So get her a makeover." Chelsea shrugged nonchalantly.

"You hired her, you do it!" Alex ordered, somehow managing to keep his voice a low whisper. Then, much to his chagrin, for the second time that day a female defied him.

"Sorry, I was officially on maternity leave as soon as I introduced you two. So, have fun getting acquainted. Tessa's out at Rita's desk manning the phones. You won't be disturbed. I'm out of here!" Chelsea shot her brother a wicked grin as she departed.

Alex turned back to look at Julia. It would be just like his sister to find him the strangest looking temp in D.C. Once again his sister had managed to stay a step ahead of him. He had expected Chelsea to play matchmaker with the temp by getting him someone beautiful, single, and in her twenties. He hadn't expected someone who looked like a fashion reject.

Alex let out a long breath. Proper appearance was very important to him, and obviously Chelsea had hired this particular temp just to needle him. Still, in these lawsuit-happy days it was probably better for him to tolerate Chelsea's sick joke for the next three weeks.

Despite the fact the Julia's back was toward him, he could tell she was thumbing through one of the many financial magazines on the coffee table. Coffee. Coffee would be good right about now.

"Julia?" Alex called. Julia turned toward him, and again Alex blinked. For one moment her fluid, graceful movement revealed a long, Grecian neck. As her pale face looked at his, an unidentifiable shudder replaced Alex's momentary burst of intrigue.

He must be imagining things. Stress supposedly could cause hallucinations, and he had to admit he was on stress overload, especially from the Florida problem. "Julia," Alex asked again, "would you like some coffee? Chelsea took the liberty of ordering lunch. It'll be sent up so we can get right to work."

"No, thank you."

With her short answer Alex now felt even more perplexed. What was it about this woman? "No-thank-you to what? Coffee or lunch?"

"Oh, coffee. I don't drink coffee." Julia regained her vampish poise and smiled shyly, revealing perfect white teeth. Her brown eyes twinkled slightly, accenting bronze outer rims, and Alex felt a wave of disorientation sweep over him. He couldn't put his finger on it, almost a déjà vu of some sort. But that was impossible. He knew he had never seen Julia Brown before.

Disturbed by his gut-churning reaction to her smile, Alex studied her openly. The black plastic glasses looked like something from the late sixties. All they needed was some masking tape on the bridge. He checked his snobbery.

Despite Chelsea's practical joke mentality, his sister knew how crucial the next few weeks would be for the company. So, if his sister said Julia could type then she probably would be okay, despite her strange look.

For the first time in his life, Alex searched to find a common footing with a woman, and coffee seemed to be the way to do it. "So, you don't drink coffee? That's impressive. I can't live without several cups a day."

"I can't stand it. I don't like mocha flavoring, so I never even saw the need to even try a cup." Julia shrugged and the blazer's ill-fitting collar scrunched up even more.

Well, there went the Seattle-grunge coffee bar theory for her appearance, Alex thought.

"Don't worry, Mr. Ravenwood. I lived with my brother for a year after I graduated from college and I can make coffee. He drank pots of it. Just tell me how you like it."

"You don't have to make coffee. The cafeteria makes pots of it and brings it up every morning at scheduled intervals. They even bring up food, so you won't have to worry about feeding me. We're a twenty-first-century company here, Julia. Secretaries aren't personal servants." Surely a temp knew that? And why was she a temp if she'd graduated college? Maybe she'd meant secretarial college.

Again he felt strangely flustered. Alex perched himself on a chair and ran a finger under the starched collar of his tailored dress shirt. For some odd reason the shirt was bothering him. He would have to tell the cleaners about it.

Julia waited for his attention before she spoke. "If

you're really sure I don't need to make coffee, then I guess I won't. Mrs. Meier told me I was to assume all of Rita's jobs and that included making sure you ate lunch. She, Mrs. Meier I mean, wanted to be sure that I took very good care of you while Rita was gone. I promised her I would do whatever it took.'' Julia pursed her lips, making her vampire look seem almost innocent.

He shoved his hands into his gray trouser pockets. What was wrong with him? A childhood thought popped into his brain as he suddenly remembered *The Ugly Duckling,* the A. A. Milne play his eighth-grade English teacher had made him read. Only one prince had been able to see the beauty in the ugliest princess alive, and his love had broken the spell and returned her to the most beautiful woman in the land. But Alex knew he wasn't a prince any more than Julia was a princess in disguise.

Julia smoothed down the front of her skirt, and Alex observed that her hands were lithe and graceful, which was at total odds with the bloodred talons at the tips.

Alex tried to relax by clenching his fists, counting to ten, and then slowly releasing his fists. It didn't help. He still felt stressed.

He pacified himself with the thought that, unlike Rita, who could sense his moods, Julia was just a temp. She'd never met him before and therefore was oblivious to the workings of his mind and body. Alex hopped up off the edge of the sofa and went over to the wrought-iron serving cart that hosted the coffee urn. Although already wired enough not to need the caffeine, he carefully poured himself a cup of the black brew.

He turned back to Julia. ''So, any questions so far?''

''Well, yes. Mr. Ravenwood, some employers keep

lists of people they allow to be sent automatically through when they call. I need to know if you have one of those lists.''

Julia's look was earnest as Alex took a long sip of the hot black liquid. Although not even noon, he wished he could have a beer. Normally unflappable, he still tried to place why he was so off-kilter today. Blinking he tried to concentrate on what Julia was saying.

''I wouldn't want to offend any of your business associates or lady friends by not putting their calls through. My previous employers were adamant about it, and sometimes concerned that I might reveal the wrong thing. So, I just wanted to tell you not to worry, Mr. Ravenwood, I appreciate discretion. I've never been one to kiss and tell.''

Alex practically spit out his coffee. He choked the remnants down, gasping for air as the offending liquid tried to burn an escape path through his nose. Dropping the cup with a clatter onto the tray, he grabbed a napkin and, turning away from Julia, he wiped his face with the cloth. Again he fought to maintain his composure. Luckily no drops had hit his white shirt.

''Mr. Ravenwood?'' Startled, Alex jumped as he realized Julia stood right next to him. ''Are you okay?''

''Fine. Wrong pipe. Hate it when that happens,'' Alex mumbled incoherently as he stepped away from her magnetic proximity. What was it about this woman? The chemical stirrings in his body still hadn't subsided. If anything they were worse. He was now reading double entendres into her words.

Julia looked relieved and sat back down. Primly she folded her hands in her lap and waited patiently while Alex composed himself.

Alex sat down in a leather wing chair opposite her.

For a moment Alex thought of his sister. If she wasn't about to give birth, he would strangle her for putting him in this situation. He would have to see the joke through.

"I don't have a phone list," Alex told Julia, impressed that she listened with rapt attention. "It's quite simple, really. I have one line in and everyone uses it. I have a cell phone, but the only people who have the number are my family and one or two good friends. I don't give the number out to anyone, even the women I'm dating."

"I see." Julia seemed to process the information as a waiter wheeled a cart into Alex's office.

Normally Alex wouldn't be eating lunch with a temporary secretary, except Chelsea had arranged it to make Julia feel welcome. Alex glanced at his watch. So far he was still on schedule, although his appetite had vanished.

Julia, however, feasted with such abandon he wondered when she'd last eaten. Although Alex was a bit taken back with her zeal in consuming the fettuccine Alfredo, he appreciated that, unlike the model-types he dated who picked at their food, Julia had little shyness about cleaning her plate.

After opting for water with an "I don't drink soda" statement, Julia turned to her dessert and closed her eyes as if savoring the flavor. Alex simply sat on his chair and pushed food around his plate. Never had a lunch been so much torture.

Alex shuddered as his imagination shifted into overdrive when Julia's bloodred lips flexed. Vampires. No wonder people found Dracula and Lestat so intriguing, and no wonder they could seduce their prey. The simple movement of Julia's full lips had such a potent beauty to it that his libido instinctively wondered what it would be like to kiss those lips until they swelled from endless passion.

"Mr. Ravenwood, I just wanted to tell you I'm looking forward to being here." Julia gave him a timid smile.

Alex glanced over at his father's portrait on a distant wall for a moment before looking back at her.

"Ah, well, yes," Alex replied. After the phone list question it was probably as good a time as ever to outline his expectations. He set his nearly full plate on the chair's padded armrest.

"Julia, this will be a good opportunity for you, but it's going to be hard work," Alex told her. He appreciated the fact that, unlike his Miss America, Julia paid attention. "You'll have to be at my beck and call. I say jump, you ask how high. Never question my judgments in front of colleagues. If you have anything personal to discuss, we talk about it in private. In the investment industry there are rules, procedures and sensitive information. What occurs in this office stays here."

"No problem. I'm very good with secrets." She reached up with her fingers and pretended to lock her lips and throw away the key. Inwardly Alex groaned. "I'm the soul of discretion. How shall I prove it?"

By locking those lips onto mine, Alex thought, and letting me kiss you until you moan my name.

"Alex!"

The indignant screech of a female voice made him start and he jerked his arm upward. While he managed to save his clothes, the tottering plate clattered to the floor, sending fettuccine Alfredo noodles falling onto the gray carpet. Had he spoken aloud? His relief at realizing he hadn't was short-lived as he turned to face the livid, raven-haired beauty standing in the doorway.

"Alex! Did you forget we were meeting for lunch?"

Chapter Two

Julia heaved a giant sigh of relief. The first part of Chelsea's plan had worked. Alex hadn't recognized her. The second part had just walked in the door. Julia studied supermodel Lydia Olson with interest.

With her forefinger, Julia pushed the black rims back up her nose and sized up her opponent in Operation Free Alex. Trained on the catwalk, Lydia had self-assurance and poise. Despite wearing three-inch-high heels and a mid-thigh-length dress that fit like a glove, she strode effortlessly into the room. Julia frowned. Though it was a sweltering July day, a sudden chill descended over her.

"Well, I can see you've already eaten." With obvious irritation glittering in her icy blue eyes, Lydia gestured to one of the empty plates.

"Mr. Ravenwood!"

Julia turned her attention back to the doorway as Tessa, Chelsea's secretary, rushed in as fast as her petite legs could carry her.

"I only stepped away to use the ladies' room," Tessa said as she approached the sofa area. "I'm so sorry. I know you left orders not to be disturbed."

As Alex got to his feet, all six feet of him stretched

with the grace and ease of a panther. Julia couldn't help staring as he drew a hand through his wavy hair. Her heart gave a little jump. His pictures didn't do him justice.

"It's okay, Tessa." Alex took responsibility for the situation. "Julia and I were just about through, and if you could show her the rest of the ropes for me I'll deal with this mess."

"This mess?" Lydia's screech had Julia literally covering her ears. "You kept me waiting at Za Bistro for over an hour. First you humiliate me, Alex, and now you call me a mess?"

"I was referring to the dishes," Alex began, his agitation evident as he drew his hand through his hair again. Julia watched him pause briefly as if he were choosing his words.

"Lydia, I apologize for the mix-up. I checked my calendar this morning and it was clear except for Julia's arrival. Rita is meticulous with my daily agenda because she knows I'd be lost without it."

Julia noted that Lydia still didn't look pleased. Her mouth puckered as if she had bitten a lemon.

"I know I told her about lunch, Alex," Lydia insisted.

Tessa chose that moment to speak up, saving a confused Alex from having to reply.

"When I heard Ms. Olson was in here I double-checked your calendar, Mr. Ravenwood," Tessa said. "Except for Julia, your calendar is clear until three." Tessa gave him an apologetic smile.

The whole situation was almost comical, and Julia chomped down on her lip in an attempt to keep from laughing aloud. Way to go, Chelsea! Julia mentally congratulated her best friend. Plan A in Operation Free Alex had worked like a charm.

A giggle bubbled up, and Julia covered her mouth with her hand. Poor Alex. He had no way of knowing Chelsea had erased the appointment yesterday, after bribing Rita with a gift certificate to Harrods' in London. Chelsea had also told Tessa to disappear when the lobby receptionist called to tell her Lydia Olson was on the way up to Alex's office.

Julia coughed down the giggle and looked up to meet Lydia's ice blue eyes. Contempt obvious, Lydia tossed her raven tresses and curled her lips up in disgust and dismissal.

"Alex, who or what is that?"

Julia's hackles rose at Lydia's derisive tone. The woman who's going to bring you down off your high horse, Julia thought smugly, suddenly a bit gleeful for accepting Chelsea's offer. Trying to stifle the laughter that threatened to erupt at any second, Julia bent her head to her chest and coughed, but to no avail. Tears began to freely cascade down her face and as a white handkerchief came into her peripheral vision, Julia looked up.

"Julia's my temporary secretary," Alex said. Julia took the offered handkerchief. He ran a hand through his thick hair yet again and began to pace along the gray carpet as Julia's tears kept falling.

"Darn it, Lydia!" Alex barely held his temper in check. "Look what you've done! You've made her cry. She's got a hard enough job to fill in for Rita without you jumping all over her."

"I was not jumping on her!" Lydia sniffed. "I just don't appreciate being stood up for lunch and embarrassed. I'm gone three days in Alaska and—" her high-pitched tone suddenly softened as if she was aware of her audience ''—you know how much I hate eating alone, Alex. Daddy would be so disappointed if he knew you forgot me. What would he think?''

Julia recognized an opportunity to leave and stood. With her fingers she patted her tears away. Her fingertips were covered with black mascara, meaning she had smudged it. Now instead of a vampire she probably looked like a deformed raccoon.

Wanting to escape, Julia smiled weakly at Alex. He had swept his hair back off his face and was now massaging the back of his neck. Obviously the whole scene had distressed him. That was a good sign, especially since Chelsea said Alex never got visually rattled.

''Mr. Ravenwood,'' Julia called. ''Really, I'm fine. I know she didn't mean to insult me. And, since Tessa's here maybe now would be a good time for her to show me around.''

Alex's eyes narrowed and then they returned to normal. He gave Julia a gentle smile. Julia's heart jumped. ''That would be perfect.'' Alex's tone softened as he continued. ''Feel free to freshen up if you want and take a break. We'll talk later in the day. There are still a few things we'll need to go over.''

''That sounds fine. Thank you, Mr. Ravenwood.''

Julia headed out the double doors, but not before she saw Alex turning to Lydia. His tone reflected his anger as he pointed his forefinger at Lydia. ''You and I will talk. Now.''

TEN MINUTES LATER, Julia watched Lydia leave Alex's office. The tension left Julia's shoulders as relief flowed through her. Lydia's lipstick was barely mussed. Another good sign. It must not have been much of a good-bye kiss.

Julia twirled a pen idly in her hand. So far the plan was working. Alex didn't recognize her, and Lydia had revealed some true colors. The only problem was the excited chills that ran down Julia's spine every time she and Alex touched.

She thought she had prepared herself for Alex's physical magnetism, but like at Chelsea's wedding, meeting him today had blown her away.

Frowning, Julia set the pen down on the desk. Ever since Chelsea had pinned Alex's picture to her dorm-room bulletin board, Julia had had the worst crush on Alex Ravenwood.

Once slightly overweight, Julia had been a naive and inexperienced young college student, and the desire she had felt for Alex Ravenwood scared her. Afraid of her reaction to seeing the actual man in the flesh, the few times he had flown to St. Louis to visit his sister, Julia had made herself scarce. She had never told Chelsea the real reason.

Julia's brow furrowed in concentration as she mentally processed her reaction to his closeness during their time alone in his office. When his blue eyes had looked into hers Julia had wanted to lose herself and throw herself at Alex and yell ''Take me now!''

That would definitely be a mistake, Julia thought ruefully. From Chelsea's descriptions of her older brother over the years, Julia knew he never had trouble finding fields to sow his wild oats. Still, poor Alex, to be involved with someone as shallow as Lydia Olson.

Chelsea was right, Julia would be doing him a favor to expose her true colors. Her confidence bolstered a bit, she prepared for the incoming onslaught tottering toward her on high heels.

"So, you are Chelsea's hire, Morticia what?" Lydia greeted her with evident disdain. Steel-blue eyes raked over Julia's appearance as if to not miss anything.

Julia noted immediately the difference in the coldness of Lydia's eyes and the natural warmth of Alex's. The color of Alex's eyes was almost a grayish blue, and his eyes twinkled naturally. Coupled with a straight Roman nose and a perfectly chiseled chin, the result made Alex a masculine and beautiful man without a hint of presumption. Alex's core of sexiness mixed integrity with good breeding. Lydia had none of these traits. No wonder Chelsea wanted Lydia out of Alex's life, and pronto.

"My name's Julia Brown." She deliberately raised her eyes to Lydia's and began to stare the haughty woman down. Two could play this game.

"Oh, so that's it." Lydia wrinkled up her nose as if the air had gone bad. "Julia Brown, Morticia Adams, they sound rather alike don't you think? Especially since you look like something the cat dragged in."

Lydia gave an exaggerated sniff and looked down her nose at Julia. "Anyway, I am Lydia Olson. I am Alex's very significant other, and we're planning to become engaged. You did know Ravenwood took my daddy's company public? Alex and my father became very close. You do understand what I'm telling you?" Lydia returned Julia's impertinent stare with a condescending one of her own.

"Ms. Oldson," Julia mocked, her insolence matching Lydia's own as she deliberately butchered Lydia's last name, "do I look like the type of woman who could compete with you?"

"Of course not!" Lydia sputtered indignantly.

"Then why are you worried?" Julia gave Lydia a satisfied smug. "Surely your time is better spent elsewhere, doing whatever it is you do that somehow benefits the world."

Lydia's lips thinned as she attempted to control her anger. "You're quite impertinent, aren't you? Just don't get any lofty ideas in your mousy little brain. Alex Ravenwood belongs with me, not with someone who shops at Goodwill."

"Oh, dear me." Julia gave Lydia a piqued look and shoved her glasses back up her nose. "Ms. Oldson, I wouldn't dream of it. I don't shop at Goodwill. I use the Salvation Army store. Now, I'm here to do a job. One that is very important to me, I might add, so I'd appreciate it if you stop wasting my time and let me get back to work."

Using an old trick she had learned from her three brothers, Julia laced her fingers under her chin and continued to stare up at Lydia. From behind the huge black glasses, Julia fought the age-old battle with her eyes and was rewarded when Lydia blinked first. Julia felt an immense satisfaction as Lydia's face reddened. Score one for all the underdogs in the world.

Julia allowed herself a triumphant grin when, a few moments later, the elevator doors enclosed a silent, fuming Lydia Olson.

"Julia?" Alex's quiet voice made her turn.

"Yes, Mr. Ravenwood?" Julia panicked as she swiveled the chair so she could look at him. How much had he heard? Had he just heard her put Lydia Olson in her place?

"I thought I heard voices out here." Alex held a file folder and he had taken off his power tie. He had unbuttoned the top buttons of his shirt, and Julia could see a hint of the smooth, firm muscles peeking out from beneath the opaque fabric. Now totally at ease, Alex had also rolled up his sleeves to his elbow. Silky hair lightly covered his forearms.

Julia discreetly drank in his masculinity for a moment. Even though she had her hands on the bodies of some of the most beautiful actors in the world when she fitted their costumes, they had never physically affected her. Yet from anywhere in a room Alex did. She gave him what she hoped was a professional smile.

"Tessa's back at her desk. You must have just heard me talking to the computer. I'm starting on those letters Rita left." Julia could have kicked herself for the lame excuse that made her look moronic, but Alex seemed to buy it.

"Okay." Alex reached into his pocket and put on a pair of wire-rim reading glasses. The glasses added an executive, intelligent air. "I just wanted to say I'm sorry about Lydia's earlier comments. When she's about to leave for a modeling job she's a little high-strung. Speaking of Lydia, would you phone the florist I use and send her some roses? Maybe those will make her feel better about the lunch mix-up. Make sure the flowers arrive within the hour. Lydia's leaving for an assignment tonight at five."

"No problem. I can handle it." Julia nodded her assent as she filed in her brain that Lydia would be out of town for a week. "Is there anything else you need me to do?"

"No, that's it for right now." Alex glanced at the watch he wore on his left wrist. Julia noticed that instead of a Rolex, Alex wore a dial watch with a night sky backdrop. The watchband was plain mahogany-colored leather.

"Plan to come back in a little after four, would you?" Alex said. "I've got a disaster at one of the Florida regional offices and I'm running out of time. We're supposed to be underwriting some municipal bonds, and that's the least of it. Anyway, I need to concentrate, so hold all calls unless it's someone telling me Chelsea's having a baby."

"I can do that," Julia said softly to hide her feelings. She would do anything for him, but there was no way she would ever let him know that.

"Good. Thanks, Julia. I know you're going to work out just fine." Alex had already buried his nose back in the file folder and soon closed the door behind him.

Julia cued up two numbers on the computer in front of her. Bless you, Rita, for such an easy telephone directory. Julia found the number for the florist and dialed. "This is Julia Brown for Mr. Alex Ravenwood. He would like to send a dozen roses to Lydia Olson. Make sure she gets them today. Cost is no object."

"What color?" The saleslady on the other end asked patiently.

"Color?" Julia asked. "I'm a temp. He didn't specify a color, he said you would know."

Through the receiver Julia heard the saleslady give an exasperated sigh. "For the past fourteen years Mr. Ravenwood sends red roses if it's a new woman, pink to ongoing flames, white to his sister, and yellow if the lady is history or about to be. He never sends black or multicolored roses, and they always need to be buds, not opened."

"See, of course you would know." Julia chortled with glee. "She gets the yellow."

IF ONLY ALL SECRETARIAL WORK was as easy as ordering flowers, Julia thought grimly as she dropped another stack of botched envelopes into the trash. Maybe she should have actually talked to the computer. She might have had better luck.

Once again she reset the printer, adjusted the envelopes and hit print. Julia shot the printer a determined look, as if daring it to defy her again. The first time she had put the envelopes in backward. This last time, sure she had it right, she had put all fifty envelopes forward and left to make some photocopies. When she returned, she had promptly discovered that the envelopes were all printed upside down as the printer proudly spit out number forty-nine.

By four o'clock Julia was starting to question her sanity in letting Chelsea talk her into this harebrained scheme.

Just remember your bank balance, she told herself as she grabbed another stack of envelopes. After giving Kyle everything but her last hundred dollars, an easy ten thousand dollars plus her salary and bonus would mean being able to afford the fantastic New York City apartment in a rent-controlled neighborhood she had found. She would even be able to buy some furniture. Yet, despite her goal, Julia wanted to throw up her hands in despair and simply walk out.

"How are you doing?" Tessa strode over to the desk and dropped off a stack of file folders. Tessa pushed a strand of gray hair that had fallen out of her tight bun away from her face. Julia could read the concern in Tessa's green eyes.

Julia slumped forward as the printer spit out the envelopes. A quick glance revealed they were finally printing correctly.

"That good, huh?" Tessa inspected the envelopes

with a woeful expression. "You're behind schedule, want some help?"

"I would love some help," Julia admitted. "I've got to stuff all fifty of these and get them to the post office by five. And Mr. Ravenwood wants me to come check in with him a little after four."

"Such is the life," Tessa agreed whimsically. "Never let anyone ever convince you that there is anything glamorous about being an executive secretary. We do just as much little stuff as the next guy."

"Literally." Julia nodded. She continued to fold the letters into thirds and shove them into envelopes. "What's in the file folders?"

"Stuff you get to put away. Rita's got her own filing system so it may take you a while to figure it out." Tessa grimaced as Julia licked the envelope. "You'll get sick if you lick all those. Rita's got a sponge around here somewhere."

"I don't have time to dig for it." Julia fished in a desk drawer for a roll of self-stick stamps she had managed to locate during one of her earlier forays. "I've got to get these things out of here soon, providing I can find the post office."

"Two blocks south," Tessa stated. "Briskly walk and you can get there in about five minutes. Walking is faster than taking the Metro."

"Yippee." Julia's sarcasm showed as she thought of her boots. "I wore the wrong shoes for all this."

"Well, you'll learn," Tessa said, folding and stuffing faster than anyone Julia had ever seen. "Mr. Ravenwood is easy to work for. He demands a lot, but he's fair."

"That's good to know." Julia's mouth felt sticky from the glue. Despite her aversion to drinking soda, she had caved in and purchased one earlier. Now she took a sip of the lukewarm soda to wash the glue taste away. "I really need this job."

"You know," Tessa said hesitantly, "you aren't exactly the type of a person I thought Chelsea would hire."

"You thought she would get someone with more experience." Julia nodded as she licked another envelope. Only thirty more of the disgusting suckers to go. "That's understandable."

"It makes me wonder what she's up to." Tessa didn't look Julia in the eyes and concentrated on stuffing. "Don't you?"

"She's not up to anything." Julia shrugged innocently. "Really."

"Now that's a lie if I ever heard one. If you were innocent you would have asked me what I meant."

Julia gulped. Boy, she had walked right into that one. She looked up to see Tessa looking directly at her and sizing her up like a hawk. Julia withered under the intensity of Tessa's gaze. While she had fooled Alex, it was obvious Tessa was not so easy to deceive, a fact the older woman confirmed.

"I've known Chelsea Ravenwood Meier since she was twelve and have been her secretary for the past four years. She's definitely up to something. I certainly don't believe in coincidences."

"Well, if she is up to something, you would have to ask her." Julia desperately tried to remain calm. Every nerve ending was panicking and she was getting a massive headache. "I really don't know what you are insinuating."

Tessa set the last of the stuffed envelopes on the desk

and picked up the file folders. "I saw your application," she said casually.

Julia heard the panic button inside her head begin to screech. With Tessa's next words she went deaf. "In fact, I typed your employment contract. Quite interesting how you have all sorts of safety-net clauses in there, including a signing bonus and an outrageous sum if Alex fires you. Rather odd for an inexperienced temporary worker, don't you think? For some reason Chelsea obviously wanted you here for the full three weeks, and I would really like to know why."

Julia leaned back in her chair, her tongue stuck to the glue strip. Her eyes widened as Tessa thumbed through the file folders, sending a small number of papers floating to the floor.

Julia miscalculated and her chair tipped. Quickly Julia thrust herself forward in an attempt to keep from toppling completely over.

"Come on, Julia," Tessa said, with a bittersweet smile. "Chelsea is like a daughter to me. I have only her best interests at heart. I can really be a help to you, or I can make your life much more difficult. A lot more difficult. Tell me the secret. I'm trustworthy."

Julia's eyes widened in horror as she watched Tessa send more papers fluttering to the floor. The way Tessa was leaning, the entire stack of file folders looked about to topple into oblivion. "That's blackmail," Julia objected.

Tessa grinned. "I prefer to call it satisfying the curiosity of an old lady."

"Five minutes!" Julia burst out, recognizing the extent of the messes she had on her hands, and that didn't include having to play fifty-two-paper pickup if all the file folders fell to the floor. "Give me five minutes and I'll meet you in your office."

"Excellent choice." Tessa nodded her agreement, and Julia sighed in relief as Tessa put the remaining file folders safely down on the desk.

Julia was picking up the papers and placing them haphazardly on the desk when Alex came out of his office. He gave her a strange look.

"You forgot to come check in with me," he said in greeting. "So, how did the rest of today go?"

"Fine, Mr. Ravenwood. Just fine." Julia plopped the papers down on top of the file folders and leaned against the desk as if to hide the mess.

She felt Alex's eyes roaming over her, taking in her discomposure. She didn't appear as quite the vampire this late in the day. Her bloodred lipstick had faded and needed retouching.

"I'm just about done with these letters, and then I'll make sure they get to the post office." Julia looked up at him expectantly, as if willing him to go away.

He shook his head, as if in disbelief, and then he simply shrugged. "Well, in that case I'm leaving for the day. I'll be in by eight tomorrow."

"Is that when I should be here?" Julia asked, her eyes widening. Eight o'clock meant an extra hour of sleep. The apartment Chelsea had found for her was on the Metro line, but she wanted to give herself at least fifty minutes to reach Ravenwood's corporate offices in Arlington.

Alex nodded again. "That would be fine although Rita is usually earlier than me. She says she likes to beat me to the mail."

Julia smiled stupidly. "The mail?"

"Right, the mail," Alex repeated with an odd look

on his face. "It'll be dropped off early. Someone in the mail room picks it up as soon as the post office opens at seven."

"Mail room," Julia repeated.

Alex gave her another strange once-over, and Julia wanted to wither like a dying flower under his sharp blue gaze. "Yes. We have a mail room. Anything you need to mail, like those letters today, just call the mail room and they'll pick it up and take it. That's their job."

"I didn't know they did that." Even to her ears, her voice sounded far away from her body.

"Sure." Alex shrugged. "They pick it up and drop it off. That way we get it sooner, and our customers get it sooner, which is absolutely necessary in the investment business. Be sure to check the fax first thing, too, okay?"

"Fax machine. Of course." Julia smiled woodenly, furious with herself for letting Tessa play her like a fool.

"Goodbye, Julia." Alex shrugged as if a bit bewildered by his temp, yet he still gave her the trademark smile that made her breathless, before turning on his heel and heading for the elevator.

Julia buried her face in her hands, glad for a moment Alex didn't know who she really was. "Stupid, stupid, stupid!" She told herself aloud as she walked around her desk and slumped back down into the chair. She picked up the phone and dialed the number of Chelsea's digital cell phone.

"Grand central." Chelsea answered on the first ring. Thanks to the power of caller ID Chelsea continued, "If this is Julia, I'm impressed that you lasted this long."

"Well, it is Julia and I don't believe it either," Julia snapped angrily.

"Ooh, touchy." Chelsea laughed from the other end of the line. "What happened?"

"Your secretary," Julia said, "is a menace."

"Tessa?" Chelsea's disbelief was evident. "Oh, come now, Julia. Tessa is as harmless as a fly."

"Well, she's making herself just as much a pest." Julia quickly related Tessa's conversation.

Chelsea whistled appreciatively when Julia finished speaking. "Wow. I didn't know the old girl had it in her. I'm impressed."

"Well, now you know she does," Julia said sourly, doodling circles on a pad of message paper.

"Okay, okay." Chelsea was surprisingly nonchalant. "Time for Plan B. We let Tessa in on the secret. I'll call her and tell her."

"Too late." Julia watched as Tessa came across the carpet towards her. "She's headed this way now." Julia held out the phone as Tessa tapped her watch. "Phone for you."

Tessa frowned and reached for the receiver. "This is Tessa. Oh, hi, Chelsea."

Julia watched as a myriad of expressions crossed Tessa's face. Her responses were short, items like "I see," "you're sure," and "well, okay." Tessa handed Julia the phone back suddenly.

"She's in," Chelsea's voice announced. "She's miffed at me that I didn't confide in her earlier, but she'll help you in any way possible. She hates Lydia about as much as I do. Just do whatever she says."

"Sounds great." Julia felt a weight lift from her shoulders. "Alex left for the day already."

"Super. He's on his way out here for dinner. Father

insisted on one last family get-together before I go into labor, whenever that is.''

"Well, enjoy.'' Julia felt an odd sense of relief when Chelsea told her where Alex was going. As she and Chelsea exchanged goodbyes, Julia wondered why it mattered where Alex went. Surely by now she was over her schoolgirl crush on Alex Ravenwood. Wasn't she? Julia placed the phone down and frowned to herself before she looked up at Tessa. "Now you know.''

"I should have known all along.'' Tessa sniffed her disappointment once and then, after deciding to forgive Chelsea and Julia's deception, she cheered up. "But now that I do, we can begin to plan. You're going to need all the help you can get.''

"I sent her yellow roses,'' Julia said hopefully.

Tessa put her hand to her chin and stared off for a moment, as if deep in thought. "That's a start, but it won't stop Lydia. She's confrontational, she'll come in here and make Alex admit it was a mistake. Then she'll sink her claws into him even deeper.'' Tessa tapped her forefinger against her cheek. The movement made a hollow popping sound.

"She's on her way for a week in Hawaii for a shoot.'' Julia grinned, but upon seeing Tessa's expression the grin faded quickly. "I guess she could phone him.''

"No, those calls would have to go through you, and you'll tell her he's busy,'' Tessa said. She rubbed a finger thoughtfully across a file folder. She saw Julia's look of confusion. "Alex has a cell phone, but only his immediate family has the number.''

"That's right. Alex told me about it earlier today.''

"Exactly.'' Tessa tapped her finger against the folder. "Alex is a bit old-fashioned compared to many executives in today's modern business world. He doesn't want to be contacted twenty-four hours a day, seven days a week, so his standard policy is never to give out his cell phone number to anyone, including girlfriends. Rita has it, which means you have it, but that's it. That'll leave Lydia only two options, faxing him, and you'll get those, or calling him at home."

"He's not home tonight," Julia announced, proud of herself for knowing some information that might be helpful.

"Perfect!" Tessa exclaimed. It was obvious that she was deep in her own thoughts. "We need to disconnect his answering machine. Chelsea always complains that he never checks it anyway, so if the lights are on but no tape is in…"

"It'll look like it's working but that he doesn't have any messages!" Julia caught Tessa's enthusiasm and matched it with her own.

"Exactly!" Tessa smirked. "Chelsea has a key to his town house in her office. I'll get it for you."

"For me?" Julia squeaked her disbelief and sat up ramrod straight in her chair. The chair jerked and hit her in the back. "You mean me?"

Tessa raised a gray eyebrow at her. "Of course," she said matter-of-factly, "you are getting paid to do this, right? So this is your dirty deed to do. While you're taking out the tape, I'd also suggest you turn the ringers off on his phones. He won't suspect a thing."

Julia's face conveyed her pure panic. "But that's breaking and entering! What if I'm caught? What if I miss something?"

Tessa looked at Julia patiently. "You know, Julia, you'll do fine. Chelsea's idea is great, and I'll think more about it tonight. I've got some great ideas. Did you know that I once let all the air out of one of my ex-boyfriend's tires?''

Julia was suitably shocked, and she didn't feel any more relieved. The idea of turning off Alex's phones had seemed like a good one, until she had to do it. However, backpedaling now wasn't going to help.

Tessa smiled wider as she continued in her reverie. ''I discovered that after a year he was still keeping tabs on me. So that very same night I decided to teach him a lesson. I didn't want to vandalize anything, just inconvenience him. It's amazing how fast a hairpin in a valve can deflate a tire.''

''What happened then?'' Julia was beginning to realize that having Tessa as a co-conspirator in Operation Free Alex might be more than a little bit dangerous.

''Well, I guess after the shop checked the tire for damage and found none, he just pumped it back up.'' Tessa shrugged. ''I never found out. Still, can you imagine? He had to change the tire. All that wasted time. Then there was the time when I—''

''Okay. I'll go.'' Julia stood quickly before Tessa could begin the next story. Julia gathered up the envelopes and placed them in a box.

Tessa reached for the box. ''I'll take them.''

''Oh, yes. Dial extension sixteen.'' She saw Tessa's look of pure disbelief and thrust the box into Tessa's hand. Julia shrugged. ''Alex told me there's a mail room.''

Tessa shot Julia a knowing and impressed look. ''You're quick. Anyway, you really do want me on your side. I know how things work around here. Get this stuff filed while I get you Alex's key. Don't forget, you need to be in here early tomorrow morning to get the faxes.''

''Alex said he and Rita always race for the mail.''

"Yes, it's their game of sorting the mail together. It's a long-standing ritual. Alex will take all the things he wants to read. But, you'll need to get the faxes so that he doesn't get Lydia's."

Tessa straightened up the box and replaced the lid. "More than likely when she can't reach him at home tonight she'll send him a fax." Tessa moved toward her office. "She's going to be pretty upset before this is all over. Anyway, I'll be back in a few minutes. I'm going to go get that key."

Tessa walked into her office and ignored the key that was already sitting out on her desk. Instead she picked up the phone and hit the speed-dial button.

"She bought it," she said into the phone when the familiar voice said hello. "I didn't know you knew anyone so naive and simplistic."

"That's why she's so perfect." Chelsea's voice floated over the phone lines and Tessa shifted the phone to the other ear. "She's totally trusting. It's her worst fault, but in this case it's going to be her biggest strength. Just as long as she doesn't get wind that she's actually a part of something bigger we'll be in good shape. I'll keep my brother occupied tonight. You just do your part and stick to our plan and everything is going to work out perfectly."

Tessa palmed the key in her hand. She had never let Chelsea down yet. "Done."

Chapter Three

Armed with the security code, a key, and a fax that had arrived as she went by the machine on her way to the elevator, Julia slowly approached Alex's Dupont Circle brownstone. It had taken her until six o'clock to get the filing finished, and Julia had spent all of the money in her purse, including the change, to take a cab over the Potomac. She hoped that there was a Metro station somewhere close since all she had left was a fare card in order to get home.

Julia hadn't known quite what to expect when Tessa had given her the address in the Dupont Circle neighborhood. Maybe a penthouse with a uniformed doorman or a converted old warehouse loft, but not the Federal style town house she faced. It wasn't where she would have pictured one of Washington, D.C.'s most eligible bachelors living.

Still, Tessa had told her that it was quite fashionable to rehab and refurbish town houses, and that Alex had done most of the labor himself.

Alex's postage-stamp yard was fenceless, and a flight of stone steps led up to an unlocked door onto a small enclosed porch. Feeling somewhat safer inside the covered entryway, Julia surveyed the gray double doors.

Taking a deep breath to calm her racing heart, Julia pressed the intercom. After several subsequent buzzes, she rubbed her sweaty palms on her skirt, took out the slip of paper with the security code, and grabbed the key firmly between her forefinger and thumb. Once inserted, Julia turned the knob.

Except for the gasp she gave as she stepped onto the marble floor, the house was eerily quiet. From the foyer she could see the town house was beautiful, but knowing the alarm was going to be silent for only twenty seconds, Julia got moving. Heart heaving, she quickly closed the front door.

The alarm box was inside the utility closet, and Julia pushed aside a mop. Checking the slip of paper, she punched in the six-number code. The red flashing light on the alarm changed to green, and Julia gave an audible sigh of relief. It was deactivated.

Time to get to work.

Stepping out of the utility closet, Julia surveyed the kitchen and gave a low whistle.

It was a chef's delight: a triple sink, a double oven, six burners set into a huge center island, recessed lighting in a coffered ceiling, and warm cherry custom cabinetry. Julia felt as if she had died and gone to cooking heaven.

"You don't deserve this kitchen," Julia said, chastising Alex aloud as she set her things down and ran her fingers over the dark woodland green Corian countertop. "Chelsea says you can't even cook." To justify herself, Julia couldn't resist a peek in the Sub-Zero refrigerator. It was empty except for condiments, beer, a stick of butter and a small container of milk about to expire.

Shaking her head in disgust, Julia searched for the

phone, locating a cordless model hanging on the far wall next to the walk-in pantry. With a flip of the switch, she silenced the ringer. Curious, she looked into the pantry, noting it was also empty except for some cereal, crackers and pretzels. Alex must eat out often.

Julia opened the door to the basement. Upon seeing that the basement was unfinished, she headed upstairs via the back staircase.

Some designer must have had a field day when given free rein over the house, Julia decided. Never except in magazines had she ever seen furniture so wonderful and rooms so perfect. Julia gave a wry smile as she checked the last of the guest bathrooms, a room larger than her parents' master bathroom in their modest middle-class "dream home."

Oh well, time to avoid putting it off anymore, Julia thought, pushing open the double doors to the master suite.

Despite the tussled condition of the king-size four-poster bed, Julia could see that the comforter matched the burgundy-and-green decorating scheme. She picked up the phone on the bedside table and clicked the ringer off. All of the furniture was the same set. Never in her life had Julia owned bedroom furniture that actually matched.

Her gaze again fell on the unmade bed. The tartan plaid sheets were flannel. What was it like, Julia wondered suddenly, to make love to Alex Ravenwood and roll around on those warm, soft sheets? What would his skin look like when it was covered with the sheen of their lovemaking? Would he hold her close afterward?

Her skin color flushing at the thought, Julia turned and took a quick peek in the bathroom. Vaulted with skylights, the master bathroom was bigger than the living room in her D.C. apartment. Julia ran a finger over the Corian countertop as her feet clicked on what she could tell was expensive marble tile.

"Downstairs," Julia reprimanded herself as she took one last long look at the shower. Don't even let your mind imagine what it would be like in that oversize shower, or you'll never get any dreamless sleep ever again.

She left the room quickly, returning the double doors to their exact position before heading down the front stairs. The living room and dining room didn't have any phones, and Julia finally found the answering machine and the last phone in the study.

The red light was blinking. "Four messages," Julia mused aloud. "All from Lydia?" Nosy, Julia hit play.

"Alex?" It was Lydia all right, and Julia cringed at her nasal voice. "I'm on the plane to Hawaii. Did you send me flowers? I think there was a mix-up. I'll call you later." The machine announced that the time of the call had been at 4:15 p.m.

After the beep, Julia heard Lydia's voice again. She was still on the plane, but this time she gave the hotel's phone number. The time of the call was 6:15. The third call was also from Lydia, this time telling Alex to call her no matter how late. The time of the call was 6:45.

The last message was from Chelsea. "Hey, Alex, are you home yet? I'm sorry you feel sick, I forgot to tell the cook that you couldn't eat things with even the slightest bit of anchovies in them. You should have skipped the Caesar salad, bro. Sorry. I guess you'll be there soon. Call me." The tape began to rewind after the machine announced the time of the call as 7:01 p.m.

Julia's eyes lighted on an antique grandfather clock that stood by the study door. If the brass pendulum swinging was any indication that the clock actually worked, she was in deep trouble. Fingers shaking, Julia removed the answering machine tape, and promptly dropped it. Bending, she scooped it back up and slipped it into the pocket of her skirt. Anxiety building, she reached and fixed the last ringer. Done.

Heart racing, Julia moved quickly back to the kitchen and grabbed her bag and the key.

Turning toward the foyer, she belatedly remembered she had to reset the alarm. What was it again? Code backward? Julia went to the closet, pushed the mop aside and fumbled with the slip of paper.

"Okay, I can do this," she whispered aloud to herself. "Five-three-zero-zero-one-nine, and hit this activity button and done." Julia's finger pressed the button and for one second nothing happened. The light flashed to armed red, and then all hell broke loose.

"Oh, God! No!" Julia cried, the shrill sound of the alarm blasting and shattering her eardrums. In her haste to turn the alarm off, she dropped the piece of paper, and as she bent for it she thumped her head on the wall. "Damn it!" Julia cussed, straightening herself up only to collide directly with a hard, immovable wooden object.

Her last vision was of a hand punching some buttons and grabbing at her before she passed out.

JAIL WAS JULIA'S FIRST THOUGHT as she regained consciousness. Even in the fuzzy blackness she could tell she was lying on a hard, still surface. Whatever type of bed she was on was cold, the chill seeping through her clothes and along her back.

I'm in jail. Julia groaned as her head pounded unmercifully. As she regained full consciousness, all her senses began to sharpen. Slowly she became aware that she was stretched out under some sort of offensive bright light. She closed her eyes even tighter.

"About time." A distant voice cut through the blackness. "You were starting to worry me."

"Officer, I..." Julia's mouth was dry as she began to speak. "I can explain."

"That'll be the least of it," the voice droned.

"Please, let me go. I've never been to jail before," Julia whispered, too afraid to open her eyes.

"Jail?" The voice sounded suitably shocked. "Who said anything about jail? Julia, you must have hit your head harder than I thought."

Julia threw open her eyes, blinking as the harsh light assaulted her. "Mr. Ravenwood!"

"You were expecting someone else?"

Julia closed her eyes, this time more to shut out his amused expression than just the light. She now knew where she was. She was lying on her back on the cold marble tile of Alex's kitchen floor. Somehow Julia knew jail might have been easier.

"I just assumed the cops came when the alarm kept sounding," Julia whispered. She opened her eyes slowly and her eyes blinked in rapid succession before adjusting fully to the light.

"Ah, you dreamed you were in jail." Alex nodded in appreciation of her mistake. "Rather understandable, since you were in my house without my knowledge. But what would Freud have to say about that dream?" Alex appeared to contemplate it for a moment. "Anyway, you hit your head on my baseball bat."

"Baseball bat?" Julia attempted to sit up, but failed and leaned back again as an excruciating pain throbbed between her temples.

"The one I was carrying. A genuine Louisville Slugger. I thought you were a burglar, so I grabbed the bat I keep in the umbrella stand. I threw open the door, you lifted your head, and you got a trip into the black." Alex gave her a cheeky smile. "You've got a nice lump on your forehead. Sorry, freak accident. But, at least you can look on the bright side. If I hadn't checked my swing you'd be on your way to the hospital right now."

"I'm sure I'll be grateful for that when my head stops pounding." Julia sat up slowly. Her head felt as if it was going to explode at any moment.

"The lump is only the size of a dime," he pronounced. He held up a plastic bag with some melting cubes. "I looked it over when you were out cold and put ice on it. Anyway, you're going to be fine. Makeup should cover it."

Julia rubbed her fingers over her forehead, finding the lump that her forefingers likened more to be the size of a softball than a dime. "If you say so." Julia looked around the kitchen, her eyes finding the Louisville Slugger on the floor. "That's some bat."

"I've had it since I played ball in high school," Alex replied. His tone shifted suddenly and Julia knew his relief at her condition was gone. The reproach would be next. She grimaced and braced herself.

"Julia." Alex was calm, a fact Julia instantly appreciated. "Julia, would you like to explain why you were in my closet working my alarm system?"

"I... I..." Julia stammered. Now that she was sitting she could feel that the wig had slipped. She patted her hair down as she continued to stare at Alex. He had changed into blue twill shorts and a red polo shirt. A tuft of just the right amount of dark curly hair appeared at the vee of the shirt and Julia stared at it as he waited for her answer.

"Come on, Julia," Alex prodded, his blue-eyed gaze never leaving her face. "I knocked you out flat. You had me worried. I could have killed you. Even though this is a trendy area, the District's known for its crime, so please enlighten me."

"I wasn't breaking in," she pleaded sheepishly. "Tessa gave me the code. The piece of paper should still be in the closet. I was reaching for it when you hit me."

Julia watched as Alex got it and held out the piece of paper. Alex studied it and looked expectantly at Julia. "And?"

Head pounding, Julia thought fast. "This fax came in at the last minute. Help me up, please, and I'll get it."

Alex reached for Julia and helped her to her feet. Her knees wobbled unsteadily and for a moment she found herself pressed against him. After the cold floor he felt warm, and lethal. Already her body was quivering, this time not from fear, but from the desire now coursing through her.

"I can make it," she mumbled, and she pushed herself unsteadily away from him. She knew Alex was watching her as she moved slowly over to her bag and pulled the fax out. She hadn't even bothered to look at it when the machine had spit it out. Hopefully it wasn't from Lydia. Julia tried to smooth the now-crumpled fax, but Alex's outstretched hand stopped her.

"Tessa thought it might be important and told me I needed to bring it over." That's right, Julia, this was Tessa's idea, blame it on her. "I was going to leave you a note." Julia inwardly cringed at how lame her reason sounded. She handed Alex the battered fax.

"Why didn't you just call me at Chelsea's?" Alex fingered the fax but didn't make an attempt to read it. Instead he continued to look at her. Julia wished she could disappear through the floor.

"I, I did," Julia stammered. "Mrs. Meier—" somehow she remembered to use Chelsea's surname "—said you had left early. Something about food poisoning?"

Alex eyed her suspiciously. "How did you know I was at my sister's? I didn't tell you before I left."

"Tessa mentioned it to me when the fax came in. She had talked to Chelsea earlier, I suppose." Julia added another lie and crossed her fingers behind her back. That's right, Julia, she told herself. Dig that hole.

Seemingly satisfied, Alex turned his attention to the fax. Julia wasn't sure if she would suffocate from the silence or from the way Alex's hair fell over his eyebrow. She was contemplating her next move when finally Alex spoke.

"You did right, Julia." He looked up at her and his blue eyes pierced through her. "This is from Donovan in Florida. I'm going to have to call him."

"Oh." Julia stammered as relief washed over her. The liar was safe on home plate despite getting hit with the bat. "So, I can go now?"

Alex didn't appear to be listening, and Julia put the strap on her shoulder, the bag hitting the pocket with the answering machine tape. Julia winced at the muffled sound. "Mr. Ravenwood?"

Alex looked up from his rereading of the fax. "Yes?"

"Is there a Metro stop near here?" Julia asked tiredly.

"Dupont Circle," Alex said, "but I'm going to call for a cab."

"That really won't be necessary." Julia shook her head, which was a mistake. Her eyes crossed and she felt dizzy. "I've got a fare card I can use. I'm only going to the Woodley Park-Zoo stop. It's just the next one."

"That's okay. It'll be my treat. I don't want you walking, even though the sun isn't down yet. It's also the least I can do for practically killing you."

Julia suspected Alex knew the reason for her refusal. Still, a cab sounded nice. She didn't feel in that good shape to be walking anywhere right now. She noticed Alex studying her for a moment.

"What is it?"

"You were only out for a minute, but I think I need to have you stay a bit longer if you could. Besides, I probably could use you around here if you could spare an hour? You're supposed to be at my beck and call, right?"

"Right." Julia gave him a weak smile.

"Have you eaten?"

"Uh, no." Julia shook her head again and grimaced at the pain that pounded between her eyebrows.

"Well, now that everything has left my system I think pasta would be in order. Let me order some delivery. Come into my study, and we'll get to work." Alex offered, "I'll also get you some aspirin."

"Aspirin would be great," Julia answered as she leaned on his arm. She ignored the jolt that traveled through her as she followed him obediently to his study.

ALEX HAD NO INTENTION of making Julia do any work. Already the lump on her forehead was turning an interesting shade of purple and she looked the worse for wear. As he phoned the Mangia Italiana restaurant and ordered delivery, he studied his temporary secretary.

Now, hair slightly askew, Julia was clutching a glass of water in one hand and pressing an ice bag to her forehead with the other. Alex frowned slightly. She must use a lot of hairspray, he thought, to have her hair move as one piece. Shrugging, he listened as the restaurant told him the price of the fettuccine Alfredo and Pollo Marsala he ordered.

"I like your office." Julia's voice filled the odd silence as Alex set down the phone.

"Thanks." Alex gave her a benevolent smile as he took a seat behind his desk. Alex had never really paid much attention to his office as long as it was clean. "Chelsea hired a decorating firm for me. I told them what I liked, they created."

"They did a nice job." Julia attempted to return his smile with one of her own, and Alex could tell the aspiring obviously had not kicked in yet. "So, boss, what do we need to do?"

Alex shifted his weight forward and leaned his arms on the desk. "I'm going to call Donovan and then I'll need to dictate some letters. After you've rested up a bit you can use the computer and get them typed up and fax them from here."

"Fax from here?" Her tone of voice sounded strange.

"Sure." Alex shrugged. "There's a modem on the computer, and a fax program. I can send and receive, but I only send. I'd much rather receive faxes at the office. I don't do any work at home if I can avoid it. Even my e-mail goes to the office, for it takes me at least twenty minutes a day to read. I keep this place a sanctuary."

"I understand."

Alex saw the look in her eyes and instinctively his own narrowed. It was obvious she didn't believe him, and for some reason it became important for him to convince her.

"Really, Julia, I try to keep work and home separate. My father managed to do it pretty well, and it really made a difference. I never grew up feeling that I was secondary to the company." Alex picked up a Cross pen and studied it in order to avoid looking at her. "I don't have a family yet, but I would sell Ravenwood Investments before I would let it interfere with my being a good father."

"You're very unique in that philosophy, I take it," Julia commented, and Alex relaxed as Julia now seemed slightly impressed. For some odd reason it was important to him that she believe him.

"It makes me seem to the press like a playboy." Alex grinned wryly. "Alex Ravenwood never works." He put the pen down and removed some bills from the wallet he kept in his briefcase. "If they only knew the true story. It's far from it, but that would be boring. Anyway, I'm going to make a few phone calls. I'll listen for the front door."

"Do you want me to stay in here?" Julia rubbed her temples.

"No, why don't you rest? The television is in the den. I've got lots of movies you can pop in if you don't like anything on cable."

"Den? Where's that?" Julia's voice sounded like a mouse squeaking and Alex frowned slightly.

"Right off the kitchen. It's the pocket door to the right of the back door. The one that looks like a coat closet," Alex gave her a strange smile. "You probably didn't notice it because you were too busy getting thumped on the head.''

"I'll sit in there. Call me if you need me.''

"I'll bring in the food when it arrives.'' Alex picked up the phone and turned away.

After twenty minutes Alex decided he was through working and headed to the den. Finding Julia absorbed in a romantic comedy, he watched her unobtrusively for a few moments.

He couldn't figure her out. She wasn't much of a secretary. He had seen the botched envelopes and her panic over using a fax machine. Something wasn't right. Alex couldn't put his finger on it, but his instincts told him if he kept working on it he would unravel the mystery Chelsea had put before him.

"Like it?''

Julia jumped at the sound of his voice. "It's a lovely room.'' She gave him a nervous smile and uncurled her legs out from under her. "I didn't know this room was back here.''

"It's my television hangout,'' Alex said of the intimate ten-by-twelve sunroom he had converted into a den. Done in comfortable overstuffed neutrals, it was in sharp contrast to the designer burgundy-and-green decor of the rest of the house.

"I figured as much with the big-screen TV. You must like TV.''

"Not necessarily TV. I'm a movie buff so I keep all of my DVD and VCR tapes in that armoire over there.'' The doorbell chimed. "That must be the food. You stay here. I'll get it.''

"Okay.'' Julia clasped her hands in her lap.

Alex chuckled as he left the room. It was obvious

that he made her nervous. Rather a refreshing change, he mused, not to have a woman throwing herself at him.

He came back with two white bags in his hand.

"That smells good," Julia said.

"It should be. They have the best food, especially for carryout. We'll eat in here." Alex set the bags on the coffee table and began emptying them. He handed Julia a carryout dish and some plastic cutlery. He settled down at the opposite end of the sofa. "Eat up."

For the second time that day Alex watched Julia as she ate. This time he scrutinized her even more. Her story had checked out. Alex had called Tessa, who had vouched that she sent Julia after him. Even the fax from Donovan had been legit. Julia certainly didn't seem like a criminal, and now Alex felt the first twinge of guilt for searching the purse she had left in his study. Her bag had contained scissors, a wallet devoid of cash and identification, one fare card, a few other odds and ends of little consequence, and lots of makeup. Alex was used to women having makeup, Lydia being a prime example, but Julia seemed to have even more than normal. Not that her makeup did anything to improve her looks.

Although, as he studied her, he wondered if she just didn't know how to wear it. Her nose was perfectly shaped, her chin looked okay, and her warm chocolate eyes, minus those hideous black glasses and false eyelashes, might actually be pretty with the right makeup shades.

He dragged his thoughts away from her appearance. From his search of her purse it was clear she hadn't stolen anything. Alex rubbed his chin thoughtfully. He found her lack of identification strange, but in Washington, D.C., where public transport was the norm, a driver's license was unnecessary. He watched as Julia dug into her food, again savoring every bite of it. He decided she was just a conscientious working girl who was trying to please her new boss in order to get a permanent assignment. Still, Alex decided, he wouldn't let his guard down.

"The food's good." Julia gave him a grateful smile as she ate the last bite of her chicken. "I'm ready to work now."

Alex shrugged and reached for his glass of wine. He took a long sip, letting the liquid tantalize his tastebuds before replying. "No, I think I'm done for the day."

"What about Donovan? I thought he was out." Julia's brow furrowed and Alex decided it was a cute movement.

"He'll call me or fax me at the office first thing," Alex replied. "There's nothing that can't wait until tomorrow."

Julia looked at Alex with new respect. "You really don't work at home, do you?"

Alex flashed her what Rita called his trademark impish grin. "No, I don't if I can help it. You didn't believe me?"

"No," Julia admitted. "I didn't."

"Well, now you know. I believe in two things—honesty and values. I can't stand dishonesty. I'm paranoid about it. I surround myself only with people I can trust. At the same time, I have a set of values. One of those things that I value is my privacy. This house is the only place I find it, and so I guard it closely. You're one of the few people who has seen the inside."

Julia raised her eyebrows at him. The laugh lines around her brown eyes crinkled with skepticism.

"Again you don't believe me." Alex shook his head.

His dark locks cascaded over his left eye, and he pushed the offending strands off his face. "Why do women never learn? Male 101. Let a female into your house and she starts envisioning herself living there. I'm not ready to share this space with anyone on a permanent basis."

Julia stood up and grabbed the bags that were now full of trash. "Then I should get going because I'm beginning to think that you need a few plants in that empty corner over there."

Alex watched as Julia smiled. It was the first time he had truly seen her naturally smile. Her smile radiated her whole face and made her skin seem softer, more translucent than pale and sickly. For some odd reason, the vision of Audrey Hepburn as Eliza Doolittle popped into his mind. Julia could be appealing. She had so much potential hidden away. To not unlock it was criminal. All she really needed was a makeover. Maybe he should get her one.

"You know, Alex, I'm serious. A big potted corn plant would just add that touch of..."

Alex couldn't resist. Instead of letting Julia finish, he tossed a pillow at her. It landed on her chest, causing her to drop the trash bag. Sputtering, she turned to face Alex. He smiled at her indignant look.

"Did I mention earlier I was a pitcher? Once I even pitched a no-hitter." Alex raised his eyebrows in mock salute and readied another pillow.

"Really? Then did I mention earlier that I've been hit by you enough tonight?" Julia shot back.

He had to give her credit. She was quick with her retorts. "I don't think you brought that up."

Alex continued to smile, despite knowing it was an idiotic grin that covered his face. Julia looked so rumpled and ruffled. It was almost comic in a refreshing sort of way. He wasn't sure what had possessed him to throw the pillow, especially with the lump on her forehead, but he liked the result. The vampire was human after all.

Her lips, cleaned of the bloodred stain from eating dinner, were now pale pink and full. Definitely kissable. In spite of her hideous hair, Julia intrigued him. From her teasing, Alex could tell that she could dish it out as well as she could take it.

That was rare, making Julia unlike any of the women he normally dated. Julia definitely had many layers, dimensions, and sides, and he suddenly felt a fierce desire and need to explore each and every one of them.

"So, Julia, would you like me to hit on you some more and see what you think?" Deliberately he baited her and waited for her reaction.

Julia's mouth literally fell open and Alex gave her a devilish smile. He watched her snap it quickly closed before replying.

"I don't think so. My face can't take any more punishment."

Alex made a disappointed noise. "Who said it was going to be your face? Last time I hit your..." He licked his lips instead of finishing. Giving her another grin, he raked the hair back out of his face. His blue eyes twinkled. "Still, it was worth a shot."

"You've taken enough shots," Julia admonished. She reached down and tossed the throw pillow back to him. "Here. Put that away. I'll take care of the trash." Julia scooped up the white bags and disappeared into the kitchen.

When Julia returned, he was on the phone. Alex saw

the look of trepidation on her face before she quickly masked it. His brow furrowed as he set down the phone.

"I've ordered you a cab. It's my treat."

"Great. That's super." Julia's relief was evident. Alex wondered what was up with her. If her lack of money was an indication, she probably didn't like the fact she was dead broke.

When the cab arrived less than ten minutes later Alex walked Julia to the curb. He held the door for her.

"Thanks again for the cab." Julia stood in front of him and gave him a grateful smile.

"You're welcome." Alex helped her into the cab, and then leaned down to give the cabby a fifty-dollar bill. "I'll see you tomorrow, Julia." He gave her a wave.

From the back window Julia saw him watching the cab. When it turned the corner, Julia finally leaned back against the seat.

What a crazy night. She had had dinner with the man of her dreams. He was handsome, charming, and had every single one of those qualities she had always been looking for in a man. Alex had them all—honesty, integrity and sensitivity.

Alex Ravenwood was Julia Grayson's dream man. The only problem, he didn't know it was her. Not that it would have mattered anyway, she thought bitterly. Two years ago at Chelsea's wedding, Alex hadn't noticed Julia Grayson, so why would he notice ugly Julia Brown?

Her heart skittered and her stomach churned. Seeing Alex today had only confirmed what she already knew, that pictures didn't do the man justice.

No matter how many photographs Chelsea had displayed in the dorm room, nothing compared to either today or the wedding. Even two years later, Julia could still picture the way he looked the night of Chelsea's wedding.

Mere film could not capture the man. No rental tuxedo for Alex, the black Armani tux had been custom cut to Alex's frame. And what a figure it was. Unlike some men, Alex's neck didn't bulge above the white starched collar of his shirt. Instead his neck was smooth, leading up to a chiseled chin. Alex's masculinity was a subtle, underlying presence that was simply there. Men respected it, women instinctively desired it.

Julia had tried to be an exception, but instead she had stared at him the entire time during the ceremony. Because of her placement in the line as Chelsea's maid of honor, it wasn't until the reception that she first touched him. All it took was one dance in Alex's arms and she had been left tingling in ways best described in romance novels.

His grip had been firm and powerful without being crushing. Julia had felt light as a feather while he moved her across the floor with crisp, sure steps. For three blissful minutes she had rested her head on his broad shoulders, breathing in the musky scent of him and feeling like a princess.

And then the music stopped, and the wedding magic ended. As soon as his duty of dancing with the maid of honor ended, Alex had left the inexperienced Julia alone. Sure, he promised her another dance. It never happened.

Instead, when Julia watched Alex draw a sophisticated woman into his arms, she had known a middleclass girl from St. Louis wasn't good enough for a man who held beauty in the highest of regards. Hurt and bitter about her own shortcomings, she had left the reception shortly thereafter.

"Ugh!" Julia said aloud.

"Ma'am?" The cabby looked in concern at her.

"I'm fine." Julia turned her attention out the window as the cabby headed up Connecticut Avenue toward her apartment building.

No, I'm not fine, Julia mentally berated herself. *I'm still crazy for a man I can't have. Not only that, but he's paranoid about honesty and people he can trust. Now I'm neither.* Julia put her head in her hands. What had she done?

The idea of Alex discovering her deception filled her with dread and her stomach churned again. Despite having had a full meal, Julia suddenly craved chocolate, her comfort food. Luckily she didn't have any. While most people gained weight in college, with Chelsea's help Julia had lost twenty-five pounds, discovered makeup, and found some self-confidence.

"We're here, miss."

"Thanks," Julia said. She stepped out of the taxi, Operation Free Alex still preying on her mind. There was at least some encouraging news from the night. By saying he wasn't ready to share his space, Alex had indicated that he probably wasn't as committed to Lydia as Lydia thought he was.

I'll use this, Julia thought suddenly. After all, this was her purpose for being in the Capitol city. Her purpose was not to fall in love with Alexander Ravenwood, and get her heart broken again. Julia lifted her chin. No, she didn't need to be tossed aside by a man ever again, so the sooner she finished the job and moved to New York City, the better off she would be.

Chapter Four

"So, it's going fine at the office?" Chelsea forked another piece of chocolate cake into her mouth.

"Pretty quiet, actually," Julia admitted, trying to ignore Chelsea's inquisitive stare. "I type, I file, and Alex speaks to me only when he has to." Julia stretched out her feet under the patio table. She and Chelsea had just finished a late Thursday night dinner at Chelsea's, and twilight had fallen over the estate grounds. Because the July night was cooler than normal, she and Chelsea had opted to eat outside in the screened gazebo overlooking the pool.

"Well, at least he hasn't recognized you." Chelsea grinned. "In fact, I know he hasn't. That night he came to dinner he berated me for hiring him such an ugly secretary. I think he wanted Miss America back."

Julia absently pushed a loose strand of her long, blond bangs back away from her face. She was wearing her bangs down to hide the lump that thankfully had almost disappeared. "Who's Miss America?"

"The temp before you that I hired. She was a ditz. Blonde jokes didn't come close to describing her." Chelsea reached over and grabbed Julia's unfinished piece of dessert. "You were through with this, right? Junior's still hungry."

"I'm done," Julia replied. A cricket chirped somewhere in the distance.

"Thought so." Chelsea popped a bite of Julia's cake into her mouth. "By the way, I meant to thank you for coming out here and entertaining me tonight. Scott had some press club function tonight and I didn't want him to miss it."

"I'm glad you invited me. I'm going broke eating at Marcel's every night, even though they do make me feel like part of their family."

"Well, I consider you part of my family. You're going to be Junior's godmother you know."

"Thanks again for that. I'm really honored," Julia said with a grateful smile.

"Julia, you've been more like a sister to me than a friend, Chelsea insisted. "I wish you lived closer, but New York will at least be just a hop compared to St. Louis. And you know Scott said you're always welcome to stay with us."

"Who's staying with us?"

Julia froze. After four days of working with Alex Ravenwood she would recognize his voice anywhere.

"Hey Alex," Chelsea called as Alex strode across the lawn to the gazebo. "What brings you by?"

"I thought you could use some company," Alex said as he pulled the screen door open.

"Liar. You knew Scott wasn't home and came to check on me. Didn't you?"

"Caught me." Alex laughed. He tousled his sister's hair in a playful gesture. "He called me this morning."

"Well, as you can see, I'm fine. Rachel's here to

keep me company." Chelsea easily used Julia's first name.

It was apparent that Alex expected his sister to be alone, and for the first time, he turned his attention to the woman sitting in the candlelight. "Rachel?"

"My roommate? My maid of honor? Don't embarrass her by not remembering her."

Julia wanted to dart under the table, but instead she smiled and drew on every bit of acting talent she had. With her hair pulled back into a ponytail and her face scrubbed totally clean of makeup, there was no way Alex would connect her with Julia Brown, his ugly secretary.

"Alex," she said in her best exaggerated Midwestern twang. "It's nice to see you again."

"The pleasure is all mine." As Alex took a seat next to his sister, a bit of tension left Julia. At least he wasn't right beside her.

"Rachel came into town to visit and help me with the baby," Chelsea told Alex. "She arrived today. Unfortunately Junior's not following schedule."

"I hope you had a good flight," Alex said conversationally.

"It was fine," Julia replied, thinking fast. "The part of flying over the river was a bit unnerving though."

Alex laughed knowingly. "You landed at Washington National. Noise abatement laws send planes over the river."

"All I know is when I saw the guy in the fishing boat waving I really hoped there was a runway somewhere close."

A servant suddenly knocked on the door. "Mrs. Meier, may I clear some dishes and refresh your drinks?"

"That would be great, Clara," Chelsea said. "In fact, why don't I help you."

"Oh no, let me." Julia got to her feet.

"Sit down, Rachel," Chelsea ordered. "I'm pregnant. My clearing dishes was just an excuse. I was trying to avoid announcing that I had to go to the rest room. You two wait here and I'll be back. Clara, get a bottle of wine, why don't you? I'm sure Alex wants some."

Julia flushed as Chelsea hefted her bulk out of the chair and duck-walked from the gazebo. Julia's heart quivered. She was alone with Alex.

"So, how long are you staying?" Alex's deep voice sliced through the quiet.

"Um, I'm on an open-ended ticket. I've got two weeks vacation, but I don't want to impose on Chelsea longer than necessary. We both thought the baby would be early."

"Ravenwood babies are never early." Alex chuckled, a husky, sensual sound that sent shivers down Julia's spine. "I was three weeks late and Chelsea was four. I'm sure Chelsea's got at least another week to go. So, it's probably good you're here to keep her from killing her husband."

"She did finish my cake," Julia admitted with a laugh.

"Lately she's been a bottomless pit when it comes to food," Alex agreed. "She has these weird cravings, too, like anchovies and artichokes."

"I guess it's a female thing. My sister was the typical pickles and ice cream in the middle of the night. Her husband didn't get any sleep the whole last month."

"I can't even imagine how Scott does it. I've got to

give him credit—he must really love my sister to put up with her moods."

"Oh, come on now, Alex. They're not that bad." Julia giggled. "I lived with her for four years so I would know."

"I lived with her longer, but I'll give you a sainthood award anyway. You volunteered."

Julia smiled. She knew that Alex, despite his mild teasing of his sister, loved Chelsea despite her faults.

"Just tell me one thing, does she play practical jokes on you, too?"

"Jokes?" Julia frowned slightly. "Like did she short-sheet my sheets or something like that? No, she never played any jokes on me. We played a lot on others, though. Why?"

"Oh, she plays tons on me." Alex ran a thumb idly across his upper lip and Julia felt her throat go dry.

"You're kidding." She took a sip of water.

"I wish." Alex paused as Clara returned with a bottle of wine and two glasses. "Her latest joke is my temp."

"Your temp?" Julia felt amazed that she got the words out of her mouth without a hitch.

"Last time, she thrust this beautiful but stupid woman under my nose. This time I've got a female version of Dracula. At least this one can type." Alex leaned back in his chair.

"Mrs. Meier said to tell you she may be a few minutes but she'll be back out," Clara announced as she expertly popped the cork.

"At least she sent the wine," Alex said, handing Julia a glass from across the table. Clara poured both glasses and then disappeared. "Let's see how long she actually takes, shall we?"

"Oh, come on, Alex. Pregnant women live for these

things. My sister was horribly uncomfortable during her entire nine months," Julia admonished. "Guys just don't get it."

"Thank God for that," Alex said, taking her pun literally. "I'll admit, I like being a chauvinistic male if it means not having to take part in childbirth."

"If men were responsible for bearing children mankind would already be extinct."

"Truer words were never spoken." Alex laughed. "So, tell me, what did you major in? I don't remember what career path you were on."

"I've got a bachelor in fine arts, and I'm a designer. I've been working at a local repertory company in the costume department. I'm responsible for interpreting what I think the characters should wear and then designing the outfits and overseeing their construction." Julia omitted that she had quit.

"That sounds challenging. I bet you've met a lot of people."

"It's been interesting." Julia pushed the thoughts of Kyle and his overdramatized professions of love out of her head. His departure with the coat check girl and Julia's money had been the only time he hadn't been acting.

"I dabbled in acting," Alex said. "I did a few school plays, but now my interest has to be limited to attending the theater and seeing movies."

"What movies do you collect?" As soon as the words were out, Julia bit her inside lip. Stupid, she berated herself. Julia Brown knows that, not Julia Grayson. Quickly she worked for a recovery. "You do collect movies, don't you? I think I remember Chelsea saying you did."

Alex didn't seem to notice and nodded. "I do. I especially like the classics."

"Hey, you two! Look who I found!" Alex and Julia turned to see Chelsea's husband escorting her down the path to the gazebo. "Scott bailed out early." Chelsea plopped down in her chair.

"Hello, Scott." Alex stood and shook Scott's hand. "I see you're surviving."

"Barely." Scott grinned.

"Ha!" Chelsea ignored her husband's comment. Instead she pounded a deck of cards on the table. Chelsea's movement was so dramatic Julia had to steady her wineglass. "The ladies are challenging you two guys to a game of spades. We were the undefeated champs of our hall."

"I don't think we can resist a challenge like that," Alex told Scott. "Prepare to be defeated, ladies."

In the end, the girls defeated the men.

"You really need to be getting some rest now, my victorious wife." Scott leaned toward Chelsea, who was stifling a yawn.

"You're probably right. Alex, it was good to see you. Drop by more often. Rachel, Clara put your stuff in the blue guest room, right?"

"Right," Julia replied, playing along with the ruse.

The group headed up the path to the main house. "So, are you planning to see much of the city?" Alex asked her.

"I'm not sure," she admitted. "Chelsea's not up to much sight-seeing."

"You'll have to take her, Alex," Chelsea called back down the path. "I have a late doctor's appointment tomorrow, so maybe you could take Rachel to dinner and then walk the mall.''

"I've got a date with Lydia tomorrow. She's taking me out for my birthday," Alex replied. "But Saturday might work."

"Saturday then. It's settled. You can take her for lunch and sight-seeing and then have her back here for dinner." Chelsea blinked as they entered the glow from the bright lights of the living room. Scott opened the terrace doors and they walked inside.

"Really, Alex. You don't need to take me anywhere. I'm sure I can explore on my own," Julia protested. The lights seemed blinding and she felt his gaze on her. Acutely aware of how girlish she looked, Julia studied her sandals.

"No, I'd be happy to do it. It's a date."

Julia wanted to melt under Alex's trademark smile, the smile that was now just for her. Her heart thumped. However, past experience at being fixed up made her offer him a way out. "If you're sure."

"I'm sure. I'll pick you up Saturday, say about noon?"

"Noon's fine." Julia managed a smile. A date with Alex. The thought overwhelmed her, and a few minutes later when she heard Alex's car engine start, she turned to Chelsea.

"I'm going to kill you!"

"Look, I didn't plan on him showing up! I improvised!" Chelsea protested.

"Improvised! I'm going to be touring the mall with him Saturday! How am I going to be able to keep him from figuring out I'm Julia Brown if I spend any more time with him?" Julia paced the living room. "I can't do this, Chelsea."

"Oh, Julia, of course you can." Chelsea gave her friend a broad, encouraging grin. "Just act totally different. He's not going to put two and two together. Alex isn't that astute. I'm sure he doesn't even look at Julia Brown. No offense, but she's ugly."

"Will someone please tell me what's going on?" Scott interjected. He looked confused.

"Uh, um, it's a long story," Chelsea said.

"You're up to something," Scott said. "So spill it. I've got all night."

"And I don't," Julia said. "I'm going to call a cab. And since this is your fault, Chelsea, you're paying." She picked up the phone and dialed in the number that was already becoming rote.

"I thought she's staying here," Scott said as he watched Julia give Chelsea's Chevy Chase address. He looked bewildered.

"No, she's got to work tomorrow," Chelsea said, placing a hand on her husband's arm.

"Work? Work where?" Now Scott looked totally perplexed as if aliens had taken possession of his wife.

"For Alex," Chelsea said in exasperation, as if her husband should have already guessed. "She's his temp."

"When we met for lunch yesterday he told me his temp is an ugly woman with black hair…oh my God. Chelsea, what have you done?"

Chelsea smiled at her husband and slid her arm through his. "Now, just trust me, Scott. Have I ever failed before?"

Scott pulled his wife close to him as Julia hung up the phone. "We'll talk about this later."

"Sure," Chelsea replied, reaching up to give her husband a kiss. There was no way she was going to tell her husband, Alex's best friend, what was going on.

Julia smiled as she observed the scene. It was good to see Chelsea so happy. Someday she hoped to be the same way, with a husband who loved her and a baby on the way. She sighed silently. Unfortunately, she had learned that in her world someday was often a long way away.

JULIA'S FEARS of being recognized were for naught. She arrived at the normal time the next morning and Alex seemed none the wiser.

"No, that one's mine." Alex snatched the envelope from Julia's hand as they sorted the mail. "You get this one. They want money."

"And what do I do with it?" Julia studied the envelope from the charitable organization.

"Send it to our charitable contribution department." Alex snatched the next letter. "Ooh, this is personal."

"What's that?" Although it was Friday, Julia hadn't yet mastered the daily mail race thing. Every morning she and Alex would fight over the mail. It was a ritual he and Rita went through every morning, and Alex had continued it with Julia.

"A birthday card from a publishing agent I once dated." Alex tore into it and pulled out the card. "She's wishing me the best and telling me she's gotten married. Isn't that sweet?" He tossed it into the recycle bin and grabbed the next envelope.

"I didn't know you were having a birthday," Julia lied as she opened a résumé and routed it to personnel.

"Yeah, it's tomorrow." Alex shrugged. "The big three-six."

"Are you having a party?" Outwardly Julia appeared to make idle conversation, but she was curious.

"No." Alex shrugged. "Tomorrow I'm taking a friend of my sister's to lunch and then sight-seeing. Tonight I'm meeting Lydia for happy hour at the Buscholtz Art Gallery. It's a premiere for some artist I've never heard of. Then we'll do dinner."

"Sounds interesting." Julia's mind raced full steam ahead. She was certain Alex hadn't talked to Lydia, and just like last night he was working from previously laid plans.

If Julia hadn't been a participant in Operation Free Alex, she might actually have felt sorry for Lydia. Julia had been putting the woman off since Tuesday. Lydia had been angry about the roses, then furious. Now after not hearing from Alex for a week, Julia knew Lydia would be stringing more than a few curse words together next time she called. Julia had already heard an earful, even learning words she'd never heard before.

Alex tossed the last of the office mail onto Julia's desk. "Actually I expect the art gallery premiere to be boring. I'm not into them."

"Then why go?" Julia gazed up at Alex in surprise.

Alex contemplated her question a moment before answering. "I guess because Lydia arranged it for my birthday. I haven't talked to her since she left on her trip, and anyway, doing these kinds of things is expected of me. That's what I've grown up doing."

Julia scratched the top of her black wig, although it did little to ease the itch. She shrugged. "Sounds silly to me."

"Yeah, well, most things in life are, but I have a reputation to maintain and a company to run that bears my name," Alex stated dryly. "Okay, that stack's all mine."

Julia picked up a stack of mail bound by a rubber band. She had learned on Tuesday to be sure to get to the contents of his post office box first. Intensely private, Alex didn't have mail sent to his home address, and instead the mail room picked it up at the post office.

"Here you go." Julia tossed him the stack.

"You got the faxes, right?" Alex caught the parcel and he set it down before dropping some empty envelopes in the trash can.

"Yes." Julia's fingers connected with Alex's as she handed him the faxes that had arrived overnight. As always, a slight electric jolt traveled between them. Like Alex, Julia pretended to ignore it.

Alex studied the faxes briefly and handed two of them back to her. "Call Mark Brantly and see if he can get in here to see me today. His number is on the fax. Send this second one to accounting and have Jennifer Sherman get the numbers that Donovan needs pronto." Julia hastily scribbled some notes.

"Also, Edward Thompson is stopping by sometime today. Let me know when he arrives, and I'll get him in as soon as I can." Alex grabbed a bunch of papers and his cup of coffee off Julia's desk. Julia watched as Alex entered his office and closed the door behind him.

Slowly she exhaled, almost unaware that she had been holding her breath. He hadn't recognized her, despite their conversation and card game last night. She reached her fingers up to feel the lump that was now barely visible on her head. Julia Brown's wig showed it off, while Julia Grayson's bangs hid it.

Perhaps Chelsea's zeal hadn't been misguided this time. Despite Tessa's being out of the office with the flu, the week had gone smoothly. Now she just had to somehow sabotage Alex's plans for tonight. The last thing she wanted to do was hear about his hot date while they were sight-seeing. Julia sighed and twisted a pencil in her hand. Alex had volunteered part of his birthday to take her sight-seeing. He was so thoughtful, so generous. That knifed even more. When she worshiped his picture he had been just a fantasy. At the wedding he had been flesh and blood, but still a far-fetched fancy.

In her girlish mind she had equated her ideal man with a vision of Alex Ravenwood. The illusion, which she had hoped to shatter during her tenure as Alex's temp, was daily becoming even more of a noose around her neck. Alex Ravenwood was everything she had ever dreamed he would be, and more.

Julia snapped the pencil in half and dropped it into the waste can. It would do her no good to pine for Alex. She wasn't his type, disguise or no disguise.

Edward Thompson arrived later that day, a fat, balding man carrying a thin manila envelope. Edward didn't look like a typical businessman. Dressed in jeans, worn tennis shoes and a ragged New York Yankees T-shirt, Edward looked distinctly out of place in the posh corporate office.

"So you're Julia Brown." He gave her an appraising glance.

"That would be me," she quipped as she buzzed Alex's office. Alex had Julia usher Edward right in. Edward was only in the office for five minutes before he came back out again. The envelope was gone.

"That was fast," Julia noted. She blinked at him through the thick black flames.

"It was a pretty open and shut case." Edward

shrugged as he headed for the elevator. "Tell Chelsea this one was free."

"I'll relay the message. Have a good day," Julia called after him. Soon Mark Brantly arrived. From the fax, Julia knew that he was a writer for a financial magazine. Unlike Edward Thompson, Mark Brantly wore a three-piece suit. He was in Alex's office for two hours before he left.

"Well?"

Julia started at the sound of Tessa's voice.

"Don't do that!" Julia snapped in exasperation, dropping the bologna sandwich she was eating while at her desk.

"Do what?" Tessa came around.

"Sneak up on me. You should know I'm a bundle of nerves." Julia groaned. "This is harder than I thought."

"Well, excuse me if I had a cold since Tuesday. I figured staying home would be a wise thing to do. I'm sorry my fever wouldn't let me get back here soon enough to help you save your precious hide. By the way, what happened to your head? That must have been quite a lump."

"Alex's baseball bat happened," Julia snapped, and then anger slightly abating, she filled Tessa in on the whole story, including the night before at Chelsea's house.

"But that's not it," Julia groaned. "Sorry, Tessa, I didn't mean to be snobby. It's not you. I just don't know how much more of this duplicity I can take. It's been okay while things have been rather quiet, but Lydia arrives back tonight and Alex is meeting her at an art gallery."

Tessa tapped a pencil against her palm thoughtfully.

To Julia, Tessa's movement sounded like a drum. "How many faxes did she send?"

"This one is hot off the fax," Julia replied, pulling it out and handing it to Tessa. "With Alex walking out Mark Brantly, I haven't had time to read it."

Tessa snatched it from Julia's hand and studied it for a long moment. "You're in luck, Julia. This gives her phone number, apologizes for canceling his birthday outing, and asks him to call her. It looks like she won't be making it after all. The shoot's been extended for another week."

"So now what do I do?" Julia's jubilation was mixed with her nervousness.

"You call her." Tessa shrugged.

"What?" Julia's tone was incredulous. "I'm not going to talk to her. Every time I call her she cusses at me."

"You're calling the hotel," Tessa chided. "You'll get some hotel attendant. She's working, remember? Leave her a message that Alex got her messages and that he's tied up in meetings all day and he'll call her again soon."

"That's a lie," Julia protested. "He won't even know. He expects to still meet her at the art gallery tonight."

"Give me some time to work on that."

Julia wondered if she should be concerned that Tessa didn't appear worried. "What are you planning?"

"Nothing yet, but I'll come up with something. Better yet, why don't I make the phone call to Lydia? After stranding you this week, I probably owe you so I'll deal with it. Oh, and you do know there is a small lounge you can use on this floor if you want to eat lunch."

Julia shrugged. "I know. But it doesn't matter. I've

been busy manning phones and ushering in visitors. I doubt I could have escaped if I wanted to.'' Julia handed the appointment book over to Tessa.

"I see Edward's been here,'' Tessa remarked.

"Yeah, for about five minutes. Who is that guy?'' Julia tossed the remains of her sandwich into the trash.

"Alex's private investigator. He's the one who's been busy uncovering the situation in Florida. But if he was in here for only five minutes it's more than likely you were his subject.''

"Alex had me investigated?'' Julia felt dumbfounded. "Me?''

"Yes,'' Tessa confirmed with a knowing nod. "He probably put Edward on it after he found you in his house. That would be how Alex works. He still doesn't know if you're trustworthy.''

"He had me investigated!'' Julia's panic was evident and she slid her chair back from the table. "Investigated.''

"Of course,'' Tessa's voice failed to soothe Julia's ruffled feathers. "You're an unknown entity. Corporate espionage is big business. Who knows what you were looking for when you were in his house?''

"What am I going to do?'' Julia slumped back into her chair, ready to concede defeat. "He knows. He's got to know. I mean, my real social security number is on my job application. There's no way the investigator missed that.''

"Julia!'' Julia jumped as the her phone buzzed and Alex's deep voice boomed through the intercom.

With a furtive look at Tessa, she pressed the button. "Yes, Mr. Ravenwood?''

"Come in here please. Pronto.''

"Yes, sir.'' Julia gulped and rose unsteadily from her

chair. This must be how a condemned man felt, she thought.

"Julia!" Tessa was attempting to say something, but Julia ignored her and, footsteps heavy, walked toward the wooden doors.

"Oh, for goodness' sake." Tessa shrugged her shoulders and rolled her eyes. "Amateur. As if we wouldn't have expected this, too." With a disdainful sniff she headed back to her own office.

AS IF IN SLOW MOTION, Alex stood up from behind his desk. Despite her concern, Julia's subconscious reacted to his smooth grace and her heart raced.

"Julia? What's wrong?" Alex set the file folder down on his desk. He reached up behind to rub his neck before taking a step toward her. "Are you feeling okay? You look a little peaked."

Whatever Julia had been expecting, it wasn't for Alex to be concerned. "No, I'm not okay." Julia choked on the words. Perhaps, if she confessed now, he would go easy on her.

For a moment Alex looked confused and he stared at Julia. "Ah. Edward. Actually, that's why I called you in here. I'm sorry you found out before I had a chance to tell you that I have everyone investigated. Standard policy. Anyway, I called you in here so you could see your file. I don't believe in secrets, so I thought you might want to take a look."

Julia felt her hopes sink, and she hoped Alex couldn't tell her knees were shaking. "Really, that's okay. I don't want to see it. Maybe it's for the best." She hovered over his desk, keeping her hands to her side to keep them from trembling. How he must hate her.

Alex's blue eyes narrowed, and the silence grew

heavy in the room. Then he shrugged. With an elaborate flick he tossed the file folder onto the edge of the desk nearest her. "There's nothing to it. Sure you don't want to peek? Unless there's something you're hiding that you want to tell me?"

Was he toying with her? Waiting for her confession? Unable to bear his look when she confirmed his suspicions, she decided the file folder route was best. She picked up the folder and scanned the report quickly.

She caught a deep breath and her chest heaved with relief. She calmed down and put the sheet of paper back. Now she understood why the P.I. had given her a message for Chelsea. The report made no mention of Rachel Juliana Grayson. Edward had only confirmed the facts listed on Julia's employment application.

Julia exhaled slowly. "Okay," she said finally. "You were right."

"Julia." Alex's voice called her back.

"Yes, Mr. Ravenwood?" Julia turned slightly but made no move.

Alex stared at her oddly for a moment. "Nothing, Julia. Nothing at all. Get Scott Meier on the line for me, will you?"

"Certainly." Her nerves frayed, Julia left the office, wondering why Alex would want Scott. Well, they were best friends and Alex probably wanted to check on Chelsea.

Julia was grateful the rest of the day passed without any more excitement, and at four o'clock she foraged a candy bar from her purse and headed for the lounge. When she returned fifteen minutes later, she found Tessa perched over her desk like a mother hen.

"I've dealt with Lydia." Tessa announced without further ado. "I left a message that Alex got her call."

"Thanks. That's a relief." Julia settled back down into Rita's comfortable chair. "I appreciate it. Two more weeks of this sounds like an awful long time."

"You'll be fine." Tessa rolled her eyes. Julia knew Tessa thought Julia was a wimp. "Really, you need to have more of a stomach for these things. You're such a baby."

"You try having your cover almost blown."

"Well, it wasn't. Chelsea knows her brother well enough. We prepared for everything."

"I don't want to know about it." Julia cut Tessa off and leaned forward to doodle on a memo pad. "I'm beginning to believe this job isn't worth the money at the cost of my sanity."

"Think of it as a good cause." Tessa smiled encouragingly. "You'll free Chelsea from having Lydia as an in-law. That's got to be worth something."

"I guess. She's gotten me out of a few scrapes." Julia threw up her hands and tossed down the pen. "So, did you tell Alex that Lydia canceled already?"

"Uh, no. Not yet. I was going to let you do that, but you'd vanished."

Julia glared at Tessa in disbelief. "I was in the lounge."

"Well, you could have told me where you were going." Obviously Tessa was miffed.

"Tessa, Just give me the fax so I can go tell Alex." Julia said. She couldn't believe this.

Tessa held out the fax and Julia snatched it. She entered the office, took a look around and strode back out.

Tessa looked sorry. "Uh, Julia, he's not in there."

"That was obvious." Julia spun on her heel, sending the layers of black beads around her neck flying. "Where did he go?"

"He left while you were on break." Tessa studied her fingertip. "Don't worry, I fixed it so the fax looks like it came through minutes ago."

"For what good that's going to do me. He's not here to read it!" Julia shrieked, incredulous.

"No, you'll have to take it to him." Tessa looked pitiful, but Julia didn't feel sorry for her. "Really, Julia, I'm sorry. It's the only way."

Julia mentally cursed, using a few words learned from Lydia. "Fine. Where is the Buscholtz Gallery anyway?"

"It's not too far. You'll be in and out in a flash. Let me get some petty cash for a cab."

Julia heaved her shoulders in disgust and reached for her purse. She had planned on spending a quiet evening reading and watching old movies. The last thing she wanted to do was track Alex down at some ritzy art gallery while dressed like a pauper.

"Here," Tessa said, pressing a wad of bills into her hands. "Don't worry about a receipt. It's the least I can do."

Julia headed for the elevator, muttering under her breath. "The very least."

Chapter Five

Located near the Smithsonian Museum and the Mall, the Buscholtz gallery was an unassuming building from the outside. However, Julia knew that as soon as she stepped through the doors she was in for one of the worst moments of her life.

With a deep breath, Julia smoothed down the multi-colored gauzy gypsy skirt that fell to the ankles of the black combat boots that had become her staple. She was wearing the same black blazer she had worn on her first day over two brightly colored tank tops. Strand after strand of black beads layered around her neck and her chest. Julia Brown certainly did not look like any of the District's elite. A bit self-consciously she adjusted the huge black drawstring bag and clutched the fax.

Taking another deep breath, she grabbed the heavy wooden door and pulled.

Cold air-conditioned air assaulted her on its quest for the July heat, and although the temperature inside the building was twenty degrees cooler, Julia still felt herself sweat as she entered.

A young, beautiful blond woman dressed in a blue power suit looked over at her, and Julia could feel the woman's immediate disdain as she approached.

"Hello, miss?" The blonde's silky voice was curt yet brutally polite. Julia was only slightly relieved at not being thrown out on her ear already.

"Brown, Julia Brown," Julia offered, steeling herself.

"Are you on the guest list?" The woman reached for a clipboard that rested on a marble-topped table. Julia glanced into an anteroom, but there was no sign of Alex.

"Actually, I'm not." Julia smiled, but it didn't quite reach her eyes. The wig itched, and Julia reached up to scratch her head. The woman looked at Julia as if she were waiting for the dandruff to fall. "I'm Alex Ravenwood's secretary and I need to speak with him."

"Really now." The blonde became openly contemptuous. The sneer on her face radiated her disbelief. "That's definitely a new one."

"Yes, I'm sure it is." Julia's tone turned haughty. "But since it's the truth, why don't you just run on in there and tell him Julia Brown is standing here and see what he says, hmm?"

The woman looked down her nose at Julia. Julia bristled. How many times had she received the same looks before she met Chelsea? Bitterly she wondered what the woman would say if she came back sans her Julia Brown disguise.

"Look, I promise I'll stand right here," Julia offered sarcastically. "Or is there a room you'd rather hide me in?"

"Why don't you wait right over there." The woman set the clipboard down and gestured to a small, antique wrought iron bench. "I'll go have someone locate him."

"You do that." Julia gave the snobby woman a trite

smile. The woman walked over to another equally well dressed woman and whispered something in her ear. The second lady appeared surprised at being disturbed. She looked at Julia with derision, sniffed, and then turned and disappeared into the back of the gallery. Julia assumed she must be the gallery owner. The first woman returned to managing her clipboard. Still Julia felt the woman keep an eagle eye on her as if she were afraid Julia was going to escape from her seat on the uncomfortable bench and mingle with the upper crust. Yeah, right.

"Julia! What are you doing here?" Alex's voice cut across the foyer. Julia turned to the lady and gave her a self-satisfied 'I told you' so smirk. The woman made a show of studying her clipboard.

"Mr. Ravenwood." Julia gave him a professional smile as her stomach dropped. She hadn't seen Alex in a tuxedo since Chelsea's wedding and the effect made her knees go weak. "This is becoming rather old, but neither Tessa nor I could find your cell phone number. You've got another fax and I'm afraid this one is bad news."

The two women hovered nearby as Julia handed Alex the fax. Now that Alex was beside her she felt bolder, and so she turned up her nose at them and deliberately toyed with her beads. "I'm sorry, Mr. Ravenwood, but I thought you would want to know. I hope I did the right thing by bringing it to you."

"Bad news, Alex?" The gallery owner slunk up next to him. Julia studied her makeup, and decided the woman was wearing way too much of it. Julia, with tons of theater makeup on to give her a washed-out appearance, ought to know.

"Yes, Angela. Lydia's shoot in Hawaii was extended

for a week. We were going to meet here and then go to dinner, but she won't be able to make it.'' Alex said. He missed the delighted gleam that crossed Angela's face, but Julia saw it and felt ill.

"How efficient for your secretary to let you know,'' Angela said, linking her arm through Alex's. "Did the fax just arrive?''

"Looks that way. Lydia says she's been at the shoot all morning and this was the first break she got. I guess it's about lunchtime in Hawaii.'' Alex studied the fax again.

"Well, you must let me make it up to you,'' Angela purred into his ear. "I'll make sure I personally introduce you to everyone.''

I bet you will, Julia thought derisively. She wrinkled her mouth disdainfully at Angela's obvious come-on. At least the clipboard snob, as Julia had dubbed her, was checking in some new guests and had left the scene. Enough of this madness, Julia decided and she coughed.

Both Alex and Angela turned to her in surprise. "Mr. Ravenwood, if there is nothing else?'' Julia queried with a bored expression on her face.

Alex turned and looked fully at her and Julia saw a wicked grin appear on his face. "Not unless you want to see the art, Julia? I'd be happy to show it to you.''

Angela's face mirrored her horror at the thought of Julia stepping foot amongst the haute couture. Julia could almost hear Angela's thoughts—gypsy trash among the elite. Angela regained her composure and smiled benignly at Julia. "I'm sure she'd rather go home, Alex. Wouldn't you, dear?''

Alex ignored Angela. "Oh, come now, Julia, wouldn't you enjoy a little culture?''

"Not really.'' Although her heart flipped, Julia refused to accept Alex's bait. However she did have to admit to herself that the thought of grunging among the elite attached to one of the area's most eligible bachelors did hold great irritation potential. "I don't spend my leisure time on this stuffed shirt stuff. Rather boring. Remember we talked about it just this morning."

"I remember." Alex's amused smile sent quivers down Julia's spine.

"Well, it's a pity Lydia couldn't make it, but we just won't let that spoil your evening, Alex," Angela interjected, obviously relieved at Julia's refusal of the invitation. "Go ahead and run along dear. I'm sure you're off duty now and have friends you want to catch up with. The Smithsonian stop is just around the corner."

Julia gave Angela a saccharin smile. "Thank you. I'd hate to get lost. This just ain't my digs, you know? Besides, with all the crime and stuff I'd hate to be around here after dark."

Angela looked suitably horrified.

"Do you have money for a cab today, Julia?" Alex sent her a dubious look that barely concealed his mirth. Julia shot him a glance that told him she knew he wasn't laughing at her, but with her.

Julia couldn't resist the bait he was dangling this time. "Oh, yes, Mr. Ravenwood. I stole all the petty cash funds before I left. I'm planning on treating myself to dinner with the leftovers."

Let him fire her, she thought as she saw Angela's mortified expression. She was going crazy anyway! She should be spending her three-week vacation on the beach or in St. Louis with her family, not playing secretary!

"Oh, so you're buying?" Alex disengaged himself gently from Angela's arm.

"That's right," Julia said proudly. "Bud's Beer and Bowling has a Friday night special. All the pizza you can eat, pitchers of brew, and a bowling ball to boot. I'll have to travel over the tracks to get there, but…"

"Well, how can a man resist a place like that?" He leaned over to peck Angela lightly on the cheek. "It's been a great show, Angela, but Bud's is in a rather seedy part of town. Since she's the most efficient secretary I've got, surely you understand why I can't let her go to Bud's alone with all of my petty cash. Come on, Julia."

With that, Alex ushered Julia past the shocked faces of the two women and quickly out of the art gallery. The July heat enveloped them immediately.

"You know, you've got guts," Alex said approvingly.

"Thanks. I just couldn't let them go unchallenged. People shouldn't be judged on appearances." Julia let out a long breath. Now that the adrenaline rush was over, she didn't feel as gutsy as she followed Alex toward the Metro stop.

"So, is there really a Bud's?" Alex turned to her as they waited for a walk sign.

"I don't know. I made it up," Julia replied. "Why?"

"Because the way I see it, your delivering this fax has been a lifesaver. And since Lydia has cheated me out of dinner, I think I'll just have whatever you are having."

"I, uh." Julia found herself being guided down the escalator and into the coolness of the Metro stop. Alex paused at the fare card machine and bought two tickets. Soon he had both of them seated on the blue line headed north.

"So, Julia my rescuer, why don't you show me someplace where you enjoy going and where I can just be like the normal, everyday Joe?'' Alex's hand was dangerously close to hers as they both held on to the metal bars. All of the seats were full. ''What's your favorite restaurant?''

''I've only been in town a week,'' Julia answered, trying to keep her balance. ''But I've eaten a couple times at Marcel's, a place on Connecticut across from my apartment.''

Alex put his arm on her back and ushered her off at Metro Center so they could transfer to the red line. Julia felt tremors from his hands and from his words. ''Sounds ideal. We'll go there.''

''JULIA! *MON AMI*!'' Marcel himself greeted Julia as they entered. ''What have you done to your hair? It's....'' The elderly French man fingered the hair that was normally blond when she came in.

''Black,'' Julia finished for the portly man who had long outgrown the tuxedo he wore with pride. ''Drop it, Marcel, or we're leaving.''

Marcel dropped the strand of black hair and turned to see the person Julia was referring to. Alex saw the surprise cross the man's face.

''Bella! You have a date! You grace us when you come alone, but to bring a man to Marcel's, I am so honored!'' Marcel beamed as Alex stepped into view. ''Ah, and he wears a tux! Such class you bring to Marcel's! I give you your favorite table, *oui?*'' Marcel led Alex and Julia through the small one-room restaurant that hosted twenty-five tables and an open stone oven in one corner.

Marcel grinned like a proud, approving papa when Alex pulled Julia's seat out for her. Marcel had seated them opposite the oven, and he clapped his hands and gestured to a waiter.

"Peter, Julia's here with a date! Make sure you treat her extra special tonight." Peter nodded as Marcel continued. "Go get them a bottle of the burgundy and start them on bread." Peter walked off as Marcel continued to smile delightedly at them.

Alex stared at the man strangely. Marcel, in his tight tuxedo, looked like an oddity, but the restaurant itself was even odder. All the tables in Marcel's were covered with red and white checkered tablecloths, white cloth napkins, a votive candle, wineglasses and silverware. The three waiters dressed formally, the restaurant being a gaudy attempt to imitate an opulent French café. Yet, despite the fact that no menus were in evidence, everyone around seemed to be eating. Some patrons were even happily drinking at the small wooden bar.

"I am serving roast duck," Marcel said, and Alex snapped to attention. "You'll love it, Julia, and I'll even leave off the mushrooms, but only for you." He eyed Alex skeptically. "You eat the mushrooms, *oui?*" Alex nodded his confused assent. "Good. Mushrooms are Julia's one flaw, but I digress. After the duck I surprise you with dessert. Peter will bring you everything you need. Enjoy your feast!"

And with that he left them.

"I take it we're having roast duck." Alex felt slightly disoriented. He had never been to a restaurant where the waiter told the customer what they would eat.

"I've heard it's one of Marcel's favorite things to cook," Julia confirmed. "Everyone lines up when he has roast duck. You'll start to see the wait begin as soon as those last two tables fill up. We're on the early side."

"Is he cooking anything else?" Alex's voice came out sounding slightly strangled.

"No." Julia shrugged as if it was of no consequence. "Marcel cooks whatever he feels like and you eat it. That's half the fun. There's always a crowd, and when you get the bill you'll die at how reasonable it is."

"I see," Alex said, although he really didn't. In fact he had lost track of seeing things clearly a while ago, but he couldn't put his finger on exactly when.

"Just remember," Julia chided him gently from across the intimate table for two, "you wanted to go where you could be an average Joe. This is it."

"I just find it odd that you've become such a fixture here when you've only been here a couple of times?"

"Well, tonight makes four. Marcel's is very good, and my apartment is just over there."

Alex leaned back in his chair as Peter brought a carafe of burgundy wine and a basket of baguettes. Peter disappeared as fast as he had come.

Julia grabbed one of the loaves of bread and put it on her plate. With dexterity she placed her napkin in her lap, reached for her knife and began to cut into the roll. "These are homemade." She pointed to the basket with her knife and grabbed the butter and began to unwrap the little packet. "Marcel's wife, Marie, does all the cooking and baking."

Alex shook his head in disbelief. Feeling warm, he shed his jacket. He placed it over the back of his chair and began to undo the bow tie. "You don't mind, do you?"

"If I did, it's a bit late," Julia replied, stuffing her mouth with another bite as Alex rolled up the shirt-sleeves. The dark hair on his arms glistened in the candlelight.

"Wine?" Alex reached for the carafe and poured her a glass. He proceeded to pour himself one and then held his glass up. Julia was already in mid-sip.

"Oh, sorry." She set her glass down and wiped her lip with her napkin. "I didn't know you wanted to toast." She retrieved the glass and held it up.

"To an intriguing two more weeks." Alex watched her face flush. "I have a feeling that they are not going to be boring."

"I'll drink to that." Julia clinked her glass to his before taking another sip. "So, Mr. Ravenwood, you've never been to a place like Marcel's?"

"Call me Alex, Julia. And no, I can't say that I have," Alex replied as he began to butter his bread. "I like it. It's comfortable."

"No paparazzi." Julia gave him a warm smile. "Just people who eat here all the time. See those two over there?" Alex picked out an elderly couple sitting at a table for two next to the wall. "That's Mr. and Mrs. Johnson. They eat here every night. Mr. Johnson hates his wife's cooking, but he desperately loves his wife, so they're part of what Marcel calls his extended family. They've been in here for at least five years. Others in here have been coming for longer. I've only been coming in less than a week but already I'm welcome. It's homey. Marcel knows everyone. He's a fixture in the neighborhood. Everyone knows everyone and everyone knows Marcel."

"Wow! This is good." Marie's baguette melted in Alex's mouth. Impressed, he took another bite.

"Told you." Julia pursed her lips. "This time you didn't believe me. Just because food is inexpensive doesn't mean it tastes terrible."

"Ah, the snob factor you rescued me from tonight."

Alex gave Julia a cheeky smile. "How can I ever repay you for saving me from the clutches of those women?"

"Eat," Julia commanded.

At her command Alex swore he saw Julia blush. Despite the paleness of her skin, he was able to see the tiny bit of rosy color spread across her cheekbones. In fact, in the candlelight Julia's face seemed a little less ashen and sallow. Alex took another sip of the wine that was surprisingly quite good.

"So, Julia, this restaurant is one thing that makes you tick. What's another?" Alex bit into a roll.

"Like what?" Julia looked slightly flustered.

"Hobbies. Interests? You know, stuff like that." Alex set his bread down on the plate in order to give Julia his full attention.

"Well, I'm into movies. I love them. I always thought I would like to write a script someday, but that's just a pipe dream. Anyway, my favorites are usually romantic comedies both old and new, although I will go for a good action flick occasionally."

"Favorite actor." Alex leaned back to study Julia. As she talked about movies she had gotten animated and he wanted to keep the adrenaline going.

"Harrison Ford." Julia gave a wistful sigh, and Alex inwardly groaned. She made sighing seem sensual. "He's someone I would love to meet someday. I mean, he's in my top ten actors of all time, right up there with Cary Grant, Humphrey Bogart, Jimmy Stewart and John Wayne."

"I like his movies." Alex surrendered an approving nod. "So we have something in common." He watched as Peter unobtrusively put salads in front of them.

"I like all of them." Julia dug into her salad as if she hadn't eaten anything for days. Either that or she was nervous. Alex couldn't tell. Everything Julia did, for some reason, confused him, and he was a man who didn't like confusion one bit.

"Actually," Julia said as she finished her bite, "I guess I'm a rabid Harrison Ford fan. He was very sexy to a young impressionable girl who had rented all the movies he ever made one weekend."

"You really did that?" Alex chuckled. Julia was definitely a refreshing enigma.

"Sure." Julia shrugged. "What else was I to do when everyone was at the junior-senior prom except me?"

"Surely you didn't miss prom?" Alex felt his chest tighten. Her admission surprised him. No one sat at home during prom night, did they?

"No, not my senior year. My senior prom was the only school dance I ever attended." Julia chewed on her salad and swallowed. Alex waited for the rest of the story as Julia's gaze shifted to study the stone fireplace.

"I had already gotten a dress when my boyfriend broke up with me, so two of my friends fixed me up with Karl Choate. I was on the newspaper staff with him and he was just a nice guy. After prom we stood on my doorstep and talked. Just when he was about to kiss me, my mom came out and told me to stop leaning on the doorbell. It was rather embarrassing."

Alex could feel every bit of her terrible teenage awkwardness, and it pained him. He didn't like that Julia had suffered, and deliberately he switched the subject, moving it away from Julia's sad memory. "My most embarrassing moment was when I had my first date and forgot to zip my fly. It was open the whole evening."

Julia stopped looking at the fireplace and turned to smile at him. Her smile made his revelation about himself worth it. Her mood lightened and she giggled, making a sound like silver bells. Alex was glad he had cheered her up. Then she shocked him with her reply. "You know, Alex, that could have come in handy at the end of the evening."

"Julia!" Alex exclaimed. His skin prickled.

Julia shot him a wicked look and sipped her wine. Her lips poised seductively on the glass and his heart raced. "Ah, if the shoe fits," she mumbled mischievously.

"You may find that shoe where you don't want it," Alex retorted easily, again back in control.

"I'm trembling." Julia faked a quiver of fear and her shoulders shook.

"Ooh, that's it." Alex put his hands together and applauded. Finally Julia's true personality was coming through. He knew she had a sense of humor lurking under the surface. "Go ahead, Julia. Show me how it's done."

Julia's mouth dropped open. She was speechless. Alex grinned, satisfaction pumping through his veins.

"Gotcha!" Alex quipped as Peter set down plates of roast duck, roasted potatoes, and a vegetable medley. For once, he had managed to confuse Julia instead of it being the other way around. "Don't mess with a master."

"I'll have to remember that." Julia said, still trying to regain her composure before bursting into laughter.

Alex gave her a knowing look and laughed with her. "Be sure that you do."

Julia stuffed another bite in her mouth to save herself from a retort. Alex grinned. He definitely appreciated a woman who knew to quit when she was ahead.

Marcel followed the roast duck with a sinful chocolate confection drenched in raspberry sauce, and when their stomachs were stuffed absolutely full, Julia and Alex finally made their way to the door.

Dinner had been good; no, it had been great, Alex decided. Despite his initial reservation about her, Julia was turning out to be one of the most intriguing and interesting people he had ever met. There was a freshness to her, a novelty that was lacking in the sophisticated glamour women he usually associated with. Not quite the girl next door, she was a multilayered beguiling mass of contradictions and inconsistencies. Marcel obviously doted on Julia, making one last disapproving comment about her hair before Julia and Alex left.

"It's just a short walk," Julia told him as they crossed Connecticut Avenue and headed the one block to her apartment building.

Julia's apartment building was rather plain from the outside, but Alex knew it was still a fashionable and moderately expensive address. He was a bit surprised by her housing choice. "You live here?"

"Yes. I sublet. It's a close walk to the Metro and I've got a great view of Rock Creek park. I haven't seen the whole parkway, but the view I've got looks pretty neat." She blinked at him through the thick myopic lenses.

"I'll walk you to your door."

"No, really, it's very safe, once I'm in the building," Julia said, declining graciously. "Besides, the Marriot's right over there." Julia pointed up the hill at the next building over, and Alex saw the brightly lit hotel. "They don't put Marriots in dumpy areas. Besides no one's bothered me yet. Just ignore the graffiti on some of the buildings on Connecticut. It's pretty old."

"Well then, good night." Alex watched as Julia

turned and went through the glass door into the foyer. He turned to leave as she headed for the elevators.

Alex smiled to himself and stood there long after she had disappeared. Tonight had been a success. He had begun to scratch the surface of what was turning into an intriguing mystery. Julia was worth getting to know. He brushed a piece of dust off his sleeve as he turned to leave, when it was obvious she wasn't returning to invite him up.

He shook his head. What was he planning to do if he went up to her apartment anyway? Hadn't he decided she could keep her secrets a little longer? A wicked thought suddenly crossed his mind as to what they could be doing. He brushed it aside as he headed up the hill to the Woodley Park-Zoo Metro stop. He really was a cad.

THE NEXT DAY JULIA watched out the window as Alex drove his black Corvette convertible into Chelsea's driveway promptly at noon.

"I can't believe you did this to me," Julia whispered to Chelsea as the latter pushed the curtains back into place.

"Yeah, right." Chelsea's disbelief was obvious in the smug grin she wore. "I saw you pining over his picture during college. Go and enjoy yourself. Besides, you're the decoy for his surprise party tonight. He's clueless, and you don't look anything like his temp. She's got stringy black hair, sickly white skin and nerd glasses. You're a natural blonde with a healthy tan. It's a great disguise and this will be a great ruse to get Alex out of here for a while so I can get everything set up."

"If you say so." Julia didn't mirror Chelsea's confident attitude. "And, for your information, I didn't pine over his picture."

Chelsea patted her tummy and gave Julia a dubious grin. "If you say so."

"But what if he recognizes me?"

"Then kiss him and make him forget."

"Chelsea!"

"Well?" Chelsea laughed. "It works when I need to distract Scott!"

"This is not the same situation."

"But it could be." Chelsea rubbed her tummy again. "Then you could be my sister-in-law with babies of your own."

"Fat chance." Julia grimaced before smiling to herself. Despite Chelsea's silly comments, Julia knew the risk of discovery was worth it. Her dreams were a reality. She would be spending all day with Alex, and that would be enough. Then, when they returned to Chelsea's house, he would be greeted by family and friends yelling "Surprise."

"Hey, there you are." Alex strode easily into the room. Julia shivered at his dominating presence. "Are you ready, Rachel? I'm starved."

"I'm ready." Julia grabbed her purse, ignoring the downside of being called Rachel all day. It was more than tolerable since it meant she could be herself with Alex all day. She had followed Chelsea's advice and dressed casually in shorts and a knit top. He wore khaki shorts and a polo shirt, and she swallowed at the sight of his muscular legs.

"Well, we've got a great day. It's only in the eighties. I see you're ready to do some walking."

"I am," Julia replied as she glanced at her dirty white Keds.

"You two have fun," Chelsea said. She gave Julia a hug and whispered in Julia's ear so that only she heard. "Don't bring him back before five."

"I'll try," Julia promised aloud.

"Of course we'll have fun." Alex grinned as he misinterpreted her words. "I've never let anyone down yet."

After stopping for lunch at Union Station, Alex bought a one-use disposable camera and proceeded to give Chelsea's best friend the whirlwind tour of Washington. They drove by the Capitol. They walked the entire Mall from the Smithsonian buildings, past the Washington Monument, and the reflecting pool. Both were slightly out of breath by the time they raced each other to the top of the steps to the Lincoln Memorial. After taking a half a dozen photographs, she still hadn't lost her energy.

Watching her was amazing. Her excitement was so contagious Alex had had to resist kissing her under Abe's watchful stare. For a moment he wondered what would happen if he did. Would she tell him what she was running from? Would she open up and reveal her secrets? He wanted her to. He needed her to be honest with him.

He frowned slightly, feeling the crease across his brow. Although he valued honesty, he normally didn't care what a woman kept from him because he never saw anyone long enough to worry about it. He had been deceived once, when he was in college, and the experience of almost being trapped into marriage had made him twice shy. Even with Lydia he still kept his emotional distance. With her modeling career she kept geographic distance, too, which was probably why he kept seeing her. She warded off the other Mrs. Alex Ravenwood wanna-be's.

But there was something about Rachel that was different. Something that drew him back and made him want to be with her. Even everyday scenes he took for granted were novel when viewed through her eyes.

They descended the steps and walked to the Vietnam Memorial, where she choked up when she ran her finger over some names etched on the black stone. Later she oohed and aahed over the White House even though no tours were available and all she could see of the mansion was through the wrought iron fence.

She had even listened to some protesters on Pennsylvania Avenue before Alex had pulled her away from their propaganda under the guise of doing some shopping.

Yes, it had been a great day, Alex thought as the wind played with his hair. He had dropped the tan top of the Corvette, and he watched as she leaned back against the leather seat and let the warm breeze tousle her blond hair. Rachel reached forward and pushed a strand back, and then stuck her hands straight up and out into the full force of the wind as Alex headed north up Connecticut Avenue.

Alex pressed the gas pedal a little harder, the g-force pushing her back into the light oak leather sport seat. She brought her hands back inside the car and laughed.

"I take it you like my car."

She turned her head toward him, her childlike exuberance obvious.

"I love it!" After digging in her purse, she pulled out a hair tie and drew her golden hair up into a ponytail. Alex couldn't see the expression hidden behind her sunglasses, but it was obvious she was having fun.

"How you avoid getting speeding tickets is beyond me. I'd always be driving flat out."

Alex chuckled. Her exhilaration was infectious. This had been one of the best days he'd had in a while, and it had to be the company. More and more he knew he had deluded himself these past few months. While image mattered in his business, it wasn't everything. Even before this week he had found himself questioning if he and Lydia belonged together, if it was worth keeping her around just because she fit in when he needed her.

Once he may have thought so, but now things had changed. He had changed. He wanted the emotional satisfaction he saw in his sister's marriage, not the emptiness he so often saw in other marriages.

His current companion's reaction to his car was an excellent barometer of image. Lydia considered his expensive car a required part of the perfect society image she projected. Rachel enjoyed his car for what it was, a powerful driving machine. A wicked, decadent thought crept into his consciousness, and Alex allowed it to take root. He glanced over at Rachel. She had leaned her head back and was feeling the breeze play with her face. Her blond hair framed her from the way the wind plastered her against the seat.

Time to loosen her up.

"So, have you ever driven one of these?"

"I wish!" She sighed and pressed the button that cycled the twelve-disc CD changer. Instantly a barrage of screeching rock blared out of the Bose speaker and amplifier system.

Alex laughed as he saw her quirked eyebrow. "Okay, so I secretly listen to heavy metal. Don't tell anyone. You'll ruin my reputation. They think I just like Bach and Beethoven."

"Alex Ravenwood listens to Metallica." Rachel giggled. "I wouldn't have believed it if I hadn't heard it for myself."

"Just because I turned thirty-six today doesn't mean I'm dead," Alex protested. "I only found three gray hairs."

"You don't have any gray hairs." She rested her arm on the black leather divider between the seats and put her head back to listen to the thumping bass.

Alex glanced at her fingers, tapping along with the beat. Her hands were long and slim, and her short fingernails naked of all polish. He frowned slightly, wishing that he had purchased a stick shift. Then he could downshift at the light he was approaching, and slide his hand over hers when they came to a full stop.

He gripped the steering wheel tighter in his right hand and placed his left arm on the door's armrest as he braked the car and waited at the light. It would be so easy to reach over, switch the ride control from sport to tour, and then place his hand over hers, but that would be a mistake and he knew it.

Chelsea's wedding reception had sent enough danger signals to his brain where Rachel Juliana Grayson was concerned. When he had danced with her he had discovered there was something fresh and tantalizing about Chelsea's elusive roommate. One dance had sent him running back to the safety of his own date, for when he touched his date he wasn't overcome with fireworks and sparks. There had been only one woman who had ever charged him with enough electricity to power a small city. And because of Chelsea's scheme, she was once again in his life.

Alex pressed the accelerator with a new determination, and quickly cut over to the left lane. The car's movement jolted Rachel, and she looked up at him expectantly.

"This is my secretary's apartment building." Alex pointed it out as he pulled into the circular driveway.

"Is there a reason we're here?"

"Yep." He leaned over to her and pressed the release button on her seat belt. "Change of plans."

Chapter Six

Alex had never seen such panic before, but he knew he had to continue.

"I don't understand."

Her lip quivered and Alex reached out a finger to silence it. The shock that ricocheted through him was almost his undoing, but he managed to pull his hand away and unstrap his own seat belt.

"Trust me." He gave her what he hoped was a reassuring smile.

"Alex!" She looked scared. The car was still running, and Metallica still blared, louder now that there was no wind resistance to carry the sound away.

He laughed as he climbed out of the car and came over to the passenger door and opened it. She was so fresh, so novel. It was heartless to tease and torment her like this any longer. "You're getting your wish. Get over there and drive."

"Drive? Me?" She put a hand to her throat in disbelief and Alex saw the graceful swan neck tighten in anticipation.

"You. Drive me." Crazy, Alex didn't add as he reached for her hand and helped her out of the low-slung seat. "Get on over there. Seat adjustments are on the left side."

Following his command, she seated herself in the driver's seat. She looked over at him. "Where to?"

"Down Rock Creek Parkway. We're not supposed to be back until after five, right?"

"Uh," Rachel stammered, and Alex shot her a knowing smile.

"Believe me, this party is one I know about. Chelsea may think she can fool me but she's always failed. I've always discovered every scheme she's tried to pull over on me. So get going."

Foot down, she floored the accelerator. With a squeal of tires, the car's V-8 engine propelled the car forward. Alex flew back against the seat with thump. He grinned as she looked at him, her blond ponytail bobbing, her hands gripping the steering wheel with a pleasure almost impossible to describe. He had wanted to give her a taste of heaven, and he had. Letting her drive his car was the safest, most viable option available to him given the circumstances, although any onlooker might think differently seeing how she wove in and out of the sparse traffic. As the car sped down the tree-lined parkway, Alex relaxed and enjoyed the glorious view of the creek and the bluffs.

THEY ARRIVED AT THE PARTY at six-thirty. Chelsea was waiting on her pillared front porch when Julia brought the car screeching up the circular driveway. She braked, sending Alex forward then crashing back, and unbuckled her seat belt and waved at her friend.

"Alex let me drive! All the way down Rock Creek then back up George Washington, and then, what was that highway?"

"Four ninety-five," Alex filled in as he got out of the car.

"Then 495 to whatever the road is back to here." Julia tossed Alex his keys and pulled her hair loose. Running her fingers through her mane, she tried to get it into some sort of order. "We're not too late, are we?"

Alex ambled up to his sister and gave her a kiss on the cheek. "You told me to be sure she had fun," he teased. "And I think I succeeded. So where do you want us to go?"

"The back patio," Chelsea said, her miffed mood not lifting yet. Alex left them and headed through the house.

"I just followed directions." Julia approached Chelsea. "I hope the party's not ruined."

"No, I just was worried you'd eloped." Chelsea scratched her abdomen. "I can't believe Alex let you drive his car. He won't even let me drive it."

"It was so much fun!" Julia tossed her sunglasses and purse onto a table and scampered toward the back patio, too high from the experience of driving a Corvette to worry about Chelsea's mood change.

She heard everyone yell "Surprise," heard the party horns, and as she stepped onto the patio she got covered with confetti.

"Hey, chariot driver," Alex said, grabbing a glass of champagne from a passing waiter and handing it to her. "You're not driving anymore, so enjoy."

"Thanks." She put her lips on the edge of the glass of bubbly, aware that Alex was watching her through hooded eyes. He had shed his sunglasses somewhere, and his baby blues seemed to pierce through her. Julia took a bit of a longer sip than normal, the bubbles popping and tickling against the back of her throat.

"It's good," she said for lack of something better.

Regretting the stupidity of her words, she took another sip.

"It's Dom Pérignon."

Julia coughed a little and held the champagne flute out as if afraid it would spill on her. Alex laughed at her stricken expression.

"This is expensive!" She sputtered as she found her breath. "All we used to drink in college was the cheap stuff."

"Sorry, not this time." Alex reached out and grabbed an elbow to steady her. Julia felt the warmth from his fingers flare through her body, and coupled with the champagne, she flushed. "Come on, there are people I want you to meet."

By eleven o'clock Chelsea's Southern barbecue surprise party had been declared a rousing success. Although she and Alex were the only people in shorts, Julia felt oddly comfortable. Alex had made a big issue of telling people that she had been his kidnapper. He had also pretty much attached himself to her side the entire evening.

It gave her a light, fluttery feeling in her stomach.

"Why, there you are!" Julia turned to see Michael Ravenwood approaching. "Been looking for you all evening once Chelsea told me Alex brought you. Where's my boy been keeping you?"

"I've been right here." Julia smiled as Chelsea's naturally overbearing father came to stand beside her.

"So, it's your first time in D.C. Like it?" Being six foot three, Michael towered over her, yet Julia had never been intimidated by him. He had visited Chelsea often enough that Julia looked upon him as almost a second father.

"It's been fine," Julia said honestly. "I've gotten to do some sight-seeing."

"With Alex," Michael prompted.

"Yes. He took me around today."

Michael made a snorting sound. "'Bout time my boy found himself a woman like you instead. I'm tired of those supermodel types that only care about what they look like. Plastic, every one of them. Alex needs a wife who'll provide him with lots of babies."

"Having fun?" Alex's voice tickled her ear and she jumped a little.

"Oh!" He was smiling when she turned to face him.

"Now don't monopolize her, Dad," Alex chided. "She's got other guests to mingle with."

Michael gave another of his trademark snorts. "Bah. You're the one with monopoly on your mind. Good seeing you, dear." Julia said goodbye and gave him a peck on the cheek.

When she was alone with Alex, he repeated his question. "So, have you had fun? With the exception of my father cornering you, of course."

"I've had a great time tonight, and I love your dad. I saw him more than you."

"Well, that couldn't be very hard considering when I came to town you conveniently disappeared. It was enough to give a man a complex. One would think you were purposely avoiding me."

Julia blushed, glad the dark shadows hid most of her face. Oh, how she had avoided Alex! She had been afraid, afraid of falling in love with him then. Now, face-to-face with him, she knew she had reasons to still be worried. She was falling deeper and deeper in love with him every day. Time to change the subject, and quick. "Thanks for introducing me to so many people. They've all been really nice."

"Of course. You're Chelsea's best friend and no one wants to offend the hostess."

Alex must have seen her horrified look because he instantly put his fingers out and touched her chin.

"I'm teasing," Alex said gently. As he removed his fingers she trembled. "They liked you for you. Old Mrs. Cusack actually came to me and said 'young man, I like this one.' And she doesn't like anyone or anything."

Her mind reacting to Alex's touch, Julia felt safer scanning the remaining crowd for Mrs. Cusack. The band was finishing a song, and many couples were still dancing. "She was the one in black?"

"Right. Her husband died twenty years ago but she still wears black. I'm trying to convince her not to leave her estate to her poodle."

Julia laughed. The moment had lightened a little, although Alex's proximity made her nervous. "I guess I should be honored then."

"Definitely. By the way, this is the last song. Would you care to dance with the birthday boy?" His eyes twinkled their invitation, and Julia gulped.

"Really, it's getting late, and I…"

"No excuses. You've only got to go inside to be home." Alex leaned forward to whisper in her ear. His voice was deep, husky and oh so tempting. "And if I remember right, you still owe me a dance from the wedding."

Julia blinked. Her voice came out a mere whisper as she pretended she had forgotten the promised dance. "I do?"

"Yes. You only gave me one. I told you I would be back, but you disappeared after dancing with Will. It was pretty funny watching him try to impress you, but I can imagine he got on your nerves.''

Julia giggled. Her voice sounded nervous as she tried to find safe footing. ''He kept insisting I looked nineteen instead of twenty-three. He was sweet for a seventeen-year-old. No matter what, his flattery was good for my ego.''

With Alex's reply, her safe footing vanished.

''Well, now it's my turn to flatter your ego.'' Alex reached for Julia's hands, and Julia couldn't stop herself from trembling as Alex led her to the terrace area set aside for dancing.

He pulled her to him, wrapped his arms around her and slowly led her through a slow song.

Heaven had never been this kind to Cinderella, Julia thought. She closed her eyes and leaned against the firmness of Alex's broad, steely chest. She could feel and hear his heart beating, the firm thump-thump. Julia sighed and nestled closer into his arms. His grip tightened, his step on the stone terrace sure. Julia heard the last notes fade away, and drew her head up, away from the warmth of his chest. ''Thanks for the dance.'' Her voice was barely audible.

''No, thank *you*,'' Alex said. Julia noticed his voice was a little deeper than usual.

Recognizing the end of the moment, Julia gave him a wry smile. There would be no glass slipper magic for this pretending princess—just the ordinary dingy Keds of one who was broke and leading a life of dishonest duplicity. Julia managed to somehow find her voice.

''I should go in, and you should say goodbye to your guests.''

''A waste of good moonlight.'' Alex appeared wistful as some guests approached him to say good-night.

With Alex's attention diverted, Julia seized the opportunity and slipped off down the path toward the gazebo. While she knew she should go inside and up to the guest room she was supposedly staying in, her thoughts were causing too much inner turmoil for her to sleep. With a long sigh she took a seat in the gazebo and listened to the tinkling of glasses and distant choruses of goodbyes.

Two more weeks. The thought hit her out of the blue. Two more weeks of her double life. Even Alex the movie buff wouldn't understand her deception and her deceit. Julia sighed again, her joy of the evening feeling like a bittersweet pill she had to swallow. Alex, the man of her dreams, had finally shown some interest in the real her, only she wasn't able to enjoy the reality of her fantasy.

Honesty and privacy. Julia could hear Alex's words about what he valued. As a lone mosquito buzzed somewhere on the outside of the screen, she allowed herself a resigned smile. To dance in his arms, just even one more time, had been wonderful. She had felt light as a feather, free, and for one moment, like a princess.

"I wondered where you went." The screen door opened and Alex entered the dark gazebo. "Party's over, but your bedroom door was wide-open and no one was home."

"I wasn't ready for sleep," Julia admitted. In the faint glow from the one nearly exhausted candle, she saw Alex take the seat next to hers. "The night was too magical to end. Except for Chelsea's reception, I've never been to an event like this where waiters walked around serving such expensive bottles of champagne."

"Except for college frat parties, it's all I've ever known," Alex said. In the muted darkness Julia couldn't see his expression. "So tell me, what do the St. Louis folk do?"

It was a safe topic. Julia knew she should feel relieved but she didn't. "Well, I can't speak for the upper crust, but we common folk like to hang out, barbecue and drink beer. We toss Frisbees, play washers and go to Cardinal baseball games."

"Sounds rather laid-back."

"It's nice," Julia said fondly. Despite her family's lack of riches, she had had a great upbringing. "It's going to be an adjustment when I go to New York. New York is the city that never sleeps, and I've never been away from home before."

"Yeah, I remember your one attempt at a Midwestern drawl the other day," Alex teased. "It's gone by the wayside. You just sound normal, as if you've lived here."

"I guess," Julia said. The darkness hid her fear of the big what-if. What if Alex recognized her voice was the same as his temporary secretary's? Not only that, but had she just contradicted her earlier story by telling him she was moving to New York?

He didn't seem to notice her voice or her slip of the tongue. Instead he turned the conversation another direction. "Chelsea's really enjoyed having you visit."

"I've had fun being here. Thanks for showing me the District today. With her baby scheduled to arrive I didn't know if I'd get to see anything." Julia's stomach knotted. Sitting in the candlelit darkness with Alex was destroying her equilibrium. Never had Alex seemed so much larger than life, and never had she wanted him more. She hoped she didn't sound nervous.

As if sensing her mood, Alex's hand snaked out and covered hers. His fingers wormed between hers, sending pulses of desire radiating up her arm. Julia's breath caught in her throat, and the spent candlewick wavered in the glass jar as the flame flickered for oxygen.

"I wanted to tell you I've enjoyed your visit, as well." His voice sounded closer, and Julia gasped. The candle flared and died.

In the darkness there was no more need for words. Julia had waited for what seemed like forever for her dream, and as Alex's lips claimed hers for the first time, Julia's whole world shattered into a billion slivers of light. All of her fantasies of kissing Alex had never come close to the dazzling reality.

His lips were tender, gently tasting and teasing hers. She felt his hand snake behind her neck and up into her hair. With a tug he loosened the tie and her hair cascaded to her shoulders. His tongue nudged her lips open, and Julia trembled with anticipation as his tongue slid slowly inside.

"Rachel? Rachel? Are you out here?"

At the sound of Chelsea's voice Julia jerked away from Alex. She turned her head away and stood quickly, knocking into a chair. Her knee immediately hurt with sharp pain.

"Damn." Julia let the rare cuss word slip as she felt the bruise begin.

"Are you okay?" From the sound of his movement she could tell Alex had stood.

"Fine." Julia gritted her teeth, pushed the door open and headed up the path, practically running into Chelsea.

"Hey," Julia greeted her friend. "I was in the gazebo. Is everyone gone?"

"Everyone except for you and Alex." Chelsea's gaze was speculative, and Julia looked away. "Father headed home already, and Scott and I are about to turn in. We wondered where you were.''

"Thinking about my lie, I mean life." Julia amended the Freudian slip quickly. She began to walk back up the path to the house, grateful Chelsea kept her mouth closed when they both heard the roar of the Corvette a few moments later.

IT HAD BEEN THE BEST WEEKEND, Julia mused. Her gaze landed on Lydia's happy-birthday fax. Without reading it, Julia fed the fax through the shredder and watched Lydia's message to Alex become slivered strips. Sorry, Lydia, Julia thought, but this one isn't getting through, either. Especially after the magical kiss. Julia allowed herself another blissful smile. She had been smiling a lot lately. But who wouldn't be?

Even though she knew the magic would never be repeated, she wouldn't trade the enchanted memories for anything. Unlike Kyle's paper-dry kisses that she thought were love, Alex's kisses had been pure magic. His lips had sparked a fire in her long dormant, and for the first time Julia had experienced the passionate hint of love's potential.

Julia sent a few more papers through the shredder. When she turned off the machine reality crashed in.

She hadn't seen Alex since Saturday night, having spent her entire Sunday morning making lists to help her keep her personas and their knowledge of Alex straight. Rachel knew Alex had a Corvette; Julia didn't. It was a confusing mess.

Although it was ten in the morning, Alex was un-characteristically late, his father taking him to some power breakfast with potential clients.

Unable to help it, Julia pushed reality aside. Spending

Friday evening with Alex in her Julia Brown persona had been fun, but spending all day with him Saturday as Rachel Grayson had been pure bliss.

After leaving Chelsea's early Sunday morning, lists in hand, she had spent the day in almost a daze. She had shopped on her own for books in Dupont Circle, and then walked the rest of the way up Connecticut Avenue to her apartment. The long walk had been invigorating, and when she had settled in for dinner at Marcel's she had had to give him an explanation of her hair. Yes, definitely a great weekend. Even working for Alex was turning out better than she expected.

"Hi. How are you this morning?" Alex's husky voice made Julia jump.

"Fine." Julia appraised him as he strode in. How could he look so good for a Monday? "You like sneaking up on me, don't you?"

"It's been providing me endless amusement," Alex confirmed. He grinned at her discomposure.

"I figured as much." Julia sighed in resignation, secretly pleased. "Anyway, it's been rather noisy around here today. You've got at least a dozen messages on your desk from people wishing you a happy birthday."

"Ah, the well-wishers. Reminding me that I'm one step closer to the grave." Alex nodded his approval.

Because Alex was now studying her, Julia flipped the switch and sent a blank piece of paper through the shredder. She hoped she looked productive.

She knew what he thought of her wardrobe; many times she had read it on his face when he thought she wasn't looking. Today's ensemble wasn't exceptional in its shock value except that it was large. Because of the bruise from hitting her knee on the chair, Julia had made sure to cover up her legs entirely. The navy pants were baggy, hanging on her like clown pants. The only fitted piece of clothing she wore was a black tank top, but even that was hidden beneath the navy jacket that Julia wore buttoned up despite the July heat.

Alex stepped into the small workroom, and as he came closer Julia shredded another blank piece of paper.

"Are you done in here?" Alex asked, and Julia's heart fluttered when his blue eyes darkened.

"Yes." Julia hesitated. "Is there something you need?"

"My birthday present." Alex stepped even closer, so close Julia could inhale his clean, masculine scent. "You do have a present for me, don't you, Julia?"

"Present?" Julia stammered the word, her senses reacting to his musky aftershave. He smelled wonderful.

"You did remember to get me a present, didn't you, Julia?"

"Uh," Julia began as a good excuse failed her.

"Then you'll just have to improvise." Alex stood next to her and she could feel the vibrations flowing between them. The tremors traveled directly to her body as if she were molded to his instead of being four inches away.

Her eyes focused on the closeness of his lips. Having tasted the honey of his mouth once, Julia knew how delicious a delicacy it was. "You want me to improvise?" She couldn't believe what she was hearing.

"Exactly." Alex nodded and lowered his head until he could whisper in her ear. His warm breath tickled and sent a shiver down her spine. "Are you able to improvise, Julia? Tell me the truth. Tell me what I want to hear."

The only thing Julia was sure of was that he wanted to kiss her. Oh, yes! Julia's thoughts raced inside her head, overriding the inner warnings of exposure and danger. She ignored the slight tenseness of his tone. All it would take was one small turn of her head and she could relive again the reality of the lips once felt only in her dreams.

But why would Alex want to kiss his secretary? The thought hit Julia out of the blue and she frowned. Reality scattered when she felt the two pads of Alex's fingers reach out and gently turn her face toward his.

"Penny for those thoughts."

"I'm not good on improvisations."

Julia felt her knees go weak as Alex held her chin for a moment and studied her face. She wanted to be in his arms. She wanted his mouth to claim hers and feel his tongue trace the outside of her lips.

A discreet cough made both of them start. Quickly they drew apart. Alex stepped back and Julia simply shoved a stack of blank paper in the shredder as Tessa fully entered the room.

"Happy belated birthday, Alex." Tessa gave her an inquisitive look and Julia knew to expect the third degree later. "I didn't know you'd arrived."

"I was going over the messages with Julia." Alex covered swiftly.

"Of course. Sorry I missed your surprise party. I hope it was good." Tessa pretended that she didn't notice the fact that neither of them held any pink message slips. She set a piece of paper on the photocopier and pressed ten copies before turning to face Alex.

"By the way, Lydia called and wished you a happy birthday. She also said she was sorry she missed you and hoped you'd forgive her for canceling the other night." Tessa collected her copies.

"It worked out fine," Alex said. Julia knew he was

staring at her, but she studied her left boot instead of looking back at him. "Julia, I've got nothing else. Check in with me about one, okay?"

"Sure." Julia gave him a weak smile as he left the copy room.

"I didn't know kissing him was part of your plan," Tessa started the interrogation the moment Alex was out of earshot.

Julia simply put her face in her hands. "It's not. I mean, I didn't. Nothing happened."

"I see." Tessa's gaze narrowed. "By the way, you jammed the shredder." Without another word she left a surprised Julia in her wake.

Julia pounded her fist, venting her frustration on the uncooperative machine that remained silent. Who did Alex Ravenwood think he was, asking her if she could improvise? Sure she could, she thought angrily. He'd been baiting her, all right, and as a matter of principle it was time to fight back. She left the shredder without attempting to fix it and hurried after Tessa.

"Tessa?" Upon hearing her name, Tessa turned and Julia hurried up to her. "Will you watch the fort for a while? I've got to run an errand to the bakery. It's business. Honest. I'll be back by one. I'll get a cookie there and skip lunch."

Tessa gave a humph. "Sure. By the way, get yellow cake and I'll even call maintenance for the shredder."

"Thanks," Julia waved her appreciation and darted for the elevator.

ALEX WALKED OUT of his office, and the person he was looking for wasn't where she was supposed to be.

"Where's Julia?"

"Lunch," Tessa offered. She shrugged. "I told her

I'd man the fort. It's been rather quiet, though. Did you need anything?''

Alex turned away, and then turned round to face Tessa again. "Tess?"

"Yes?" She looked at him.

"Do you notice anything odd about Julia?" He hesitated slightly, as if not sure how to proceed. "As if she's hiding something?"

Tessa stared at him blankly for a moment. "No. Not, not really. I think she's missing a few brain cells, but she seems really sweet. Why?"

"No reason." Alex ran a hand through his hair. "You did see her employment file, right?"

"Of course I did, Mr. Ravenwood." Tessa gave him a thin-lipped smile. "I typed it. Was there a problem with it?"

"No." This wasn't going the way he planned, and for some reason Alex knew he had lost the opportunity to find out answers. Of course, asking his sister's co-conspirator was probably like asking Woodward and Bernstein to reveal who Deep Throat was. "No, Tessa, I just wondered. That's all."

"If there isn't anything else?" Tessa inquired, her gaze narrowing slightly.

"No, not now." Alex turned and strode back into his office. Once he closed the double doors behind him he let out a silent curse, went back to his desk, and dialed the phone.

"Scott Meier." The voice on the other end greeted him crisply.

"Any luck on your end?"

"Alex, my man, good to hear from you. And so soon. Didn't we just talk Friday afternoon? And Saturday?" Alex could tell that Scott was laughing at him.

"This situation is driving me crazy." Alex picked up a pen and doodled on a sticky note.

"What? Rachel, Julia or the scheme?"

"All of it!" Alex groaned. "They're all the same. I mean, come on. When's she going to confess? I keep trying. I even let her drive my car." Alex omitted the fact that he had kissed her.

"Just let it play itself out," Scott advised. "Chelsea wouldn't tell me all of what she's up to, even after I tried to kiss it out of her. Hey, that's something you could try."

"Kissing my sister?" Alex stared at his scribbles. He never doodled, and absently wondered why he was starting the habit now.

"No, not her. And I know you aren't dense enough to know who I mean." Scott gave a throaty laugh. "See you later, bud, I've got a meeting in two minutes. Try the kissing. I'll have to do a lot of it myself when Chelsea finds out I squealed, but we guys have to stick together."

"A lot of help you were," Alex said with a growl as he put down the phone. "Try kissing." Although, after the time they'd spent together this weekend, maybe that's exactly what it would take.

"Right on time," Tessa observed dryly as Julia emerged from the elevator. "You've got four minutes to spare, which is good considering your makeup is sweating off. By the way, Alex came looking for you."

Silently Julia berated herself and headed to the bathroom. After reapplying the pale makeup to her tan skin, she headed into Alex's office.

Alex looked up from the computer as she entered. He

studied her for a moment. "Didn't I have any messages?"

Julia threw up her empty hands in horror and felt a crimson stain appear on her face. "I forgot them! I'll be right back."

Embarrassed, Julia returned with the messages.

Their fingers connected when Julia handed the papers to him, and again she felt the frisson of shock that occurred every time they touched. Alex lingered his touch, or had she imagined it? He was studying the slips without glancing in Julia's direction, and she took frantic notes as he made comments and returned many of the slips to her. Then Alex dismissed her with a wave.

"Oh, Julia." She was at the door, her hand on the doorknob when he called her back. "I'm going to be on the phone for a while, and I need that Alliance report on my desk by three. Also, when you finish typing those letters, don't hesitate to bring them in."

"Yes, Mr. Ravenwood," Julia agreed. "Anything else?"

"No." Alex had already turned his attention back away from her and Julia felt just a bit disappointed as she left the room. She brushed the feeling aside.

AT TEN UNTIL THREE, Julia was squirming in her chair. At five until three she was drumming her fingernails on the desk. At two minutes until three she was about to chew them all off when the elevator doors slid open and Alex's "improvisations" arrived.

"I'm from Joe's Deliveries." The tuxedoed female carrying the black helium balloons and a box approached Julia's desk.

"You're right on time." Julia rose and gave the older woman a smile. "Let me show you in."

Julia knocked on the door and entered. Alex had his back to her and was gesturing to himself as he talked on the phone.

"Look, just get it done by five. I'll be waiting for those numbers." Alex turned and placed the receiver down. "Julia. Do you have the report?"

"Uh, no." Julia gave him an apologetic shrug.

"Then what are you doing in here?" Alex seemed irritated.

"I'm improvising, Mr. Ravenwood. Just like you told me to do." Julia stepped aside as the woman entered the room.

"What?" Shock covered Alex's face as the woman handed him the black balloons and the box before she left.

Julia watched Alex hold the box in one hand and the helium balloons in another and wished she had brought her disposable camera. The look on his face was price-less, unmistakably something she and Chelsea could laugh about for years to come. Julia had done the impossible; she had managed to upend Alex's equilibrium.

"Didn't I have to tip her?" he asked, finally coming out of his shock.

"Taken care of at the time of order."

Alex set the cake and the balloons down and the "over the hill" weight allowed them to float slightly before holding them steady.

"Julia, what is this?" Alex ran a hand up the nape of his neck.

"It's your birthday present. A cake. And here you thought I'd forgotten."

"You did forget." Alex reminded her. He took his reading glasses off and set them down. The movement was somehow sexy.

"So I did," Julia admitted, pushing the ugly black frames back up her nose to hide her nervousness. "But remember you told me to improvise. And of course I must follow your orders. You say jump, I ask how high and all that. I distinctly remember you issuing me a challenge. Besides, at my other office secretaries were in charge of cakes. You also get this."

She held up a card. Alex's blue eyes held hers for a moment, the outer rims seeming to darken. For a moment Julia felt as if time had stood still. Unconsciously she put a hand to her throat.

"So, hand it to me."

Julia's heart jumped and she wondered if Alex could see it pounding beneath the layers of clothing she was wearing. With determination she squared her chin and stepped closer to Alex's awaiting fingers.

He smelled good, no, fantastic. She inhaled his clean, wholesome scent as she placed the card into his hand, her fingers feeling cool and tingly. "Open it."

"In a moment."

Julia swallowed, her body suddenly feeling a bit hotter. She wondered how silence could sound so loud. All around, her senses buzzed. Her heart was pounding in her ears, a sped-up thump-thump that she was sure could be heard in Virginia.

Alex stared at Julia strangely, watching as she began to fidget and back up toward the office doors. Alex set the card down on his desk and began to cross the short distance between them. As if hypnotized, Julia froze.

Alex stopped in front of her, barely inches away but still not touching. "This is one of the nicest things anyone's ever done." His voice came across sounding husky and she blinked. The black glasses slipped a little down her nose.

"Really?" Her voice squeaked as the word seemed to catch in her throat.

"Yes," he replied. Even though he was still not touching her, he could feel her skin prickling from his proximity. "It came from the best of motivations, Julia. Although it might have been sort of an order, you gave it to me without strings."

"Except for the balloons."

"Except the balloons," he agreed. This was working out better than he had expected. Just one little challenge had the real Julia coming forward. He decided one more push couldn't hurt. "Come here, Julia."

Just one step. He could see the debate in her eyes: longing mixed with the apprehension. He could see that Julia didn't want to take the step, knew she shouldn't make it. Ready to take Scott's advice to heart, he decided to help her along. He reached his arm forward and Julia's feet moved as if of their own volition. The next moment Alex had her in his arms.

God, holding her close felt good, and that didn't even begin to describe it. Never before had he felt that he had found a missing piece to his life. No other woman had ever made him feel like this. Julia gave a little breathless sigh, and Alex reached up to pull her glasses off. With his forefinger he rubbed the bridge of her nose. A warm flush crept across Julia's face.

"You don't need these," he said softly as he tossed the ugly black frames aside.

"No," Julia agreed breathlessly. She looked up at him, and he could feel that her body was already on fire. Her lips parted softly, already anticipating the ecstasy of the moment when his lips would touch hers.

Not yet, my pet, Alex thought as he leaned down and placed a chaste kiss on her lips. Still, he felt her shake from the sensation of that one quick kiss. Her eyes were wide-open, and unable to tease her further, he brought his lips down to press against hers. He kissed her as soft as a butterfly's landing, and time seemed to stand still. Scott was right. Kissing was definitely the way to go. He drew his lips back for just a brief millisecond before he reconnected with her eager mouth and deepened the kiss.

Julia trembled as he expanded the kiss, shooting his tongue lightly inside her lips. The fire in her body raged as his hands caressed her arms. His tongue slid over her teeth, daring them to part and let him totally inside. A low, wanton moan rushed out of her lips and suddenly Alex's mouth captured hers. Totally. Fiercely. Possessively. Julia felt his tongue slip inside her mouth and practically died from the pleasure. No one she had ever kissed had raised her passion as Alex did just by teasing the roof of her mouth.

He drew his lips away from hers just enough to murmur. Julia strained herself to hear him, but she couldn't make out his words.

But she realized the implications and the moment shattered. Reality was Julia Brown kissing Alex Ravenwood, in his office. Even if Alex never uncovered her deception, this would never be her world. No matter how much she wanted it to be, she was Rachel Juliana Grayson and he was Alexander Ravenwood.

She was the girl who could quote Jeff Foxworthy and David Letterman; he could quote Plato and Socrates and read Latin. She had dropped Spanish after two days. They had nothing in common, not even heavy metal music and Corvettes.

With all the strength she possessed, she pushed him back away from her.

"Alex, I can't. It isn't right. Whatever this feeling is, it isn't right." Her chest heaved and her heart broke as she blindly stayed her course of action.

Alex drew a hand through his hair. Obviously agitated, he began to pace before he stopped and simply threw up his hands in frustration. Julia cringed at having hurt him.

"Surely you see that there is something going on here! Something between us! Don't you think we owe it to ourselves to be honest with each other and find out? Don't you?"

"It's hormones. Close proximity," she lied shakily. Somehow she had to maintain her cover. Somehow, she couldn't let him find out. Not knowing how, she turned and stepped toward the door, just as it opened and Tessa stepped inside. A group of people stood behind her.

Tessa's eyes missed nothing, but she only said, "The gang's all here for cake."

"Over there." Julia pointed as she rushed out the door, not stopping as Alex's "Julia" got lost in the chorus of "Happy Birthday."

Chapter Seven

Julia had discovered the small bookstore near the Dupont Circle Metro stop on Sunday. She had always loved bookstores, finding them a haven in which to hide from the world, even if for just a little while. And this bookstore, with its neighborly feel, was just what she needed after the birthday disaster in Alex's office. So upon rushing out of Alex's Arlington office she had taken the Metro home and immediately stripped off the disgusting clothes, gone into her small bathroom and taken the cold cream to her face.

She had scrubbed off every bit of the sickly white pallor until her face was a rosy pink. She freed her blond hair from the hideous wig, letting it fall like silk around her shoulders. Taking a brush, she straightened the strands and started to pull them back up with a clip. Then she let it fall to her shoulders again. She had been growing out the shorter haircut since Chelsea's wedding.

God, she was such a fool. Hadn't Kyle taught her anything? He had been a costly lesson, the swindling fraud. He proved she didn't understand men at all.

So at the bookstore, more than two hours after leaving work early, Julia was curled up in a big leather wing chair reading the latest John Grisham novel and attempting to forget Alex Ravenwood. A cup of hot chocolate and a chocolate-filled pastry rested on a table by her side.

Engrossed in the story and forgetting her troubles, she almost missed the shadow that crossed over the pages. Until it became a permanent blockage of the light. She looked up to find Alex staring intently at her, and she gasped.

"Hi, Rachel." Alex gave her a devastating smile. "I thought that was you, but I wasn't sure. How do you like the book?"

A tumult of emotions ran through Julia and she stared at him blankly. He still had on the suit he had worn at the office, giving him a young, professional air. She managed to find her voice but the words came out slurred.

"Uh, it's good. I've liked it. So far." Julia held the book possessively against her chest.

"So, what are you doing in my neck of the woods?"

Relief flooded Julia. He hadn't put two and two together. If he had, Julia was certain she wouldn't be drowning in those baby-blue eyes with the outer rim of dark blue. Instead she would be drawn and quartered, and Alex would ship her home on the first plane to St. Louis.

"Chelsea's nesting and told me to get out and enjoy myself. I've spent the day at the Smithsonian, and I just didn't feel like heading back yet." Julia kept her face a pleasant mask. Just when had lies become so easy to tell? She didn't like the fact that she was becoming such a professional at it, and she took a sip from the cup. The now-cool liquid did little to wet her parched throat. She drained the last of it and shook the empty cup before setting it down. Alex was still watching her, and she squirmed a little.

"I was just about to get a cup," Alex said. "Would you like me to get you more coffee? Regular or decaf?"

"I—" Julia stopped herself before the "I don't drink coffee" rolled off her tongue. "That's sweet, Alex, but no thanks. I've got to get going."

"I'll drive you back. I live right around the corner so we can get the car. I'll even let you drive."

Julia panicked and hastily grabbed her trash. "No, Alex. Really. I'm not going to make you go all the way out and then back. Especially in rush hour."

Alex frowned and rubbed his neck. He didn't appear pleased with her answer, but Julia didn't feel like worrying about it. She just had to get away from him. "If you insist."

"I do." Julia nodded.

"Well, have a good evening then."

"You, too." She watched Alex head for the café. When he was out of sight, she picked up her fanny pack and the cup and headed for the check-out counter. Within moments she had slipped onto the Metro for the ride one stop northwest to her apartment.

ALEX WATCHED HER LEAVE. So this was how it was going to be. He had guessed she would play it this way, but he had been hoping she wouldn't. He had to admit it, he was disappointed. He thought there might be more, something there.

No wonder he had never gotten married, he thought as he took his coffee from the salesgirl with the blatant come-hither look, which he ignored. Women.

Maybe that's why he had kept Lydia around, because she never was around for long before she took off modeling. He sipped the black liquid and walked over to the business journals.

Of course, she had been dropping lots of hints lately. He'd have to do something about that, of course, but using a fax machine or voice mail just wasn't his style. He grabbed a journal and settled into the chair she had vacated. It still felt warm from Julia's presence.

Alex frowned. He would need to do something about her, too, but if this was how she was going to play it, well so be it. He allowed himself a momentary ego massage. He'd never lost to his sister yet. And he wasn't goint to start now, especially when the results of winning would be so pleasurable, so rewarding. He had felt the sparks, and he wanted the fire. And he would have it. All he had to do was have a better plan. And then Rachel Juliana Grayson, also known as Julia Brown, had better watch out.

"JULIA!" ON FRIDAY at three-forty, Alex strode out of his office holding a briefcase. "We're leaving. Grab your purse, a laptop, and come with me. The plane is waiting."

"Plane?" Julia was grabbing her stuff as Tessa appeared. "Plane?" she repeated stupidly.

She and Alex had hardly spoken all week. Ever since the kiss and the incident in the bookstore, she had avoided him. She'd hidden behind the ugly black frames and checked in with Chelsea daily in case Alex was planning to visit Chelsea's house.

Not that he did. Alex seemed to be avoiding Rachel as well as Julia. He even stopped sorting the mail with her.

"Plane." Alex repeated Julia's parroted word. "We're flying to Panama City right now. If all goes well we'll be able to come back late tonight, but don't plan on it. I know it's Friday, but this can't be helped. If you need to cancel a hot date or have someone take care of your cat you can call from the plane.''

Lugging a laptop, Julia found herself in the elevator. "I don't have a cat or a date.''

"Good, because I know we won't be back tonight.'' Alex punched the button for the ground floor. "One of our branch managers has been skimming profits and doctoring books. We've just gotten the proof we need, right before the office is to underwrite municipal bonds. I'm going to have to remove him from his position and try to keep the bond deal afloat without losing the firm's reputation. This whole thing has the potential to be a public relations disaster if not handled correctly. Anyway, the lawyers are already there, but Father always said the president is the one who must handle things like this. That's me now, so we go.''

"We go,'' Julia repeated quietly. Alex had warned her that first day. *You are at my beck and call. I say jump, you say how high.* An odd feeling came over her as the elevator descended. Within moments Alex bustled her out and into the waiting limousine.

They were hardly seated before the limo pulled away from the curb.

"Don't worry, Julia, I'll make sure you get compensated for your trouble. Chelsea or Rita usually handles these types of things, but obviously neither one is available. So you're it.''

"Oh,'' Julia said as Alex reached into the small refrigerator and took out a bottle of spring water.

He handed it to her and took out one for himself. "We'll take the company jet to Panama City and we'll be in meetings all evening.''

Julia knew he was watching to see her expression, but her black wig hid it as she sipped her water.

"As for clothes," Alex continued, "I've arranged for the hotel where we're staying to open its boutique no matter how late we arrive tonight. I want you to buy whatever you want, regardless of the cost. And, not to sound crass, but get something modern that doesn't look like you're attending a rock concert, okay? You need to look corporate for this assignment, and I expect you to do it. I always keep clothes on the plane, as does Chelsea, so see if you can fit into hers. She won't care. She can't wear them anyway."

"Yes, Mr. Ravenwood." From years of rooming with Chelsea, Julia already knew she could wear her clothes. She leaned back against the seat as Alex opened his briefcase and removed a report.

It was a nasty dilemma to be in, and after the plane took off Julia finally gave in to the inevitable when the captain announced it was safe to move about the cabin. Julia glanced at Alex. Comfortable in the plush seat, he was engrossed in a report and not paying much attention to her movements.

Julia sighed at the irony of it all. While she only had the clothes on her back to keep her disguise, even under stress Alex managed to look good. He wouldn't need to change; what he was wearing was fine. Julia decided she really liked his wire-rim glasses. As his firm fingers turned a page he glanced up at her. Being caught staring, she quickly averted her eyes.

"Clothes are in that closet," he said, before returning his attention to the report.

"Thanks," Julia covered. She got up, went to the closet and pulled out the first suit she found. She would show Alex Ravenwood that she wasn't a total loser, she

vowed to herself. Just you wait, Alex, she told herself
as she entered the lavatory. You want corporate? I'll
give you corporate.

With new determination Julia removed the annoying
wig. She freed her natural blond hair and ran both hands
through it. For five minutes she massaged her scalp until
it felt better. Then she took cold cream to her face and
removed her makeup.

For a moment or two she enjoyed seeing her normal
face again, and then she got serious about making Julia's new corporate image. She pulled the scissors from
her bag and trimmed four inches off the wig, bringing
it up to her shoulders. She brushed the edges under,
replaced the wig, and tucked up her hair. When she
reapplied the theater makeup, she made herself a shade
less pale and added some rosy color to her cheeks.

Instead of using the black liquid stick that made her
eyes appear sunken into her head, Julia deliberately
used a soft jade eyeliner that accented her eyes. Makeup
done, she dressed in Chelsea's blue power suit and surveyed the results. She frowned, and dug in her bag.
After pulling out a pair of gold wire frames, she popped
them on her nose. She hated the annoying black ones,
and with a flourish she dropped them into her bag.

Now she looked totally professional, not like the rock
concert groupie Alex thought Julia Brown must be. Provided she didn't get wet she would be in great shape.
Well, Alex, she thought with satisfaction, let's see what
you think of your temp now.

Pride filled her as she stepped out of the lavatory. As
if waiting for her, Alex's head snapped up from the
report, and his blue eyes instantly darkened. Julia felt a
momentary pang of panic, but it eased as all Alex could
do was simply stare, speechless.

Julia walked across the carpeted floor to her seat and crossed her legs the moment she sat down. The skirt came to above her knees, revealing her toned, firm muscles. Alex jerked his eyes away from her thighs and looked up at her face.

"You cut your hair. It looks good." Unconsciously he bit his lip.

"I just followed your instructions." Julia purposely shifted her position by planting her feet apart, and bringing her knees together.

"Thank you." Alex put the magazine down and, with a flick of his wrist, removed his glasses. "You look perfectly corporate. I appreciate it."

"Well, I've appreciated your efforts to pretend otherwise. In fact, Lydia told me I was quite hideous before she left. From the way you looked at me when I walked in I thought you felt the same. Anyway my hair-color job got botched so it's pretty bad, I know. But I always carry scissors, thread and makeup in my bag." Suddenly uncomfortable, Julia stood up so Alex would have no insight into her thoughts on the matter. "Is there something around here to drink?"

"You don't do soda, but I can provide bottled water," Alex told her. "There's also a full bar, or you can have juice."

"What do you want?" Julia went to rummage behind the bar.

"Bottled water."

For not knowing the plane, Julia moved with superb efficiency. She brought back two bottles of water and handed one to Alex. "How long until we land?"

"Over an hour. We'll eat whatever has been catered in for the meeting. If you're hungry there should be some snacks in the cabinet."

"No, I just wondered, that's all." Julia took a sip. The cold water soothed her parched throat.

"Sorry to just rush you off." Alex put away the report and gave Julia his full attention.

"You did warn me." Julia's fingers felt chilled from the ice-cold water, and she set it down on the table. Her fingers collided with Alex's as he did the same with his drink. She gave him an apologetic smile. "Static. Sorry."

Alex's disbelief was obvious but he remained silent. He let her remark go unchallenged.

"So." Julia spoke to fill the silence. "Tell me what to expect tonight."

Briefly he explained the situation, and then to Julia's surprise, he appeared amazed when she actually had some suggestions that sounded better than his own.

"You're staring again." Julia leaned forward slightly and waved her hand in front of Alex.

"I was thinking about what you said." Alex shook his head as if shaking off a daydream and he snapped to attention. "You've hit on some valid points."

"Lawyers are always so legalistic. I know you have to be legalistic when you fire this man, but make sure you're still compassionate." Julia took a deep breath. "Even though what he's done was illegal, he's still a person with feelings. He's just ruined the way of life he knew to pay for his wife's cancer operations and to give her the things she dreamed off before she died." Julia set down her empty bottle.

Alex nodded. "Any other thoughts?"

"Well," Julia began.

Almost two hours later the plane landed in Panama City. Alex had listened to Julia and bounced ideas off her. Julia smiled to herself. She had impressed Alex, and it felt good.

The plane taxied to a stop, and before the captain announced that it was safe to move about the cabin, Alex stood. "Julia, are you ready?"

"As I'll ever be."

Without questioning his decision, she unclicked her seat belt and moved to join him in the aisle. "I'm looking forward to seeing you in action...oh!"

It was like watching a slow-motion horror show that tried to be funny. Julia cried out in alarm as her unfamiliar blue heel became caught in the strap of the purse that lay at her feet.

Thrown off balance, Julia landed in her seat. The purse, launched like a rocket, flung wildly into the air and headed the opposite direction. Cosmetics crashed to the floor and ricocheted off the thin carpet, and Alex's foot crunched down on Julia's makeup. A cloud of light beige powder poofed up and adhered itself to his pant legs, just as his other foot caught a round tube of lipstick.

Now himself off balance, Alex lunged for support. Finding none, he lost the rest of his footing, knocked into the table, and landed with a thud on Julia's lap.

The air left both of their lungs with a whoosh, but it wasn't from the sharp impact. It was from the force and position of impact.

When Julia turned her head, Alex's lips were mere inches from hers.

Julia had no idea what Alex was feeling, but her body burned. The weight of his chest pinned her arms flat against her sides. Every nerve ending on her body was alive and singing.

Through the thin blue fabric of Chelsea's suit, Julia

could feel every one of his firm muscles, and with each breath she inhaled the masculine scent so uniquely Alex Ravenwood. He smelled delicious, and she wanted to run her lips over his skin. A spark surged through her and Julia knew there was no way she could blame it on static. Agonized, she closed her eyes.

"Julia?"

Julia opened her eyes to find his blue ones so close their noses were almost touching.

"Are you okay?"

"I think so," she replied, trying to stop her lips from quivering. What would it be like to just reach forward to kiss his mouth? To taste it again?

"Good. I hate to do this, but I need to press against you in order to lift off. Are you ready?"

Although Alex was holding his body still, his touch had reduced her to jelly.

"I'm ready," Julia lied. She would never be ready when Alex was involved.

"Okay. We'll do it on three. Ready? One. Two. Three." Alex's hands pushed against her shoulders and his thighs pushed against her legs. Within seconds he was standing, and the warmth covering Julia disappeared. "Let me help you up."

Alex reached for her and strong fingertips linked with hers to pull her to her feet. Julia looked in dismay at the remains of her cosmetics. Powder was ground into the carpet. Eyeshadow containers had broken open and the contents had shattered. Even Alex's clothes hadn't been spared.

"I'm so sorry!" She moaned in agony as she looked at the mess. "Your pants! Alex, I'm so sorry. I can't believe this. I'll pay to have it cleaned. I mean, it's Armani. Just send me the bill."

"Shh." Alex put his right forefinger to her lips. "I've got another suit, remember?"

Julia nodded. Alex's finger on her lips was doing even worse things to her equilibrium than when he had sat on her lap. Desire trembled through her. She wanted to open her mouth and slip his finger inside and suck on it just slightly.

With a jerk she pulled her face away from the temptation and dropped to her knees and began to scoop up cosmetic cases.

"Julia, stop." Alex pulled her up to her feet and brushed some powder off her suit jacket. "I'll buy you more makeup. Just don't get yourself dirty. We need to go directly to the meeting, and Chelsea doesn't have more clothes. I do."

"What about your suit?"

"I'm going to change right now. Do not, and I repeat, do not clean this mess up. Promise me." Alex stepped toward the closet that held spare clothes.

"I'll just carefully get what I need." Julia squatted down. "I won't get messy. I promise."

"Good." Alex lifted a suit out of the closet and disappeared into the lavatory.

Julia turned and surveyed the mess. Her powder was destroyed. Five powdered eyeshadows had cracked and were now useless. She twisted up the bloodred lipstick Alex had tripped over. It broke off and fell to the floor. Almost everything had suffered some damage.

Julia scooped up the few things that hadn't broken and put them back in her purse just as Alex returned. With her purse on her shoulder and the laptop case in hand, she successfully disembarked down the plane steps.

"Just be sure you get makeup when you buy some

clothes tonight," Alex said as he waited for Julia to climb into the waiting limo. "Makeup is easily replaced, right?"

Julia slid in the limo without answering him. Of course it was, unless it was theater makeup.

IT WAS ONE-THIRTY in the morning before Alex and the lawyers declared it quits for the night and one-forty before Julia dozed off in a chair in the hotel clothing shop.

Alex watched her sleep. For a moment he debated whether to wake her up, and then, deciding that fate was giving him an opportunity, he picked out the clothes himself. Tomorrow she could protest his choices. Tonight he was sure the only thing concerning her right now, besides sleeping, would be having fresh underwear, a toothbrush and paste, and a pillow to collapse onto.

"Even though it's Saturday, we're back on at eight-thirty tomorrow morning," Alex told her as the elevator halted at the penthouse suite. Julia nodded, and Alex watched her with amusement.

Julia Brown certainly wasn't a vampire. In fact, she hardly made a decent zombie as she groggily made her way through the suite to her bedroom. The bellhop wheeled the rack of her new clothes into the living area, and disappeared after Alex generously tipped him.

Alex was still on an emotional rush as he shed his clothes and stepped into a robe in the privacy of his bedroom. The advice Julia had given on the plane ride had been dead-on.

The meeting had been emotional, with the branch manager often in tears, but it had gone better than he had expected. After the lawyers adjusted for the embezzlement, Ravenwood would finish its presentation to the city regarding the bonds. Alex headed out into the living area of the suite and noticed the rack of clothing was still where the bellhop had left it.

"Julia? Your clothes are out here. Do you want them?"

When there was no answer, Alex eyed her door. It was wide-open. Frowning slightly at her lack of response, he pulled the rack behind him, stopping outside her door. "Julia?"

Still no answer. Alex poked his head around the door frame. Julia had collapsed facedown on the bed, and she was sound asleep. The makings of a grin crept over his face. He felt suddenly like an adolescent schoolboy catching a girl changing.

Her skirt had ridden up slightly, giving him an even better view of her legs. She definitely had great legs, he noted. Checking his lustful, boyish thoughts, he wheeled the rack in and went over to stand beside the bed.

Unabashed, he gazed at her a minute before waking her, pausing as he caught a glimpse of one strand of hair that seemed out of place. It was sandy blond, certainly a sharp contrast to the jet-black color.

He smiled to himself and decided to let sleeping secretaries lie. Pun intended.

"Julia? Julia?"

"Uh-huh?" Julia propped herself up on her elbow and turned and blinked at him.

"Get ready for bed," Alex ordered. "You've got clothes to sleep in on the rack."

"Right." Julia got up and drunkenly grabbed her purse. "Gotta take off my makeup, too."

"That's right, sleepyhead. I'm having breakfast sent

up for us. I'll see you in a few hours.'' Alex smiled as he watched her go into her bathroom and shut the door.

Turning, he walked out of her bedroom, closed the door and walked over to his. As he brushed his teeth, he thought over the evening. Julia was truly an enigma.

It had taken all the control he had mustered to stop himself from kissing her when he landed in her lap. And Chelsea had been worried about him firing her. No, now that Alex was enjoying Julia's game of duplicity, firing Julia wasn't the problem. Not hardly.

There was a reason Rita was his secretary. She was old and married. Definitely not available. Definitely safe. Definitely not a distraction.

Not so with Julia. Alex got a sexual shock every time he touched her. It was a feeling totally foreign to him. Sure, he had desired women enough to enjoy their freely offered bodies, but with them he had never felt a chemical stirring, as if two halves had been made whole. It was an odd sensation to want a woman this way, a woman who could offer him nothing but herself.

Julia was beautiful and desirable, and became more so every time he saw her. Yes, it was time. Time for her to end this farce and admit there was something happening between them. Alex smiled to himself as he stripped and slid beneath the cool, crisp sheets. He sure hoped Julia liked her clothes.

MORE MODERN? Was this what Alex had meant when he insisted she update her wardrobe? Julia studied the clothes hanging on the rack. There was nothing more about any of these clothes. There was nothing to them at all.

The only two semiprofessional secretarial dresses were sleeveless with short hemlines. Julia would have felt more comfortable wearing them to a happy hour at one of Lydia's fancy art galleries than to the reorganization of an investment branch.

And of course everything else was even less. Much less. There were two bikinis that Julia was sure would barely cover a size A woman. There were lacy bras with matching panties that probably belonged on a Victoria's Secret model, not her.

There were cool sleeveless shirts and shorts that she might be able to use. The short satiny nightgowns with spaghetti straps, well, definitely not for a woman whose idea of sleepwear was an oversize T-shirt.

Then there were more casual beach dresses, a long black sleeveless cover-up for the beach, and two slips, literally, that pretended to be evening dresses made just for dancing. Alex had provided every item she needed, including costume jewelry and shoes to accessorize all the outfits.

Julia adjusted her wig. Without all of her makeup the disguise was falling apart. Her face looked more and more like her own. Still, she did the best she could to disguise her looks and headed out to breakfast. To her relief Alex didn't seem to notice much except that the dress fit.

"Great. I'm glad it fits." Alex set the morning paper down and reached up to take off his glasses. "I figured if you fit into Chelsea's suit you must be her size, so I bought everything in her size."

Julia felt his eyes slowly peruse the black linen dress. The V-neck sleeveless dress came to just above her knees and had black buttons all the way down the front.

"It's not quite corporate." Julia sat down at the table opposite Alex and reached for a croissant. "You didn't buy me anything with sleeves."

"Well, this is Panama City. Even fancy hotel shops don't sell many corporate suits." Alex grinned. He took a sip of coffee and watched her over the rim of the cup. "Besides, it's a lot more casual here than in the District. By early this morning everyone will pull off their ties and coats, just watch. It's Saturday."

"Still, this dress is sort of short for a secretary," she protested. Alex lowered his gaze to rest on the tops of her exposed breasts and Julia felt her face redden. She knew she would be scarlet if Alex knew which set of lacy underwear she wore.

"Well, if nothing else you'll serve as a great distraction to a bunch of overworked men." Alex's grin was unmistakable. "Of course, if you prefer, I could ask them to send up your only other alternative. It's a T-shirt that reads 'I had Sex on the Beach at Joe's.'"

Julia caught the teasing in Alex's tone and pretended to consider his suggestion for a moment. Then she looked up at him covertly through her long lashes the way she had seen done in the movies. "That would be lying. I haven't had sex on the beach."

"Really?" Alex's eyebrows shot up quizzically. "I could remedy that for you."

Julia had the decency to blush at Alex's seductive, take-me-now look. Well, two could flirt. "Really."

She popped a grape into her mouth and pursed her lips into an O before plucking another grape from the bunch and repeating the process. "Would I have to let you call all the shots?"

"Absolutely," Alex drawled, his voice deep and husky. "I'm sure it would take at least three times in order for you to fully experience it."

Julia watched Alex shift slightly. The lower half of his body was hidden beneath the table and impishly she wondered if she was arousing him with harmless banter about alcohol.

Julia rubbed a finger absently over her lips the way she had seen in R-rated movies. "What if I decided that it wasn't enough? That I wanted more?" Her voice was now husky, sensual.

"Parts of you could be sore the next morning," Alex rasped.

"Hmm…" Julia reached out for the pitcher and poured herself a tall glass of water. Leisurely she took a long sip. "I'll have to consider it. When would this adventure begin?"

"In the darkness of the night." Alex reached for his cup of coffee and drained it in one swallow.

"Hmm…" Julia said again with as much poise as she could muster. The thought of having Alex between her sheets was sending illicit shivers up her spine. She studied her croissant as if she were memorizing each flaky layer.

Upon looking up, she saw that Alex's blue eyes had darkened to almost one solid color. She had affected him. Womanly triumph that she could tease a man of Alex's caliber filled her with joy. She had wanted Alex for so long. Her full lips opened to speak.

"I'll answer it." Julia stood and walked over to the phone, which had begun shrilling at the most inopportune time. She picked up the receiver, listened for a moment and set it back down. Alex's eyes had returned to normal, meaning the moment had passed. She checked the sigh as she issued the order to begin work.

"The limo is here, Alex. We need to go right down."

THE ORDEAL OF REORGANIZING the office wrapped up at seven-thirty that night. After what seemed like the longest nonstop Saturday Julia had ever had, lawyers and accountants packed up their briefcases and began shaking hands with Alex.

Julia slumped back in her chair. Absently she flexed her fingers. They hurt from typing on a laptop all day. Amazing how good she had gotten just from working at Ravenwood Investments. Because no one was paying her any mind, she idly watched Alex. He was standing with some of company lawyers, and he was deeply intent on what they were saying.

Free to run her gaze unnoticed over him, Julia treated her eyes to the delight his six-foot frame afforded her. He was gorgeous. Julia found herself frowning slightly. It didn't make sense. She had worked with beautiful people at the theater. She had touched their faces, applied their makeup and styled their hair. Superficial beauty had long ago stopped being appealing. Kyle had seen to that. Thank God, she had wised up before he had gotten into her pants. Julia shuddered involuntarily. She was lucky all he took from her was her money and a sliver of her pride.

Julia stared openly at Alex, noticing how even a rolled-up Calvin Klein suit looked superb on him. She had seen a different side of Alex today. He had been compassionate with the fired employee, somehow allowing the man to retain his pride and dignity. Alex had never raised his voice, never threatened, and never made the man feel like dirt. Instead Alex had been gentle yet firm, kind yet nonapologetic for the deed he knew he had to do. When the man had crumpled into tears, Alex had been ready with a linen handkerchief.

Chelsea was right; Lydia didn't deserve him. Alexander Ravenwood was a deep, complex man who valued integrity and honor.

And Julia knew she had neither. Every time Julia lied to Alex about who she was, she felt terrible, and she lied every day. Alex wanted honesty above reproach, and Julia's deception had to be the lowest of lows, despite the eventual good intentions behind it.

Not only that, but what would Chelsea do if she found out how much Julia wanted Alex? That had been Chelsea's whole purpose behind the silly, hideous disguise. Not only would Julia lose Alex, but she might lose her best friend, as well. Julia and Alex making love was surely not part of Chelsea's plan.

But Julia wanted to do it. Luckily the phone had interrupted her at breakfast. She had actually been about to proposition Alex. Julia shuddered. How many women propositioned Alex? Dozens probably. Despite his teasing her about alcoholic shots, she knew he wasn't serious. Men were never serious where she was concerned.

And then there was Lydia to consider. Alex might not be serious about her, but Lydia thought he was. She had left fifteen messages yesterday, and Julia was sure she would have left more if the office had been open. Alex hadn't called her in two weeks.

Julia rapped her fingers lightly on the table. Alex the movie buff was going to age as gracefully as the movie star he somewhat resembled. She had seen every Robert Redford movie ever made. Looking at Alex, Julia wished she didn't love Robert Redford movies as much as she did. After Alex they would take on a whole new meaning.

"I'll give you a nickel this time for your thoughts." Suddenly Alex was standing in front of her and Julia jerked in surprise. Her eyes widened in horror. No, she hadn't spoken aloud. Slowly she exhaled, letting the tension leave with her heated breath.

"I," Julia faltered as she grasped for the right words. "I was thinking about Robert Redford movies."

"Ah." Alex smiled. "Trying to find the likeness? People have sometimes said I look like him, except my hair isn't blond. So, was that why you were staring off into space?"

"Well, not exactly." Julia quickly regained her composure. "I was just thinking about his movies."

"Which ones?" Alex settled himself down in an empty chair next to him. "You know I'm a movie buff. I really liked some of the earlier movies he did."

"I liked most of them, so I guess we have something in common." Julia gave a low whistle and looked at Alex with appreciation.

"Oh, I never doubted that we had things in common." Alex smirked a little and Julia blushed. How could just one look from him send her reeling? "So you like your men old enough to be your father?" Alex teased her suddenly. "You're what, twenty-seven?"

"I'm twenty-six," Julia corrected him. "Older men are more mature, not that I've ever dated any."

"Well, I'm ten years your senior. So do you think I'm more mature?" Alex's eyes glittered dangerously, but Julia couldn't tell with what.

"Definitely one foot in the grave," she quipped. "Thirty-six is so over the hill. Why do you think you got black balloons the other day?"

"It makes me very experienced," Alex steadily replied.

"Exactly." Julia ignored his retort. "Look at how you handled yourself tonight. Now what do we need to do next?"

"We go to dinner. And fly home tomorrow." He slouched down in the chair and leaned his head back. "I'm too tired to fly across the country tonight. Firing people is intense." He closed his eyes briefly and then opened them to look at her.

"Julia." His voice was husky. "I couldn't have done it without you."

Julia blushed at his warm compliment. "Sure you could have. You're the boss."

Alex leaned forward and grabbed her hand. Immediately it tingled.

"Stop saying that. I'm being serious. All that stuff you mentioned on the plane about pride and principles. It made sense. Anyway, I'm hungry. Are you up for dinner and dancing?"

"Uh…" Julia was shocked. "I thought you were tired?"

"I just want to avoid jet lag, and you have no excuses where clothes are concerned. I know you have a dress. I've made reservations for nine o'clock. That'll give you plenty of time to rest up. Ready to head back to the hotel?"

Julia nodded mutely and pushed her chair back. "My job is to follow you anywhere."

"Good girl."

Alex gave her the trademark smile that Julia had seen over and over again in Chelsea's photos. It was the same one that at eighteen had claimed her heart and given every boyfriend thereafter the impossible standards Julia never let them reach.

Alex reached for her hand and pulled her to her feet. Her body ached from his simple touch.

"I'm calling the shots, remember?" He raised his eyebrows and waited for her response.

Julia's head snapped around, and she relaxed as his wicked grin told her he was teasing. "After you, then," Julia quipped.

Alex shot her a cheeky look. "Oh, no. Ladies first. I insist."

Julia had the distinct impression he stared at her bottom the whole way to the elevator.

Chapter Eight

The night was perfect. By 9:05 p.m. they were sitting at a private table in a foliage-surrounded outdoor gazebo. Burbling trickles from a five-foot man-made waterfall next to their table made a pleasant backdrop for conversation. In the distance Alex could also hear the sounds of waves lapping the shore.

Except for the waiters that hovered now and again, he had left orders that they were to be left pretty much alone throughout dinner. Soft tiki torches and a candle had provided the romantic light he wanted for their dinner. When the last vestiges of daylight had vanished, the night had come in on little cat feet and had stolen around them, creating the illusion of intimacy.

Alex watched as Julia polished off the last bit of strawberry shortcake and leaned back in satisfaction.

''You're staring.'' Julia caught Alex watching her, although his expression was unreadable. She looked at him in playful exasperation.

''Get used to it,'' Alex said gruffly. ''You're a sight for sore eyes compared to Rita. Besides, you have hardly any makeup on and it looks good. Extremely good,'' he added softly.

When he had picked out the white spaghetti-strap slip

dress he hadn't realized that it would be so completely sexy. The silk hugged her curves, and let those beautiful legs be seen from mid-thigh down.

Julia seemed to focus on the candlelight dancing through the last sips of Riesling in her wineglass. "It's the light," she said flatly.

"No, I don't think so." Alex shook his head in disagreement. "You don't give yourself enough credit, Julia. You don't need a lot of makeup."

She swallowed the last of the wine in her glass. "Well, I'm sure you remember that most of my makeup broke on the plane. And, since you are a connoisseur of beautiful women, I'll take your advice and not replace it."

"Good, although I'm not as much of a Casanova with women as the press makes me out to be. Most of my reputation is all smoke. No fire."

"Men always think that," Julia contradicted, her voice sharp. Didn't they?

Alex's eyes narrowed slightly. He didn't think she was referring directly to him. "Sure, but because I'm a rich, eligible bachelor, all a woman needs to do is stand by me and the rumor says I've bedded her. Now, I'm no saint, but I'm not a Don Juan, either."

"I didn't mean that."

Alex recognized Julia's attempt to backtrack, but this time he refused to let her escape. Alex decided to test the waters.

"Yes, you did. You're wondering how I could kiss you the other day when I'm supposedly dating Lydia."

Julia's mouth had dropped open a little, and she snapped it closed. Alex gave her a wan smile.

"Lydia is one of the things I'm going to have to take care of when I return. But enough about her. Tell me about you. From your conversation it sounds like you had a bad run-in with someone else.''

''You could say that.'' Julia's fingers tightened on her wineglass and she twirled it idly in her fingers. ''He was interested only in notches on his belt, or bedpost, or wherever he kept them. He may have taken all my money and part of my pride, but he didn't make me a notch.''

''That's good to know. Pride and lack of money are both things a person can fix. Self-respect is a lot harder.''

''That's what I keep telling myself,'' Julia replied quietly.

Alex filed her admission away in his memory and decided to change the subject. With a flourish he snapped his fingers. ''I'd almost forgotten.''

''Forgotten?'' Julia's tone sounded curious as she reached for her water glass. ''Forgotten what?''

''This.'' Alex leaned back in his chair as a waiter appeared carrying two shot glasses on a tray. The waiter set one in front of Julia and one in front of Alex and then discreetly disappeared.

Alex revealed nothing about what was in the shot glasses. Instead he waited until Julia looked at him expectantly. Her milk-chocolate-colored eyes were luminous in the candlelight, and he filled her in on the secret.

''I just wanted to wait until you were full. I promised you sex on the beach.''

Julia practically spit out her water. Alex could tell it was all she could do to keep the water from gushing out her nose. She coughed several times.

''Are you okay?'' Alex leaned forward to grab her hand, sorry he had rattled her this way. ''Julia?''

''I'm fine,'' Julia choked out the words. She wiped

her face with her napkin. Alex's throat constricted. The pressure of the cloth on her lips had just made them fuller. "You blindsided me."

"Good. You've done it to me several times. I'll consider us even." Alex chortled with merriment now that Julia seemed fine.

"When have I blindsided you?"

"Bottoms up." Alex lifted his shot glass in a salute and ignored Julia's question. He waited while Julia did the same. "Ready? You can do it. Like college. One. Two. Three."

In unison they downed the fiery liquid. Alex stifled a grin when Julia had to rinse hers down with water. She was definitely a novice.

"What was in that? I feel like it's racing through my veins. At least I think that's what this feeling is."

"Oh, Julia." Julia delighted him with her naiveté. "Our conversation today was just too precious to pass up. You've just had Sex on the Beach. It's vodka, amaretto, peach schnapps, cranberry juice and orange juice." Alex felt like the Cheshire cat. "So, how was your first time? Did you like it?"

"It was good. It feels warm and fuzzy. Somewhat liberating."

"We're going to do one more of those delectable shots to celebrate two successful weeks of working together."

"Oh." Julia's eyes widened as a waiter bearing two more shot glasses magically appeared. Alex noted that she slammed the next one back without a problem.

"No more." Julia held up her fingers in a stop gesture.

"No more," he agreed. "I don't get ladies, especially my secretaries, drunk." He watched as Julia took a long sip of water. He could almost see the water slide down her throat. "Come on, time to go."

"Where to now?" Julia rose unsteadily to her feet, and Alex enfolded her arm in his.

"Dancing," Alex replied, feeling the warmth of her creamy skin next to his. "Then we'll take a short walk on the moonlit beach before we call it a night."

Alex grinned when Julia quickly masked her expression of alarm. So he had rattled her. Gotten past the smooth one-liners that she threw at him to keep him off balance. "Don't worry, Julia, I won't pounce on you. I just like to kick off my shoes and walk on sugar white sand. Don't tell anyone, though, because I'm supposed to be a suave businessman."

Relief showed on her face for just a moment and then Julia allowed him to lead her over to the poolside terrace where other people were dancing.

"No problem," she said. "I'll keep your secret."

"That's right," Alex agreed smoothly. "You told me you don't kiss and tell." *But will you kiss me?* He left the rest of his thoughts unspoken, already certain by the look of shock on Julia's face that she had caught his subliminal message.

DANCING IN ALEX'S ARMS was pure heaven, Julia decided. She felt as if she floated on air, especially when her soft body was crushed protectively against his muscular chest. How peaceful. How perfect.

"I could stay here forever," Julia thought…aloud.

"What did you say?" Alex reached forward to tilt up Julia's chin. His blue eyes were murky and Julia felt as if he could see through her. "Something about forever?"

"I…I've loved the beach forever." Julia recovered.

Inwardly she cringed at her stupidity. Alex's eyes were veiled with his dark lashes, and she couldn't tell if he believed her or not. Another lie, she rationalized. *My whole relationship with him is a lie. Even when I've been myself I've been lying. He hates liars and that's what I am. Hands off, Julia. Hands off.*

She pushed against him slightly, to give herself more distance, but Alex pulled her back to his chest as the band began another slower song. Julia relaxed and gave in.

There were reasons she was afraid of him, afraid of destroying the fantasy that could never come true. Again her body rhythms began to move in sync with his own. She fitted so nicely in his arms, just like the other night.

The song ended and the band began to pick up the tempo. Reluctantly Julia let Alex go and followed him back to a small table at the edge of the terrace. Alex waved off the waiter and turned to Julia.

"Ready for that walk?"

"Not yet," Julia said honestly. Not until the alcohol and desire stopped flowing through her veins, she thought. If she didn't wait, she would have Sex on the Beach, this time in the biblical sense. She wondered if Alex could tell what he did to her equilibrium. Two dances and Julia again wanted to toss aside her pride and her reputation.

She surveyed Alex. He had shed today's suit for a dressy short-sleeved shirt and fitted twill pants. Casual, yet with an aura of pure class. Her gaze lingered at the raven curls peeking out from the vee formed by his first few unbuttoned buttons. Darn. He was everything she had ever wanted. Everything she had ever dreamed of. Everything she could never have—except temporarily.

Still, maybe when it was all over, maybe at the end of three weeks, maybe then there might be a right moment. She could let herself succumb and give in to the longings that coursed through her body like Florida wildfires. Then, later she could hide in New York City and start her new life licking the wounds that she knew would come from the burn of having loved him.

"If you aren't ready for the walk, shall we go dance some more, or would you rather sit out?"

Julia started from her reverie, not sure of the second part of Alex's statement. "Certainly." She saw his look. "Dancing's fine." She had heard him mention dancing, and dancing was safe.

Other couples again filled the terrace, enjoying the band and the atmosphere created by tiki torches, small hidden strands of white lights, and lily-pad candles that floated in the pool.

Julia allowed Alex to lead her back onto the dance floor. This time the song was a faster salsa number she didn't recognize, so Julia followed Alex's lead and allowed him to whirl and twirl her around. More couples crowded the floor, and Alex pulled Julia closer with each spin. Heat surged through her every time her body pressed against his for the briefest of moments before he twirled her away.

"Watch out." Alex guided Julia around a couple that was dancing with drinks in hand. "I wish people would have more common sense."

"Or just courtesy," Julia added, her eyes following the couple careening drunkenly around the dance floor. "But they are having a grand time."

"Bully for them," Alex replied stiffly. "She's sloshing her drink on the tiles and he almost collided with that elderly couple by the pool."

"Well, not everyone can dance with the finesse that you have."

Alex frowned, as if he was unsure of the intent behind her words.

"Seriously." Julia pacified him. "You are a wonderful dancer. I feel like a ballerina in your arms. You know exactly how to lead a girl." Julia shivered as Alex adjusted his hand on her bare back.

"Really?" Alex's wicked grin was back and Julia stared at his full lips. "Where would you like me to lead you? Perhaps on that walk? In fact, I think I'm ready to take it."

"It's my job to follow you wherever you lead," Julia reminded him softly, her meaning clear.

For a moment neither of them moved. Then Alex simply changed his position and guided Julia toward an open escape route. "This way," he said huskily.

Julia nodded unsteadily. Her head felt light. By now the alcohol had fully traveled her whole bloodstream, but that didn't affect her decision. Her decision had been made years ago. Trembling slightly, she focused on walking over the ceramic tiles.

The band began an even faster number, but Julia didn't notice. Intent on following Alex, she concentrated as he threaded her through the now-crowded terrace. She knew the escape route he headed for circled the pool and led to the boardwalk and then to the sand and surf beyond.

Alex's hand was on hers, leading her single file, and Julia almost lost her balance as she found one of the wet spots from the woman's drink. "Idiot." She silently cursed the woman for her clumsiness and then she cursed herself for wearing spaghetti strap heels that didn't provide traction.

"Careful, it's wet," Alex called over his shoulder.

Julia, busy watching the conga line that was coming to claim her, didn't hear him. "What?"

"I said be careful, it's—"

The tug on his arm knocked him off balance. Alex skated on the tile and worked to regain control.

The loud splash was the only indication of Julia.

"Julia!"

With more speed than a *Baywatch* lifeguard Alex jumped into the pool after her. Most of the candles in the pool had inverted with Julia's decent, plunging the pool into an eerie semidarkness. Alex grabbed for what he thought was Julia's head. "Julia!" He pulled on her hair to get her face up out of the water. With a cry of anguish, he discovered he had ripped off her head.

No, he had ripped off her hair. A sinking feeling came over him and frantically Alex treaded water for a moment as his eyes searched the murky darkness. "Julia!"

"I'm over here. Shallow end." Julia's voice was flat.

Alex looked up as the terrace lights flashed on all around them. Gaping people lined the edge of the pool. Julia stood in chest-high water with her arms across her chest. He looked at the mass of black hair in his hand and then back at Julia. Her wig was in his hand and the moment of truth had finally come at last.

Julia Brown and Rachel Grayson were one and the same, and there was no way she could hide it anymore.

"WELL, IT'S GOOD TO KNOW chivalry isn't dead," Julia said wryly as Alex waded up the pool toward her.

"Yeah, but my watch is," he shot back, struggling to maintain composure as his wet clothes clung to his body. He held up her hair on his finger. "You lost something."

Resigned to the inevitable, Julia gave a long sigh. "First my makeup, then my hair. You have a strange way of destroying my disguise."

Alex walked up toward the steps and tossed her hair in a mass up on the tile. He wasn't quite sure how to handle this situation. Did he shout at her for concealing her identity all this time, or let it slide and wait for her to explain? He wasn't sure.

Besides, he had never jumped into a swimming pool fully clothed to rescue someone who didn't need saving. Already he could see a waiter appearing with a load of white towels. He turned back to Julia as he stepped out of the pool and grabbed a towel. "Coming?"

"Uh, no," Julia replied, her voice still flat. Alex ran a towel through his hair and looked at her in confusion.

"Come again?" Alex asked, checking to see if he had heard her correctly. Julia was still standing in the water up to her neck.

"I'm wearing white," Julia told him, "and I'm not moving until everyone else goes back to whatever they were doing and you throw me one of those towels."

Finally understanding, Alex spurred into action. "Okay folks, thanks for your concern. She's fine." Alex waved to the crowd gathered at the edge of the pool and then turned to the waiter standing next to him. "Kill those lights." Within moments, the lights flickered out and people, realizing the show was over, headed back to their tables or to the dance floor where the band was now beginning a slower number.

Alex tossed Julia a towel and watched it slowly sink into the water near her. Hands still crossed over her chest she walked over to retrieve it.

"Lousy shot," she called to Alex. "I thought you were a pitcher."

"Not of towels. Besides, beggars shouldn't be choosers," Alex retorted. "I promise I'll wrap you in a dry one when you get up here. Juan said he'll take us in the back way so no one sees what wrecks we've become."

Julia moved to waist-high water, the wet towel dripping. "Help me," she called to Alex. "I can't walk in these shoes."

Once again Alex stepped into the water, Bruno Magali loafers and all. Well, they were already wet. As was his wallet, his watch, his white shirt.

Alex saw Julia's eyes widen as she took in the full effect of Alex's wet white shirt. It left absolutely nothing to the imagination. Alex faced Julia, shielding her front, and expertly swapped her wet towel for a dry one.

He had covered her in the dark, but still, for just the briefest second Alex had seen why Julia hadn't wanted to get out of the water. Her itsy bitsy silky white slip dress was worse than a wet white T-shirt. Alex tucked the towel in, hiding Julia's figure from himself and the world.

"Come on." Alex led her after Juan and within moments safely ensconced Julia in the penthouse suite.

Julia's teeth chattered the whole way.

"Let's get you warmed up," Alex rasped as he tipped Juan fifty dollars in wet money and shut the door to the suite behind him. "Come to my room."

Julia turned to look at him frantically. Her brown eyes were large and luminous and her wet blond hair hung in clumped strands around her face.

"What?" she stuttered, her teeth chattering.

"I have a Jacuzzi tub, and you're getting in it." A

cherry flush stole over Julia's face. "Alone," Alex clarified with a wistful smile. "Now."

TEN MINUTES LATER Julia found herself deep within frothy bubbles, warm jets massaging her aching limbs. The tub was huge, big enough to seat at least four people. Julia kicked her legs slightly, enjoying the feel of a tub big enough to swim in.

This tub was so much nicer than the standard five-foot tub in her apartment. Eyes closed, Julia stretched her arm forward, only to connect with a hard cloth object. Her eyes shot open and she jerked her hand back from Alex's thigh.

"I brought you some brandy." Alex offered her a glass from where he was sitting on the edge of the tub. "Don't worry, you're safely out of view beneath all those bubbles. And, as much as I am tempted to hop under there with you, it might be wise if we didn't do anymore swimming tonight."

Julia reached forward and took the snifter from his hand. She took a long, deep swallow as Alex reached forward to lift a strand of her real hair.

"So, Rachel Juliana Grayson, would you care to explain why you're my secretary and why you were in disguise?"

Julia closed her eyes as the hot liquid burned down her throat and sent fire through her veins.

Hands gripped her shoulders and pulled her up slightly. Alex's face loomed closer, and in defense Julia brought the brandy snifter between them. "It was Chelsea's idea. Honestly."

At the mention of his sister's name, Alex let Julia go and she slid deeper in the water, almost heading under.

She lifted herself back up, managing somehow not to spill a drop. Grimacing, she took another sip of brandy.

"Of course it was." Alex's voice was sharp and Julia's eyes widened. "For two weeks I've been trying to figure out what kind of game Chelsea's playing. So, now that it's over, why don't you tell me the truth?"

"Could we talk about this later?" Julia asked. She was acutely aware that beneath the bubbles she was stark naked. "I'll get dressed and we can talk."

"I want an answer now." Alex's anger was evident in the lines that creased on his forehead. "I've been waiting for you to come clean for a while, so tell me!"

Julia shuddered. "Just one question first. How long have you known?"

Alex regarded her with hooded eyes. "I knew something was up when Chelsea hired a secretary who was ugly. Then suddenly Chelsea's best friend is also in town. After Thursday evening I had Edward Thompson run two checks, one on you, and one on Julia Brown. You only saw the one on Julia Brown. Then I did what any normal man would do. I called Scott and he confirmed everything. So, to answer your question, I knew for sure Friday before you came to the art gallery."

The enormity of it hit Julia. For the first time Julia understood the depth of Alex Ravenwood. "Oh my God," she whispered. "I didn't know."

"You should have. I've been giving you opportunity after opportunity to confess and come clean. Your and Chelsea's mistake was that you both underestimated me. So why did you do it?"

"Chelsea said you have a weakness for beautiful women," Julia replied, drinking more brandy. The heat traveled through her already alcohol filled veins. "I was the best qualified for the job she wanted me to do, but she was afraid that if you knew I was even a little attractive that, well, we might have an affair and not do any work. In fact, you did find me attractive, didn't you? You kissed me.''

Julia didn't wait for Alex to confirm or deny. ''Anyway, Chelsea didn't want you to think she was matchmaking or that I was trying to lure you into a relationship. Anyway, I needed the money, so I became Julia Brown, your temp. I'm in between jobs.''

Alex's eyes showed his skepticism. ''Really. I still find this a little far-fetched. You told me you were on vacation.''

Julia was very aware of the hard, muscular thigh perched next to her face. ''I am in between jobs. I'm headed to New York in two weeks to work for the House of Viscountie as an entry-level designer. I couldn't work at my last job any longer, especially with everyone feeling sorry for me.''

''Why would they feel sorry for you?'' Alex asked.

''Because I dated this guy named Kyle.'' Julia let the water hide her shaking. ''He told me he loved me, and then when his show ended he hit the road with all my cash and the coat-check girl. Poor naive me.''

''So you created Julia Brown to fool me.''

''No, Chelsea did, but not just to fool you. My name is Rachel, and that was what was on Chelsea's wedding program. We knew you only knew me by my first name, but no one ever calls me that. Because my mom's name is also Rachel, I've always gone by my middle name, except on official forms. Anyway, the Brown came from an inside joke from college. Chelsea and I used to call each other Julia Brown and Suzy Smith when we would go out. Guys believed us. As if...'' Julia drained the last of the brandy. She was probably tipsy, but she didn't care. The truth was out, well, at least most of it, and she felt as if a giant weight had been lifted from her shoulders.

"I should have guessed." Alex shook his head, anger still evident. "Only a good friend of Chelsea's would go along with any of her games. And admit it, you played along."

"Sure." Julia handed him her brandy glass. "I needed the income and playing secretary was fun. It was better than taking Chelsea's loan, which really would have been a glorified handout. Besides, there's nothing between us. I know whatever you thought you felt for me wasn't anything but safe teasing. I looked like a vampire, for goodness' sake. Even Lydia called me Morticia."

"She said what?" Alex looked horrified.

"She said I looked like Morticia, you know, from the Adams Family." Julia softened it slightly. "Of course, I took it as a compliment. I was supposed to be unobtrusive, and I didn't want her to feel threatened."

"Why would she be threatened?" The tone of Alex's voice sounded odd.

"Women are often afraid of losing what they perceive as theirs, and she told me she expects to become engaged to you in a short time."

Alex grunted. "We've never even talked about being engaged so I don't know where she's gotten that idea from."

"Maybe not, but she expects it just the same. Anyway, I'm not Rita."

"No. That's for sure." Alex's voice was low and husky. Julia felt his gaze run over her. Damp curls clung to her face, and the jets produced bubbles that gave him only a teasing glimpse of her cleavage. "Without your makeup and wig, you're one of the most naturally beautiful woman I've ever seen.''

"I am not," Julia denied. "I've never been beautiful, and I've always had to work even to be pretty. I'm not fishing for compliments, either. It's the truth. I didn't even know how to apply makeup until Chelsea showed me. She took me to one of those salons that find your perfect style.''

"That's not the truth," Alex insisted. "The truth is that even in your disguise you tripped up my libido like no other. How do you think I figured it out? Every time I touched you I felt something between us. My instincts didn't lie, and there were too many coincidences between Julia and Rachel. All I had to do was kiss both of you to be one-hundred-percent certain. Julia, you're an unsuspecting temptress, and you've definitely tempted me.''

Julia flushed. Between the combination of alcohol, warm water and his intense stare, she was overheating. "I'm pretty warm now. I should get out."

Alex didn't move.

"That means you need to leave." Julia waited, but it seemed that leaving Julia was about the last thing Alex could do at that moment.

"I've changed my mind," he said gruffly.

She looked up at him in complete bafflement until his next words dawned on her.

"I've decided that I need to go swimming again."

Water flowed over the tub and onto the floor as Alex tossed himself into the huge Jacuzzi. His clothing floated as he brought his face to hers. Julia waited, longing for the kisses she craved.

"No towel to hide behind this time, Julia," he murmured softly. "That wet dress showed it all."

"You promised not to look." Julia whispered as his face came closer to hers. Like a moth to a flame she simply waited, paralyzed with the desire of what she knew was to come, what she knew she had been waiting for, praying for.

"No, I didn't." Alex's lips found hers and he gently teased her mouth. "I promised to wrap you in a towel." With his statement finished, Alex pressed his lips fully to Julia's, capturing her mouth in one tumultuous movement.

Julia felt as if she was drowning. Alex rested his weight on the floor of the tub and he kissed her with abandon. Firm, persuasive lips coaxed Julia's open, and stars exploded as his tongue collided with hers. Julia drank in his essence, tasting brandy on his own tongue, and she let herself give in to the passion that was running through her body.

"Chelsea was wrong," Alex murmured against her neck as his lips trailed downward. "From our first meeting I've been wanting you to nibble on my neck. You may have looked like a vampire, but I was ready to offer you all my blood if that's what it took. The only time I've ever felt literal sparks in my life was when I danced with you at the wedding, and when I touched my vampirish temp."

He bit her neck playfully, but not hard enough to leave any marks. Julia shuddered from the sensation.

Expertly Alex lifted Julia's body up onto the ledge until the bubbles barely covered her breasts. "Do you know what you have been doing to me? Do you know how much I've wanted you? Every time I touch you, you drive me crazy."

Julia gasped as his mouth found one of her nipples. The sensation of water and Alex caressing them was almost too much. Her whole body quaked and shuddered, and suddenly she found herself lifted slightly as Alex used a free hand to raise her buttocks to his awaiting fingers.

"That's right," he soothed, shifting his mouth to her neglected nipple. "Let go, Julia. We can be so good."

Julia's mind struggled for sanity as his fingers entered her femininity, causing an explosion inside her body. She trembled, and as much as she didn't want to, she pulled away to look at him.

Alex's eyes were murky with desire, and already his fingers were working, thrusting again. Julia quivered as the rapture intensified. She arched against his fingers as his mouth encircled her breast. "Let me make love to you, Julia."

"Alex!" Julia shouted his name and shuddered as she peaked. Already his hands were roaming, causing sensations across her abdomen. How she wanted him right here in the warmth of the water. But he didn't love her. She had promised herself after Kyle she would never be used again.

And, despite his words, she would be just another woman who had succumbed to the charms of Alex Ravenwood. Worse, she would have to avoid him at Chelsea's house, and if she did see him everything would be strained. Everything would be ruined. Irrevocably.

"Alex! We can't do this." Julia pushed against him and accidentally shoved his head underwater.

"What the hell?" Alex came up sputtering. Despite her nakedness, Julia was already on her feet and grabbing for a towel.

"We can't do this. Chelsea's my friend. You're her brother." Julia hastily wrapped the large towel around her. It covered her to almost her ankles, but not before she knew Alex had gotten his first true look at her naked body.

He stood up, water dripping off his polo shirt and shorts. "A few seconds ago you wanted me," he grated. Julia could tell he was hurt and confused by her rejection, and it pained her.

"I want you," she admitted with a whisper. Quickly she averted her gaze before she couldn't control her traitorous body. "But this is wrong. I can't. We can't."

"Julia." Alex simply said her name before he reached down and forcefully turned off the bubble jets and opened the drain.

"Chelsea's my best friend!" Julia replied with a harsh cry. Her emotions had run amuck. "And then there's Lydia. I won't make love to a man who's dating someone else. Give me some credit for having morals, Alex! I will not let you use me like Kyle did. I will not be hurt again!"

With that, Julia turned, tripped on her towel once and slammed out the bathroom door.

Alex stared at the closed bathroom door. He felt slapped across the face, although Julia's hand had never once been raised against him. Whoever this Kyle had been, he had done a number on Julia, and it was deeper than just taking her money.

She was right, though, he thought as he stripped off his shirt. She deserved more. He wasn't ready to make a commitment to anyone, including Lydia, despite what Lydia might think. And making love to Julia, as much as he wanted it, would drive a wedge between Julia and his sister that would be irreparable.

Alex glanced at the clock on the counter. It was almost midnight. He shrugged his shoulders in frustration and dropped his shorts. Time for a long, cold shower.

Chapter Nine

The sound of pounding roused Julia from her uneasy slumber. Her eyebrows furrowed, she scrunched up her face, and pressed a hand to her forehead to ease the pressure. Still, the pounding continued.

Someone was at the suite's living room door. Julia hauled herself up out of bed, her eyes acclimating themselves to the darkness of her bedroom. She blinked as she saw the clock on the dresser. One-twenty in the afternoon. She had slept over twelve hours. With a groan, Julia grabbed her short robe and put it over the slinky starfish nightgown Alex had chosen. She threw open her door, blinking again in the bright sunlight that flowed into the living area of the suite. "Coming!" she shouted at the main door. "This better be good. Hold your horses!"

Julia walked to the door and threw it open wide. "Yes?"

Lydia Olson, in four-inch heels and a dress shorter than the one Julia had worn the night before pushed past her into the suite. "Where the hell is he?" Lydia stepped into the room like a cat on the prowl. Suddenly she turned to look at the blonde in the short, silky robe. "Who the hell are you?"

Julia's mouth quivered slightly as she shut the door and waited for the lightbulb in Lydia's head to dawn. Julia saw the minute it did, as Lydia's scathing look turned first into total disbelief, then genuine horror, and then absolute contempt. "Morticia? What the hell happened to you?"

"Nothing but some good sex," Julia murmured idly, reaching up to rub her forehead.

"Good sex?" Lydia snapped, her anger evident.

"Definitely good sex." Julia loosened the tangle of her shoulder-length mane. "On the beach. I'd never had it before, you know? Alex and I did it twice."

"You! You!" Lydia was so furious the unladylike curse words she had been flinging at Julia all week didn't make it out of her mouth. Instead Lydia approached Julia, hand raised. Julia wondered what Lydia was planning, but a door opened and Alex strode out wearing nothing but dark blue silk boxers. Abruptly Lydia dropped her hand to her side.

Oblivious to the scene, he walked into the room toward the table. "Julia? Was that room service with lunch? I can't believe we slept so late." He glanced up and saw Julia's odd expression. With a questioning frown, he turned to see what she was looking at. "Oh hi, Lydia."

Julia's grin widened slightly as she waited.

"Lydia?" Alex turned back to her in complete shock. "What are you doing here?"

"I could ask you the same thing, darling," Lydia gushed scathingly. Julia had to give Lydia credit, she didn't shriek or rant.

Another knock sounded, and Julia turned to let in an intrigued waiter. Alex handed him a tip, and looked at

Lydia. "We were about to have a late brunch. Care to join us?"

"If you're sure I'm not interrupting." Lydia flounced over to the table. "It's been a long flight and I was worried, Alex."

Julia noted with interest that Lydia's nasty tone had now became sweetness and light when she sat next to Alex.

"Worried?" Alex lifted a silver dome and grabbed a red grape. He popped it into his mouth. "About what?"

"I just knew the flowers you sent me were a mistake, Alex." Lydia poured herself a glass of water and Julia bit her lip to hide her disgust.

"No," Alex stated easily. "I sent flowers. Right, Julia?"

"Right," Julia agreed. She watched as Lydia nearly choked on her water.

"But Alex." Lydia's voice was almost weepy. "They were yellow."

It was over too fast, Julia decided. And right when it had been starting to get so good.

"Yellow roses?" Alex looked at Lydia. "Why would I send you yellow roses?"

Because you were in the tub with me last night, Julia wanted to blurt out. Still she held her tongue and shrugged as Lydia looked up at him.

"They were yellow." Lydia pouted. "The card only said your name. And right before I had to leave on an emergency photo shoot." Lydia looked up at Julia suddenly. Julia caught the direct venom in her eyes and wished Alex hadn't missed it. "Did she order them?"

"Who, Julia?" Alex munched some bacon. "Of course. That's what secretaries do."

Julia found her opening. "Was there something

wrong with yellow roses, Mr. Ravenwood? You didn't tell me what color, and so I just asked the florist to send the usual." She hoped she sounded penitent and professional, considering she was standing in a starfish nightgown.

ALEX STARED AT THE STARFISH nightgown, wishing for a peek of what lay beneath. He turned his attention back to the flowers Julia had sent Lydia. "Oh no, Julia," Alex told her. "You did the right thing. I didn't specify. It was all a simple misunderstanding."

One I wish I had known about earlier, Alex thought. How opportune. He looked at Lydia. Despite the ninety-degree heat outside and an obviously long plane flight, she looked perfectly polished in her blue slip dress. However, Lydia's glamour didn't hold a candle to how good Julia had looked last night when wearing her white dress. He switched his gaze to Julia. Waves of blond hair curled around her face.

Alex shook himself out of his digression. "Julia, you need to eat." Julia shook her head and her curls fell everywhere. Alex swallowed tightly.

"No, I'll just go get dressed and leave the two of you to talk." Julia smiled sweetly.

Alex shot her a dirty look. Of all the nerve, she seemed to be enjoying his discomfort. "If you insist. Just be sure to pack, because we've got a plane to catch, don't we?"

"Actually," Lydia spoke up a bit too quickly, "only Julia does." She turned to Alex and beamed. Alex felt nauseated. "After your sister told me where you were I arranged a short holiday for the two of us, Alex. I knew the flowers were a mistake. Anyway, on Friday the office told me they weren't expecting you in tomorrow, so I figured we could fly home late tomorrow evening. I'm sure your secretary would rather go home today, though. That way she can be in the office bright and early to start the week."

"Oh, absolutely." Julia smiled perfectly. Alex frowned. He didn't like what was going on. He knew he needed to step in and do something, but the least confrontational path still wasn't clear. Luckily the phone began to shrill, cutting the strange silence that had fallen. Alex slumped a bit in the chair as Julia moved toward it with an "I'll get it." How was he going to get out of this?

"MR. RAVENWOOD'S SUITE. This is Julia Brown, may I help you?"

"Julia!" Chelsea's voice traveled across the miles. "Is the wicked witch there?"

"Yes," Julia replied cryptically.

"Did she catch you in a compromising position?"

"Not exactly." Julia gave Alex a smile and held up a finger telling him to be patient.

"Damn. Oh!" Chelsea let off a string of four-letter words.

"Chelsea?" Julia was instantly worried.

"What's wrong?" Alex must have heard the concern in her voice, because he stood, but he didn't reach for the phone. Boy, those boxers sure looked great on him, Julia thought as Chelsea's foul-language tirade suddenly stopped.

"Contraction," Chelsea responded. "I'm in labor. They're rolling in my epidural now. About time. This baby had better be worth it."

"It will be," Julia soothed long-distance. "I'm on my way home."

"With Alex, of course," Chelsea said. "I'm having a baby, and I want you both in the delivery room with me. Besides, you didn't think I would let wench woman have a holiday with him, did you? Get him on the phone. Oh, here it comes."

Julia held out the phone as a string of curses assaulted her ear. "Alex, Chelsea wants to talk to you." With a sweet smile at Lydia, Julia left the room.

"HOW ARE YOU FEELING?" A few hours later Alex strode into the birthing suite so powerfully the nurse attending his sister gulped.

"Surviving!" As a contraction hit, Chelsea grimaced despite her epidural. "I've still got a way to go."

"She's progressing just fine." Despite her graying hair, the nurse gave Alex what he always considered the woman's speculative look. He ignored it.

"So, where's Rachel?" Alex sat down in a chair to the side of Chelsea's convertible hospital bed. Knowing Chelsea hadn't yet been privy to the fact that Julia's disguise had failed, he waited for his sister's answer.

"With Scott," Chelsea fibbed. She reached for her ice chips and shook the plastic cup. She put the cup to her mouth while the nurse adjusted the machine running her IV.

"So right after I talked to him, Scott grabbed her and took her to dinner," Alex said with a wicked grin. He saw his sister's look. "Now don't get angry! You knew at some point I would expose your little scheme. And she really is with Scott. He didn't want to eat by himself. He said you had sent him off on a break, and after telling Julia she wasn't missing anything, he dragged her off. So I volunteered to keep you company."

"At least you'll come in," Chelsea said as she finished her ice chips. She handed the cup to the nurse, who left to refill it. "Dad refuses. He's out in the waiting room. Said he waited outside for both of us, and he'll be in when the baby arrives. So how did you figure it out?"

Alex rolled his eyes. "The first time or when she fell in the pool?"

"She fell in the pool?" Chelsea's voice sounded incredulous.

"She fell in the pool," Alex confirmed, "and when I jumped in to save her I grabbed her wig."

Chelsea closed her eyes at the horror of it. "Don't tell me any more. I'm in labor. I don't even want to know. Just tell me you didn't yell at her and that you sent Lydia home."

No, he hadn't yelled at her. Alex brushed the memory of touching Julia's naked flesh in the tub out of his head. "Yes, I sent Lydia home. I figured you wouldn't want her hanging around."

"Absolutely not," Chelsea stated. She gave a vigorous shake of her head. "I can't stand that woman. But don't get me started. I've cussed so much today I think Scott's hair would have turned gray if they hadn't broken down and given me my epidural."

"But you're fine, right?" Alex leaned forward a little and peered into his sister's face. She didn't seem to be in much pain at this point.

"Perfect as I can be now. I'm actually more or less comfortable if you can ignore the monitors attached all over the place." She sighed. "But the end'll be worth it, as you'll find out when your wife gives birth."

The thought of his wife giving birth gave Alex momentary pause. "It seems I'm missing part of that equation. I don't have a wife."

"No, but you will. Lydia's trying pretty hard for the job, although I couldn't see her wanting to ruin her figure by having a baby. Did you know your feet grow and might not go back? Poor thing might gain an inch or two."

"I thought we weren't going to talk about Lydia."

"So we're not. Let's talk about Julia instead. You never told me if you yelled at her."

Alex lowered his lashes and looked at the paper scrolling out both the baby's and Chelsea's respective heartbeats. "I told you I didn't yell."

"Alex!" Chelsea's heartbeat line shot up. "You didn't!"

"Didn't what?" Alex frowned.

"Sleep with her! Not Julia!"

"No!" Alex's denial was indignant. Sure, he had wanted to, but he hadn't. Therefore he wasn't lying.

Chelsea relaxed back against the pillow. "Good. You'd only hurt her."

"What do you mean I'd only hurt her?" Alex didn't like his sister's opinion of him. He wasn't that shallow, nor the decimation of all women, either. He scowled slightly.

"She's not, well, experienced like you are. She's not a love 'em and leave 'em type." Chelsea rushed on, despite the protesting look Alex now sent her. "Don't give me that nasty look, Alex. If you and Julia had an affair it would create a wedge if it ended terribly. I don't want to lose my best friend."

"I didn't lose my best friend," Alex pointed out, deciding it best to ignore the love 'em and leave 'em comment, "and you married him. In the beginning things weren't all that smooth for you two."

"Yeah, but you're guys. Guys stick together no matter what."

"That's sexist!" Agitated, Alex ran a hand through his hair.

"Look, Alex, if you need any more proof the sexes are different just continue to hang around here a little bit. One's about to pop out pretty soon. I know you like Julia, but she's different. She's a real person and she wears her feelings on her sleeve. Kyle did a job on her when he ran off with her money, and I don't want to see her hurt again."

"Chelsea," Alex paused. His sister watched him expectantly, but Alex didn't know what to say. Yes, he had feelings for Julia, but he hadn't figured how deep they were yet. He had to admit the truth to himself. What had started as an attempt to expose his sister's scheme wasn't just a pleasurable plan anymore. It had become much more complicated than that.

And he hated complications in his life, and Julia was promising to be a very big one. He wanted to make love to her, yet he didn't want to allow anyone to become too close. "How about I promise I'll take care of her. Will that satisfy you?" As soon as the words left his lips, Alex knew they were true. No matter what, he would take the utmost care of Julia. She deserved nothing less.

"No, but it'll have to do." Chelsea grimaced. As if on cue, the nurse arrived with ice chips.

"Let's check you out, Mrs. Meier. If we're lucky, you're at ten and we can start pushing. Your doctor's already on his way, and I just saw your husband get off the elevator."

"I'll be outside, Chelsea," Alex said.

"Chicken." Chelsea called after him.

As Alex walked out of the room to join his father, he decided that's exactly what he was.

Chelsea delivered an eight-pound ten-ounce girl at twelve-fifteen Monday morning. It had been a long, intense day, but as far as Julia was concerned, there wasn't a more beautiful baby anywhere in the world.

Julia put her hand on the nursery glass, watching as a nurse bathed Chelsea's daughter. She had never seen an actual birth before, but she had held Chelsea's right hand while Scott held Chelsea's left. Alex had chosen to keep his father company in the waiting room.

Later, when the labor was over, it had been one of the most wonderful moments of her life, first watching Chelsea hold her newborn, and then holding little Tara herself. Alex and Michael had entered the birthing room, and the look on Alex's face when he held Tara had been priceless.

Julia could still picture it, and she gave a little shiver. The lines on his face had relaxed, and the warmth in his blue gaze had been like a million candles. He had pursed his lips, cooed at Tara, and smiled in absolute delight when she scrunched her eyes in response. It had been love at first sight between Alex and his tiny niece, and at that moment, Julia had known she was totally and hopelessly in love with Alexander Ravenwood.

Sure, she had always loved him, if only as hero worship or an undying crush from afar, but after watching him cuddle Tara, and peer into her open, alert eyes, Julia knew she loved him beyond just a simple infatuation. He was the man she would never get over, the man who owned her heart without knowing it. He made Kyle's momentary blip in her life insignificant by comparison.

Julia wiped the condensation from her breath off the nursery window. Out of view of her mom, Tara was receiving her first shots. Her little face would cry for a moment, then she would suckle the pacifier again and all would be fine.

No matter if Alex ever loved her, she had to do what was right. She had to break up his relationship with Lydia. For Tara's sake.

A long sigh escaped her. Despite Lydia's disappearance at the airport, Julia knew the dreaded woman was still in Alex's life. In fact, on the flight home Lydia had shot Julia killer looks whenever Alex turned his back, and Julia had pretended not to notice. On Chelsea's special day, she refused to let anything get her down. Admittedly she was a little miffed that Alex told Lydia that Julia was Chelsea's best friend, and that Julia's costume had been Chelsea's idea of a joke. The only thing he had left out had been the Sex on the Beach shots. That topic he had avoided.

"She's lovely, isn't she?"

Julia turned from the nursery window to face Alex, and nodded, magnetically aware of his presence. "Absolutely. She's beautiful. I can't wait to hold her again. She was so precious in my arms. I can't wait to have my own some day."

Alex's face became unreadable for a moment. "So you want children?"

"Oh, lots." Julia nodded. She gave a nervous little laugh when his eyes darkened. "I grew up in a big family. They're my biggest support system. Someday it'll happen to me. Right now I'm just happy for Chelsea. Tara's so beautiful." Julia turned away from Alex. The nurse was now rocking Tara to sleep. Alex had been standing too close, and it made her nervous. It was as if she stood before him open, vulnerable and bare.

"Well, you can visit tomorrow because we're ready to leave. Dad's tired so he's already in the limo downstairs waiting to take all of us home." Alex cupped Julia's elbow.

"I bet he's tired." Julia felt relieved that she and Alex weren't going to be alone. From the way his hand on her elbow was making her feel, it was probably better they had a chaperon. "He's a grandfather now."

"Although he remained in the waiting room, he's absolutely besotted, and I'm sure Chelsea will see him night and day now." Alex led her down the hall and into the elevator. His touch had desire shooting through her. Julia's stomach felt fluttery as they stepped out into the brightly lit lobby. The deep night was hot and muggy, and Alex opened the limo door for Julia.

"About time." Michael Ravenwood's tone was gruff as Alex followed her in. Even at sixty-six he remained a man people recognized and respected, despite his retirement two years ago. "Been wondering if you were trying to make one of your own, Alex."

"Of course not, Dad."

"Well, you oughta be." To Julia's amazement, the elder Ravenwood lit into his son right in front of her. "You sowed enough wild oats. Time to give me an heir, eh? Chelsea's marrying only satiated me temporarily, boy. I want to be a grandfather in a big way. That means you best get moving. I was thirty when your mother had you and forty when we had Chelsea. You're thirty-six now, remember? You're getting old, son, old."

Julia gazed out at the black night and put a hand in front of her mouth to keep from laughing. So this was one of the patriarch's famous lectures. Although Julia had never been privy to one directly, Chelsea had told her enough stories. She felt Alex stiffen beside her.

"Time you settled down," Michael repeated forcefully.

"I'm going to marry when I love someone," Alex said tightly, "not just to give you grandchildren, Father."

"Well, at least you believe in the institution." Michael seemed somewhat placated. "Not that you've ever given any indication before with all those women about. Even this latest one doesn't seem like the stay-home-mom type. She's rather plastic, don't you think? Like a Barbie doll. I'm not sure I like her. Now take Julia here. Why couldn't you find someone nice like her?"

A bit embarrassed, Julia coughed, seeing now why Chelsea sometimes referred to her father as a hellion. In all his visits to St. Louis, she'd never seen him on a roll like this.

"Look, son, I was faithful to your mother for thirty-five years, God rest her soul. She was a good mother to you kids. Best lady that ever walked the face of the earth."

"I know, Dad," Alex replied calmly as if he had had dozens of times before. "I'm working on it."

"Good." Michael eyed Julia. "Good. I'll be waiting. I'm not getting any younger, you know." Satisfied with his lecture, Michael turned his attention away from his son. "So, Julia, been working for my boy, eh?"

"Yes, Mr. Ravenwood," Julia replied. "I'm filling in for Rita while she is on vacation."

"Well, maybe you can get my son on a vacation," Michael snorted. "Tells me I'm retired and bans me from the office. Now he works more than I did. Damn fool.''

Julia watched as Alex rolled his eyes and looked out the window.

Julia smiled and began a conversation with Chelsea's father. It was good to see that someone occasionally got the better of Alex Ravenwood.

Without waiting for the chauffeur to come around to open the door, Julia eased out as soon as the limo parked in front of her apartment building. Alex was suddenly right behind her. "I'll walk you to your apartment," he stated.

"You don't have to," Julia said, walking up the steps to the locked community door.

"I didn't offer," Alex replied. "I stated." He reached and took the suitcases the chauffeur had removed from the trunk. "I'll bring your new stuff."

At her apartment door, he waited while she fumbled for her key, and after she passed through the doorway he stepped inside.

Julia knew what he was seeing when he put her suitcases down. The one-room studio apartment was small, minuscule compared to his town house. Having been rushed off to Florida at the last minute, Julia had never even been home to make the foldout double bed back into a futon. Instead the covers were rumpled and tossed, as if she had just gotten up.

She could see Alex's gaze roving over the room, taking in the eclectic decor. Without blinking an eye, he turned back to her.

"Good night, Julia," he said simply. "You don't need to make it into the office today at all. Take the day off. That's what I'm doing. I know I can use the sleep. Anyway, you know where I'll be if you need me, either at the hospital or home sleeping. I'll see you at work Tuesday bright and early at eight.'' He paused, as if debating something.

Julia saw his look and gave him a crooked smile. ''I'll be there, without my wig and with my more modern wardrobe.''

''Good.'' Alex nodded, as if relieved. Julia wished she knew what he was thinking. ''Sleep well and lock up tight. Chelsea would kill me if anything happened to her best friend.''

Of course, Julia thought as she closed the door and slid the dead bolt into place. The magic moments were over, and they were back to brotherly affection. With a sigh she listened to the muffled sound of Alex's footsteps, and then she moved to the front window. She watched as he entered the limousine and it slid out of sight. Julia looked at the clock and groaned. Three in the morning. She would probably sleep the rest of the day away. But it was worth it. She wouldn't have missed tonight for the world.

Exhausted, Julia kicked off her shoes and headed for bed, her dreams filled with babies. Lots of babies. Her babies, looking just like their daddy Alex.

A FEW DAYS LATER Julia wasn't sure if she and Alex had ever gone to Florida. It was as if the weekend had never happened, except for the work that had backed up in their absence.

''How's it going?'' Tessa walked up and dropped another file folder into Julia's in box.

''Slow,'' Julia groaned. It was two in the afternoon on Thursday and she had missed lunch in her attempt to dig out from the mess of letters Alex had dumped on her that morning. He was still holed up in his office, just as he had been for the previous two days. They had hardly spoken except when he gave her instructions. "What's that?"

"Sales figures." Tessa smiled and Julia knew something was up. "The boss wants them immediately."

"So why are you giving them to me?" Julia quizzed.

Tessa put a hand through her gray hair. "Because I have a feeling Alex likes your new look and you have a mission to fulfill."

"Oh, that." Julia shook her head and the sandy blond curls around her chin bounced. "I've done a lot of thinking about the job that I have to do and I'm running up against a brick wall."

"You just need to use your imagination. I've seen the way Alex looks at you, even when he thought you were Julia Brown. But if you don't want to use that, well, I'm sure you'll think of something else." Tessa shrugged. "Anyway, get this report in there pronto."

"Yes, ma'am." Julia stood. She didn't feel like correcting Tessa and telling her that Alex had known her true identity the whole time.

She smoothed down the professional black skirt. Once she had finally gotten out of bed, she had spent Monday afternoon shopping for proper work clothes.

Julia frowned self-consciously. Ever since the moment he had walked her to the door in the wee hours of Monday morning, Alex had hardly glanced at her or spoken to her except to issue directions. Even when she had seen him at the hospital, their conversation had been stilted, and the past two days at work had been almost horrible.

In fact, it was as if he was again avoiding her.

While that may be what she thought she wanted, now after the incident in the hotel suite bathroom, she wasn't so sure. Julia's face reddened at that memory. She had relived it many times.

She had never let anyone touch her like that before, and Alex had brought her to heights that she didn't think existed except in romance novels. Somehow touching him, loving him, had been right, despite her protest to end it. That had been fear, panic on her part. No, she still loved Alex, craved his touch. And now he was avoiding her. With a sigh she grabbed the file folder and knocked on Alex's door, pausing for his "Enter" before venturing inside.

He wasn't at his desk and Julia scanned the room, locating him at his computer work area.

"Yes?" Intent on typing, Alex didn't even look at Julia. She bristled.

"I've got the sales figures that you said you wanted immediately." Julia felt a bit unnerved and angry when Alex didn't even peel his focus from the screen.

"Oh. Set them on my desk. I'll get to them in a minute."

Julia made a noise that sounded like a hmph.

Alex turned suddenly. His blue gaze roved over her impassively. "You have a problem with that, Julia?"

"No, Mr. Ravenwood." Julia shook her head and her fingers whitened as she continued to hold the file folder. "I was just clearing my throat."

Alex's eyes narrowed and his lips thinned. "I see."

Julia felt like squirming as he continued to stare at her. "Do you need anything else, Mr. Ravenwood?"

Alex exhaled slowly. "No. Do you?"

Yeah I do, Julia thought. *I need things to be fun and friendly like they were before. I want to drive Corvettes and run up the Lincoln Memorial steps. I want to kiss you.*

But her thoughts remained hers as she instead stared back at him, returning his impassive look with one of her own. Then she frowned. Alex had circles under his eyes and looked as if he hadn't slept in a few days. With a bit of bitterness Julia wondered if Lydia had been keeping him up late.

"No, Mr. Ravenwood. Thank you for inquiring, but I don't have anything else." Julia walked over to the desk and set the file folder down.

"Julia." Alex called her name and Julia turned to face him again before continuing on to the door.

"Yes, Mr. Ravenwood?"

"Hold all my calls. All of them. I've almost got this finished. I'll buzz you when I'm available and then you can give me my messages." Alex had already turned back to the computer screen.

"Certainly." Julia walked out of the office and closed the door behind her.

Tessa was still standing at Julia's desk. "Not good, I assume."

"Alex wants all his calls held." Julia shrugged. "That was the extent of our conversation. Take a message, Julia, and I'll get it later."

"Interesting." Tessa rubbed her chin thoughtfully. Slowly she wadded up a pink piece of paper and dropped it into the trash can.

"What was that?" Julia raised her eyebrows as curiosity overcame her.

"I was doodling while I waited for the results of your mission." Tessa idly studied a fingernail before she glanced up again. "I'll see you later."

"Whatever." Julia shrugged. She was tired of Tessa's curiosity. In fact, she was tired of Operation Free Alex. She was tired, period. Tired of hurting. Tired of wanting what could never be hers. Hadn't Kyle taught her that?

With a slight groan, Julia thumped down in her seat and began tackling the stacks of paperwork in front of her.

Chapter Ten

After Julia left Alex hit the save key, his thoughts too far away from his project to concentrate properly.

Damn Chelsea, he thought, wishing for just a brief moment that he was an only child. Because his father was gaga over his first grandchild, Michael Ravenwood had begun a new life's quest—marrying off his son. Lydia Olson's name had popped up more than once over the past two days.

His family had made it clear they hated her without directly saying the words.

Not only that, but if they had their way they would be booking the wedding chapel for him and Julia.

Chelsea, being her most maternal self, had been the one to bring up him marrying Lydia the most, but Alex wasn't fooled. He knew there was no love lost between the two women, and that his sister hated the idea of his marrying Lydia.

On the pro side, Lydia fit comfortably into his lifestyle, and the press seemed to like her. And she was usually out of town. A lot.

But, as the past week had proved, he didn't love Lydia Olson. Far from it. And he wanted to marry for love.

Not that he was in love with Julia, he told himself. Just lust. That's what it had to be. Lust was the reason he hadn't been able to keep his hands off Julia. He nodded, trying to convince himself. But he could still see her naked, imprinted ever since she had jumped out of the bathtub, and because of it he had been spending sleepless nights dreaming of her.

Unable to face his feelings, he had decided to just avoid her, but that plan wasn't working, either. When he had asked her earlier if there was anything else she needed, he had hoped she would have said "you."

But she hadn't, so he didn't jump over the desk like in some adolescent fantasy and kiss her lips and tell her she was driving him crazy.

Alex ran a finger through his hair and began to pace. He paused only long enough to take his reading glasses off and set them by the computer. What was he thinking? Chelsea had made it clear several times that she would kill him if he had tried to seduce Julia.

Alex could still remember the conversation they had had in the hospital.

"Did you have to disguise her? It really seems rather strange. She could have been my temp without becoming Julia Brown."

Chelsea had looked at him wisely, as little Tara Marie had happily suckled on her mother's breast. "You would have seduced her."

"I would not." Alex let go a rare lie.

He had known it was not the truth, for he had done everything to seduce the woman with unquenchable fire in her veins. He had felt that fire burn at Chelsea's wedding, in the gazebo, in the Corvette, and in Florida.

Chelsea had known he was lying, and had given him her most dubious look. "Really, Alex. Look, like I told you before, Julia's my friend, and I'd like to keep her that way. I don't want her hurt.''

"I'm dating Lydia." Alex had protested halfheartedly, throwing out the name of the woman he didn't want anymore, except as a shield from which he could hide his true feelings. Those scared him, and Alex wasn't a man to be scared.

"Of course you are," Chelsea had drawled. "But when did that ever stop you before? You trade women in quicker than used videos. Even your best friend settled down before you did."

"Well, you married Scott," Alex had snapped, but to no avail.

"You're grasping for straws," Chelsea had replied easily as she shifted Tara Marie to her other breast. She pulled the cloth over Tara's head and looked directly at Alex. "Scott's my soul mate, and I'm his. The question is, have you found yours? Although I can't stand the woman, you still need to do right by Lydia. I know she wants to marry you. She's made no secret of it."

Alex brushed off the rest of the memory and grimaced. He sat back down at the computer and idly tapped his fingers on the keyboard. When the answer didn't reveal itself, he leaned back in the chair and stretched his six-foot bulk. He was tired. He hadn't slept well since he had dropped Julia off at her apartment four nights ago.

How could he have violated Julia like that? How could he begin making love to her? He had acted like a rutting animal, not like a man of honor and integrity. Guiltily Alex broke a pencil in half and tossed it onto the table.

He needed to clean the messy work area, but not today. No, tonight he was seeing Lydia, and it was time to get the disaster that was his life straightened out. He had to do right by Lydia, like Chelsea kept insisting. For once his sister was correct, and he had to be honest.

He would let Lydia know his feelings when he met her at Henrick's for the formal cocktail party. He considered himself an honest man. He needed to make her an honest woman. He owed that much to Julia.

Alex glanced at the clock. He could use a drink and he wasn't meeting Lydia until six-thirty. Well, he decided, this eligible bachelor was going to be early. That should shake the press up enough so that when he dropped his bombshell about marriage it wouldn't come as a complete surprise.

JULIA SHARPLY SUCKED IN her breath and her heart did flips as at five o'clock Alex Ravenwood walked out of his office wearing a black tuxedo. Julia scooted her chair closer to her desk to hide her body's reaction. Did he know how absolutely beautiful he was?

Of course he did, Julia pushed the thought impatiently out of her head. He knew all about his image and the need to maintain it.

And she knew she could have no part in it. Rita returned to work on Monday, meaning tomorrow was Julia's last day in Alex's office.

Her heart broke as he strode over to her desk. I can't do it, Chelsea, she thought to herself. Not even for ten thousand dollars. If Lydia made him happy, then she was just going to have to live with it. Operation Free Alex was over.

"Julia." Alex stopped in front of her desk. "Any messages?"

Julia handed him the pink message slips and Alex

slowly flipped through them. Through lowered lashes, Julia watched him as he handed them back to her.

"Great, nothing that can't wait until tomorrow. I'm leaving the office for the rest of the day."

You look nice, Julia wanted to say, but she held her thoughts in check. "Have a nice time tonight," she said instead.

Alex looked at her oddly, and then remembered the tux. "Oh, yeah, this. I'm meeting Lydia at Henrick's at six-thirty. We're attending a cocktail party being sponsored by one of the publishing companies. We handled their IPO."

"You'll be early," Julia observed stupidly.

"Well, I have to make a few stops first, but yes, I want to be early. After standing her up for lunch, I don't think she would forgive me if I stood her up again. We've had too many miscommunications lately and there's something really important I need to talk to her about tonight."

Julia nodded mutely.

"Go ahead and leave anytime, Julia. You deserve it. After all, you're free after tomorrow." Alex reached out and touched a curl, pulling it downward and releasing it like a spring. He seemed distracted for a moment as he watched the curl spring back against her chin. "By the way, if I forget to tell you tomorrow, you've done a great job. I really appreciate all your hard work."

"No problem." Julia felt wooden as she watched Alex head for the elevators. A tear threatened to cascade down her cheek and she angrily brushed it away. She wasn't going to cry again over a man.

Sure, Alex would keep more than just a sliver of her pride when she left for New York, but she had known it would happen. Right? She consoled herself with the thought that she had been desirable for once. It didn't help. Even though she knew she didn't have any hope, his choice of Lydia still hurt.

And he had chosen Lydia. He had made that much clear by saying he wanted to talk to her about something very important but he had a stop to make first. Julia buried her head in her hands. That could only mean one thing. Alex was getting ready to propose to Lydia Olson.

Julia had failed and would nurse a broken heart long into the future. And after Kyle she swore she wouldn't be hurt again. Once a fool…

"What's wrong with you?" Tessa approached Julia's desk carrying some pink messages. "You've had your head down for twenty minutes now. I've been wondering if I should come over here or not."

"Alex is making a stop before meeting Lydia." Julia found that saying the words almost brought her to tears. "He has something important to talk to her about."

Tessa put a gentle hand on Julia's shoulder for several minutes before she spoke. "It will be fine, you'll see."

"No," Julia looked up at Tessa as the first tear fell. "I've failed. I've let Chelsea down. She doesn't want Lydia as a sister-in-law and I can't blame her. But at the same time if Alex is happy with her, how can I deny him that?"

"It will be fine, Julia," Tessa soothed. "He won't propose to her tonight."

Julia flicked away a tear. "How can you be so sure?"

"Because the message that Lydia won't be there until seven-thirty is the one that I threw away earlier."

"So, he just waits a little." Julia dabbed her eyes. "She's still coming."

Tessa grinned. "Ye of little faith." She picked through the messages and thrust one at Julia. "You need to deliver this one to Mr. Ravenwood immediately."

"What is it?" Julia suddenly looked hopeful.

"The one from Lydia saying she isn't coming at all."

JULIA PULLED OPEN THE DOOR to Henrick's. One of Arlington's newest and poshest restaurants, it wasn't the type of place Julia would choose to go if she didn't have to. But she had to. Drawing in a breath for courage, she stepped into the modern, glittery interior of the restaurant.

The maître d' glanced over his horn-rimmed glasses and down his nose at her. "May I help you?"

Julia smoothed down Chelsea's little black slip dress, extended her invitation and gave him her warmest smile. "I'm meeting Alex Ravenwood."

The maître d' studied the invitation and, at his nod, Julia felt relief sweep over her. "Yes, ma'am. The party is through that hall and to your left. He's already arrived and left word that he is expecting you."

Uh, wrong, Julia thought wryly as she walked down the hall. He was expecting Lydia. Julia didn't even want to imagine his reaction when she showed up, again, in his beloved's place. At least this time she was dressed appropriately, thanks to Chelsea's office closet.

The room was packed. The overabundance of perfumed bodies assaulted Julia's nose when she stepped into the party room. There had to be at least two hundred people in here, Julia thought, as she threaded her way through the tight crowd. She searched the people who were standing, and tried to peer around them to see those who were sitting.

Julia circled the octagonal room twice. People glanced at her but dismissed her, and Julia felt her frustration mount. No Alex.

"Hey, you look too pensive." A friendly male voice intruded on her thoughts and Julia turned. The unfamiliar man grinned at her. "Come on." He grabbed a flute of champagne from a passing waiter. "There's no way anyone could stand up a beautiful woman like you."

"Well, that's not exactly it. He didn't know I was coming," she said, drinking the champagne a bit too quickly. Bubbles popped against her throat, giving her a tingly feeling.

"Then I'll consider myself lucky to be his stand-in." The man sized her up as he reached out his hand. "Tom Campbell, Campbell & Calvin."

Julia took his hand and returned his firm grip with one of her own. Her pseudonym was automatic, rolling off her tongue as if she was back in college. "Julia Brown. Grayson Designs."

"Nice to meet you, Julia." Tom drained his champagne and reached for another glass. He barely avoided sloshing it on Julia's shoes. "So, what's Grayson Designs?"

"It's my own company." The lie, honed in college, slipped off her tongue with ease. The champagne again bubbled in her throat as she took another sip. "I work mainly with theater companies."

"Really. That sounds intriguing."

Julia gave him a weak smile, realizing she might as well be stuck with Tom for a few more moments. At least she didn't look like a wallflower waiting for someone to take pity and notice her.

Julia laughed slightly at the image of her waiting and

pining for Alex and changed the subject away from herself. In her limited experience with men like Tom, they liked to talk about themselves. At least Kyle had. "So, Tom, what about you?"

"I'm a publishing agent. Mainly nonfiction."

Julia nodded and slowly finished her first glass of champagne as Tom began to detail how he chose clients to represent. Julia tuned him out and accepted another glass of champagne from a passing waiter. While Tom looked good in his tuxedo, she just wasn't interested. His golden looks didn't hold a candle to Alex. Speaking of her boss, five more minutes, she promised herself, and then he was on his own. Lydia could stand Alex up for all she cared. She grabbed some weird-looking substance off a passing hors d'oeuvres tray and realized Tom was still talking.

"So, I discovered a real winner in Ariana MacLeod, but then I'm always on the lookout for a sure thing."

"How nice." Julia ignored his line and gave him a weak smile. So engrossed in his own importance, Tom didn't even notice. Julia continued looking at anonymous faces and using her finger to circle the rim of her champagne flute.

"I definitely think a person should be on the lookout. You never know what you might find." The rich baritone voice Julia knew intimately startled her and she jerked her arm forward.

"Hey!" Tom jumped back slightly as champagne sloshed out of Julia's glass and over his shoes.

"I'm sorry," Julia apologized. "I didn't mean to."

"Of course you didn't." Alex came around from where he had been breathing down the back of her neck. "I startled you. I'm the one who needs to apologize."

"This is Julia Brown," Tom interrupted proprietarily.

He reached forward and pulled Julia toward him. "Julia, this is Alex Ravenwood, CEO of Ravenwood Investments."

"Nice to meet you." Julia stepped out of Tom's grasp and held out her hand. Alex shook it firmly. Unlike Tom's handshake, Alex's sent chills down her spine, and Julia's hand tingled long after he dropped it.

"Oh no, the pleasure is truly all mine." Alex's blue eyes glittered for a moment before he turned away from Julia. "So, Tom, what are you selling now?"

Julia cringed inwardly as Tom began to outline some of his author's current manuscripts. She stood there as if rooted, not knowing how to break in and tell Alex about Lydia. Her body was so tense she felt as if she would explode.

"Here." Alex lifted another glass of champagne from a tray and passed it to her. "You're empty. Or I could order you something else if you'd like."

"This'll be fine," Julia said. She took the fresh glass, her fingers in direct contact with Alex's.

The shock that sizzled between their flesh almost caused her to drop the champagne flute, but she steadied her shaking hand and took a small sip. She had already had two glasses on almost an empty stomach. Just where were the hors d'oeuvres anyway? Time to find them, Julia decided, and get out of this messy situation.

"Tom." She interrupted the man gently. "It was a pleasure meeting you, but I need to mingle some more." Julia smiled her warmest smile, and saw Alex's blue eyes narrow.

"Oh, Julia, I'm sorry." Tom quickly smiled his apologies. He reached out his arm to touch Julia, but she sidestepped him.

"Really, I must go." Julia clutched her third empty

glass and, with a vague goodbye smile, she began to thread her way through the crowd. Even more people had crowded into the too-small room. Julia wormed her way through the throng and toward the door. The champagne had gone to her head, but she was still functioning. Food would be helpful, she thought. Home would be even better.

Julia finally reached the door of the party and began to head for the exit. The maître d' gave her a strange look. "Leaving so soon?" he asked as he glanced down his nose at her. "Didn't you find him?"

"Of course she did." A hand gripped her elbow firmly and Alex gave the man a mocking smile. Petrified, Julia just looked up at Alex. "I would never stand Julia Grayson up."

With that, he simply guided Julia out the door. The July heat assaulted them the minute they stepped onto the sidewalk.

"Hot," Julia babbled, moving her feet quickly over the sweltering pavement. "I need to get home." Julia tried to extricate her arm and head for the Metro stop.

Alex shook his head, put a hand on her arm and stopped her flight. "I don't think so. I think you have a message to give me, don't you?" With his free hand he flipped open the phone and punched one number. "I'm ready," he said simply before closing the phone. He turned to Julia. "I borrowed Father's limo tonight."

He must really have been planning to impress Lydia, Julia thought. The thought made the hot day suddenly seem cold and she shuddered.

"I don't understand," Julia replied as the three glasses of champagne caught her full force. "I'll be fine in the Metro, really. If it's Chelsea's dress, I'm sure that no one will try to take that from me."

"I wouldn't be so sure of that," Alex said tightly as he loomed over her.

"Tessa said I should wear it," Julia rambled on, shrinking away from him. Alex caught her and held her steady. "Tessa didn't want you to be embarrassed like when I went to the art gallery. She said people talked for days."

Alex's fingers tightened on her arm. "They're about to talk more. Smile for the camera, Julia." Alex pulled her to him, and Julia found herself suddenly crushed against his broad chest. The shock of being flattened against him caused a strange reaction in her body. Her body clung to his, and only her eyes revealed the disorientation caused by him and not too much champagne. Alex's eyes had darkened to a murky blue. Julia felt as if she was flying.

"Ready? Say cheese."

"Huh?" What was he talking about? Somewhere in her consciousness she heard the whir of the flash and the click of the shutter, but she lost all conscious thought when Alex Ravenwood's mouth descended to kiss hers. Julia lost herself the moment his lips pressed down. Her body exploded into millions of fireworks as Julia welcomed the kiss. As Alex deepened the kiss, the tension left Julia's body.

His hands lifted her arms, and Julia wrapped them, as commanded, around his neck. Alex's tongue slid inside her mouth, teasing and tantalizing, and Julia found herself burning all over. It wasn't just the heat from the sidewalk that seared through her shoes. It was much more.

"Julia? Did I miss something? Is this him?" Tom's voice cut through Alex's kiss. Julia pulled away and tried to find her senses.

Alex detached Julia's arms as a discreet honk cut through the traffic. The limousine pulled up to the curb. Opening the door, Alex helped a dazed Julia enter the cool interior. He turned back to Tom.

"Sorry, Tom, it's a little game Julia and I like to play with each other. Makes life so much more interesting." Alex winked and turned to give a trademark cheeky grin to the photographer now frantically scribbling on a pad of paper.

"Julia Grayson," he said helpfully as they got into the limo. "Be sure you spell it correctly."

Chapter Eleven

In the coolness of the limo Julia struggled for composure. She failed the moment Alex slid in next to her.

"We're ready," were the blunt words Alex used to greet the chauffeur. "Remember the way to Julia's apartment?"

At the chauffeur's nod, Alex pressed the button and raised the privacy glass. "Well, Julia Brown of Grayson Designs, would you like to explain the cryptic call that I got from Tessa on my cell phone about an hour ago?"

Julia's eyes widened. "She told you I was coming?"

"Of course. Although that was about all she said. Care to explain why?"

"Because Lydia wasn't. She canceled again. I've got the message here saying she's not coming." Julia opened Chelsea's small black beaded purse, but Alex's movement stilled her fingers.

He was watching her with hooded eyes and it left Julia disconcerted. While she could drown in those blue pools, not seeing them disturbed her more.

"So you're taking her place?" Alex's words were soft, and his face loomed closer to hers. The outer blue rims of his eyes seemed almost cobalt, and Julia froze in anticipation as he reached out a finger and snaked it under her chin.

"No," Julia protested weakly. Indescribable shivers ran through her. "Tessa didn't want you to be stood up. She tried six times on your cell phone, but you didn't answer. She even called the restaurant, but now I see why they couldn't find you. The place was packed."

"That it was. Luckily Tessa reached me or I wouldn't have been able to rescue you in time. Tom Campbell is a human leech. He finds a beautiful woman and he just latches on for all he's worth." Alex's finger lightly traced her jawbone, sending a rush of desire flooding over her.

"Oh."

Alex studied her face. "I promised Chelsea the night she had Tara I'd look after you. I think saving you from Tom Campbell more than fulfills my promise, even if she did set this all up."

"Set this up?" Julia jerked her head up in surprise.

"You poor thing. You really have no clue, do you? Tessa and Chelsea set this all up."

"But Lydia canceled! And Tessa said she couldn't get a hold of you!" Julia's voice trailed off as all the pieces to the puzzle fell together.

"Tessa had no problem an hour ago, did she? And my cell phone shows that I haven't missed any calls." Alex reached into the small refrigerator and withdrew a bottle of water. He unscrewed the lid and handed the bottle to Julia before getting one for himself. He settled back against the leather seat and loosened his tie, and Julia used the silence to let his words sink in before he continued.

"You may be Chelsea's best friend, Julia, but Tessa's always been her co-conspirator. They've come up with some really great schemes in the past few years. I should have seen through this one the first day, but the disguise fooled me. I pegged Chelsea for sending me a beautiful secretary, but then she outdid herself by having you show up in that getup. Then when I figured out her best friend and my temp were the same person, the game changed again. But it doesn't matter. Whatever they're doing to Lydia and me, I know you aren't involved. You're just their pawn."

Julia's eyes widened in surprise and she took a sip of water in an attempt to hide her expressions. "Look, Alex, I'm sure Tessa didn't know about me. She tricked me into giving the secret away! She threatened to upend the file cabinet."

"Oh, Julia." Alex's tone was benign. "I can't believe you didn't see it. You lived with Chelsea for four years. Surely you recognize one of her setups when you see one, don't you? She played you like an instrument and you performed perfectly."

"What about Lydia? Did she cancel tonight or not?" Julia leaned back against the cool leather and tried to process it all.

"I have no idea." Alex tapped his finger against the water bottle.

"Then you may have just stood her up if Tessa made it all up!" Julia sat up suddenly, panic filling her.

"I may have." Alex shrugged. "It'll be the first nasty thing I've done in my life. But it doesn't matter anymore. Chelsea got what she wanted, which was for me to ditch Lydia Olson. For once I don't mind letting my sister win. It was time to let Lydia go. Besides, I'm sure Tom can take care of Lydia. He'll have a great time telling her all about us."

He lowered his face to hers and his lips grazed lightly

over hers. "I'm hungry." Julia's eyes widened fearfully as he pulled away from her. He gave her a cocky grin. "Want to order Chinese?"

"I don't think Lydia would like this," Julia protested, her lips still tingling from the brief kiss and its implications, implications she hadn't even begun to process or understand.

Alex shook his head. "No, I don't think Lydia will, but she doesn't have a choice. As of tomorrow our picture will be plastered on the front page of D.C.'s daily tabloid."

The limo pulled up in front of Julia's apartment building. "Our picture?" Julia whispered.

"The one of us kissing." Alex was already opening the door. "Lydia should see it as soon as she gets up tomorrow. I'm sure she'll get the message Chelsea wanted her to see loud and clear. My sister will be delighted with the turn of events. While it may not be the best way to deliver her message, I'm sure it'll be effective."

Alex's firm grip helped a wobbly Julia out of the limousine. "Lydia'll be furious." Julia's voice was inaudible.

"I'm not going to worry about it." Alex shrugged and he grabbed Julia's hand and practically pulled her up the walkway.

"Look, Alex, I told Chelsea that if Lydia made you happy that I wasn't going to interfere anymore." Julia concentrated on moving her feet toward the apartment building door. She needed him to understand, needed to tell him the whole story. She needed to tell him about the money.

Alex cut her off before she continued to defend herself. "It doesn't matter, Julia. You played your part. I didn't discover the sabotage to my phones until just a day ago.''

Not waiting for Julia to confirm or deny his accusation, Alex opened the door to the building. Cool air rushed out and Julia stepped inside. Suddenly overheated and dehydrated, all she wanted was to sit down on a comfortable chair.

"I'll admit," Alex said as he ushered Julia into the elevator, "it took me a little longer than normal to figure Chelsea's entire scheme out, even after I saw through your disguise. I have only one question, Julia. Even when you were in disguise and you realized you could get to me, was making me fall for you just part of the plan, or was it real?"

Julia felt sick to her stomach. When Alex reached for her key, she simply passed it over to him and clutched her stomach. Opening the door, he moved so she could step inside first.

"It doesn't matter. I called Chelsea before I went to the party and told her she won. I was going to tell Lydia at dinner tonight that it was over. So you can stop feeling guilty, Julia. You didn't do anything to force my decision. I'm a big boy, I know how to end my own affairs, even if this one's ending a bit messy."

Julia slumped down on the convertible futon as Alex maneuvered expertly in the tight quarters.

"Is there a Chinese place close?" Alex pulled off the loosened bow tie and set it on a scarred end table.

"There's one on Connecticut," Julia replied, getting to her feet. "The menu's by the telephone. You can't miss it."

She saw him glance at what served as her kitchen. In the space of maybe ten square feet she had a small refrigerator, oven and sink.

Suddenly Julia had to get out of the short dress. "I'm going to change." Ignoring Alex's look, she darted into the bathroom.

Julia stared at herself for a long time in the mirror before splashing some water on her face. She loved Alex Ravenwood. She needed to tell him that he meant something to her. She needed to tell him about the money.

He had just finished ordering the food when Julia reappeared wearing shorts and a sleeveless polo shirt.

"You look cooler," he observed from his seat on the sofa. He had taken off his jacket and the black cummerbund, and Julia noticed he had left on the custom-sewn black dress shoes.

"Can I get you anything, Alex? All I have is bottled water, but I can run down to the store on the corner." Julia bit her lip.

"Water is fine." Alex stretched his legs out and Julia felt his eyes watching her as she opened a large bottle of water and poured each of them a glass.

Julia placed the cup on the table next to Alex and took a seat in the wide-backed wicker chair. She decided to wait for a good opening.

Alex saluted her with his plastic cup. "So, Chelsea says you're really headed to New York next."

"I've got a job with Viscountie designing formal attire." Julia spoke up as the air conditioner hummed in its attempt to cool the room.

"Chelsea told me she offered to set you up in business in Washington, D.C., but you turned it down."

"I don't have the connections or the investment capital." Maybe now she should tell him. Feeling Alex studying her, she shifted uncomfortably and began twisting her hands. Catching her movements, she placed her hands in her lap. Maybe later.

Alex gave her a wry smile, and Julia knew he sensed her nervousness. "I know my sister, and Chelsea wouldn't invest in a charity case, even if it was you."

"So how will Lydia retaliate?" Julia changed the subject dramatically and deliberately avoided Alex's expression.

Alex raised his water glass to his mouth and looked at her over the rim. Julia felt his scrutiny and saw his features darken for just a moment. Then the tension seemed to leave his body and he settled back against the floral upholstery again.

"I'm not certain what Lydia will do, but you'd better watch your back. She'll probably try to claw your eyes out. If you want, you can take the day off tomorrow. With pay."

Julia gave a weak smile, her relief at Alex letting the subject change only short-lived. "Gee, thanks."

Alex shrugged. "Glad to oblige. You've been a terrific secretary, Julia." He straightened up and got serious. "I admit, I was wary about you once I discovered your motives, but you did the job. You've been the best temp I've ever had. If you wanted to stay in the District, I'm sure Ravenwood would have a spot for you."

A lump formed in Julia's throat. The last thing she wanted was to work at Ravenwood Investments day after day in a menial job just so Alex could keep her around. No, that was not an option. When her job was up, and her ten thousand dollars safely in hand, she was leaving. Hopefully her heart would still be mostly intact.

"Food." Julia rose as a ring sounded. She pressed the button on the speaker by the door. "Yes?"

"Woo Chan." The caller was obviously Chinese.

"Come on up." Julia buzzed him in the door.

Alex stood and took his wallet out of his pocket. "I've got it, Julia."

The arrival of the deliveryman gave Julia a few moments to attempt to pull herself together. After Alex's revelations, she wasn't sure why he was still in her apartment. Instead she watched as he pulled out a wad of cash and traded it for bags of Chinese food. He set the bags on the coffee table and began removing small white cartons.

"We seem to do a lot of eating, don't we?"

"We do." Julia smiled.

"I'm going to wash up."

"Sure." Julia tugged on the hem of her shorts as Alex disappeared into the bathroom. She gazed at the closed door. Behind it she could hear the clanging of her toilet, and then the running of water as it splashed in her sink. Alex was in her apartment. She didn't know why, but he was here. Thank you, she whispered aloud. *I love him. I'll tell him the truth later, after dinner. I promise.*

She grabbed some napkins off the counter as Alex came out. "I was getting napkins."

"We'll need those," Alex said, his eyes narrowing for a moment. "Let's eat, shall we?"

The room was growing darker as the sun set, and as the night wore on they slipped back into the camaraderie of friends.

"So, are you afraid of going to New York?"

"Petrified," Julia answered. She chased a piece of rice with her chopsticks. "Liam told me I was a fool to go."

"Liam?"

"My older brother. The one I lived with for a year. I've got three brothers and one sister, but Liam and I are close confidants. He told me no man was worth leaving for. But I just couldn't stay at that job anymore and take everyone's pity."

"Your brother sounds wise," Alex said. Julia couldn't see his expression because of the twilight shadows hiding his face.

"Perhaps. Although Liam dated a married woman for a while, so I usually don't take his advice on relationships. He'll be the world's last living bachelor before he allows himself to be hurt again."

"What about you?" Alex's voice was low and deep.

Julia's brow furrowed as she frowned. "What do you mean, what about me?"

"What about you. Kyle hurt you, and you're running away to New York. Are you ever going to love again?"

I already am in love, Julia thought, but she didn't say the words aloud. How could she? "I hope so," she replied after a moment's pause. "I want to be married, and I want kids."

The room had grown too dark, and Julia reached up to turn on a light. Alex gave an amused glance at the tasseled lamp shade.

"I'm subletting, so the apartment came furnished." Julia defended the tasteless decor. "Can't you tell?"

"I was wondering. Looks like late seventies." Alex gave her a warm smile and Julia's heart fluttered. With the turning on of the soft light, she felt hope flood into the room. Maybe things were going to be okay after all, and her heart would survive Alex Ravenwood. The decor seemed to be a safe topic, and Julia decided to stick with it.

"Some of the furniture's more like early seventies,

but the rent's reasonable.'' Julia decided not to mention Chelsea paid the rent, and smiled instead. Sitting in the glow from the lamp, he looked almost perfect, except for one small thing. "Alex, you've got egg on your face.''

"I've what?'' Alex questioned, as if not understanding the subject change and Julia's meaning. Julia reached her fingers forward and picked a piece of egg that had been lingering by his lips off his face. She held it out for him to inspect.

"Egg on your face. From the fried rice,'' Julia added for good measure. She flipped the offending object into an empty carton.

"I've never had literal egg on my face.'' Alex grinned. "You've saved me again. Julia, my savior.''

Julia blushed and looked down at her crossed legs. "You're a cad.''

Alex leaned over and, with a swift movement of his fingers, he lifted her chin up until he could see her face. "Perhaps.''

The intensity of his gaze scared her as he confirmed her use of the stereotype. Alex's face was mere inches from hers, and Julia forced herself to breathe.

"That's probably the perfect word for what I am. Not only did I play along with Chelsea's game, but I've just broken up with a woman by publicly dumping her. I didn't intend for it to happen this way, but I let it.'' Alex leaned forward, moving himself to rest on his knees. Slowly he stroked Julia's chin.

"You see, Julia, I can't help myself when I'm around you. I can't sleep, I can't think. I can't function. I'm know that's not what Chelsea intended, she told me as much, but you've got me totally confused, and I'm never confused.''

Julia stared at him. His lips looked even fuller, more tantalizing as he continued.

"You see, I've thought of nothing except kissing you again like I did in the bathtub, and those thoughts don't make me good husband material for Lydia. I needed her to be honest and stop deluding herself about me. Now that I've been brutally honest, you need to be as well. Don't lie to me this time, Julia. I want the truth. Was it only an act for you? Were your kisses just to make me come to my senses and dump Lydia?"

"No." Julia felt she was shouting, but her voice came out of her mouth a mere whisper. Alex's fingers burned a path across her chin, and he moved his hand to lightly stroke her earlobe. "Never."

"No act," he murmured to himself. He seemed satisfied, no delighted, Julia couldn't be certain. Her brain had short-circuited. As Alex's fingers stroked her cheek lightly, her body became one big ache.

"Oh, Julia." Alex's reserve shattered and he practically groaned her name. "Kiss me?"

It was a question, not a command, and Julia loved him for it. She barely nodded her astounded consent before Alex leaned forward and brought his mouth to hers. He gently covered her disbelieving lips, and although it was a soft kiss, unlike the possessive kiss outside the restaurant, Julia felt the passion flare immediately. Her body melted, and as if sensing she was losing her balance, Alex scooped her into his arms. He leaned her back onto the floor where he proceeded to kiss her neck, her throat, and then her ears.

Julia clung to him, her arms stroking his back. He smelled of heaven, all musky and male. Her body molded to his and instinctively she pulled his white shirt up out of his pants so she could run her hands over his naked flesh.

"Julia," Alex's murmuring of her name was music in her ear. "Do you know what you've done to me? Somehow you felt so right every time we touched." He slid his hands underneath her shirt, and in one click he had unhooked her bra.

Julia's breasts sprang forward from their tight confines, and Alex slid over onto his side so that he could caress them intimately. His hands massaged her full breasts, and Julia gasped in delight as he drew up a hardened nipple and ran his fingertip over the aching nub.

"Julia, tell me you want this or I'll stop." Alex rubbed his finger in a circular motion over the other breast and then stroked the aching tip between two fingers.

Julia threw her head back. She'd wanted him for so long. To deny herself now, she couldn't do it. Wouldn't do it. "Oh, Alex, yes." Julia shuddered and Alex brought his mouth to taste her twin charms intimately.

Julia writhed and bucked against him as the wave of sensation from Alex's tongue cascaded over her. He nuzzled and lathed, and Julia understood why men fought wars over passion.

Alex paused from his ministrations long enough to whisper to her. "Julia, I want this to be special. I don't want to rush, but I'm not sure I can slow myself from touching you everywhere at once."

A shudder of pleasure ran from Julia's chest to her toes, and she moved her hands to feel the soft hair on Alex's broad chest. Her fingers ran across his flat nipples and he groaned. With one deft movement he lifted her up off the floor and then placed her down again minus her shirt. His mouth again found the hardened points of Julia's breasts and Alex caressed and tasted until Julia cried out his name.

"You really want me," Alex whispered, his fingers on the buttons of her shorts.

"For the longest time. Yes. Oh, Alex! Yes." Her voice whimpered with desire. Waiting for the fantasy had been worth it. Tonight Julia knew she was finally going to understand the summit, the peak that women reached when they were with the person they loved. And she was with the person she loved.

Julia pushed all nagging doubts out of her head, and captured his mouth with hers. For tonight he belonged to her. Boldly she sent her tongue deep within Alex's mouth, tasting the man who had claimed her soul years ago from only a photograph.

Alex pulled his mouth away from hers and silenced her protest by placing a finger on her lips. Gently he pushed her head back, and began trailing kisses over her neck again. He paused briefly to kiss her ear before sliding down her neck, across her chest, and then down the flat of her belly.

She quivered as his tongue teased below the fabric waistline of her shorts. It was an intimate act he was leading up to, and one Julia had refused to consider with any other. But with Alex her body became almost wanton. Her dreams of this moment hadn't even been close to the reality of the waves of passion coursing through her.

Flesh teased flesh, and Alex kissed her belly button before his fingers slowly slid the zipper of her shorts down. In a direct line, Alex followed his fingers with his lips. He eased Julia's hips up, freeing her from her clothing. His hands slid under her buttocks, cupping them, and Julia trembled with anticipation and aching need. His fingers stroked inside her thighs, touching her and then Julia gasped and her body splintered into slivers of pleasure as Alex captured the center of her heat with a searing kiss.

Julia arched and cried out in pleasure, and Alex gave himself to her, stroking her until her world shattered into a thousand rays of light. She heard herself screaming out his name as he pressed his hand over her throbbing womanhood. He moved himself forward, and Julia found herself struggling with him to free him from the last bondages of his clothing. She knew not where any of it sailed, nor did she care.

She gasped with desire as she felt his hardness next to her leg. She had seen men naked before when they were changing costumes, yet never had Julia seen the full masculine glory that Alex was now revealing to her. With one well-placed thrust, Alex lowered himself to her, sinking into her heated slickness with a muted groan.

"Julia!" Alex cried out her name as he broke through her virginal barrier. Julia dug her nails into his shoulder as the temporary pain gave way to excruciating pleasure and fulfillment.

"Julia!" Alex's desire knew no bounds as Julia felt his manhood tightly sheathed inside her. She shuddered immediately as the first crest of pure bliss crashed over her. Alex moved tentatively once, stretching her newness before he thrust himself deep inside her.

"Julia, I'm being selfish. Forgive me!" Alex groaned. His manhood buried deep inside her hit her apex, and Julia cried out as Alex's thrusting quickened and intensified.

Tears brimmed in her eyes, not from pain, but from

the sheer joy of having him inside her. Her body responding to the age-old dance of soul mates, Julia clawed her nails into his shoulder and began to match his driving rhythm.

"Julia, I don't want to hurt you. Oh, Julia!" Alex cried out her name again and pulled slightly away, but Julia moved her hand around his waist and forced him back down toward her. Her body writhed with her own powerful need to claim this man, her first lover, and all the fulfillment of her new, emergent womanhood.

"Now, Alex." Julia's breathy voice whispered in his ear. "Yes, Alex, yes."

She gave a passionate cry as Alex drove himself even deeper, if that were possible, burying himself into her until he filled Julia with every ounce of his being.

Julia felt herself climaxing around him as they crested over peak after peak together. She felt Alex's final, shuddering thrust as he filled her with the last drop of his essence. Spent, he collapsed upon her.

He made a motion as if to move, but Julia tightened her arms and refused to let him break their union until the last aftershock had subsided from her still-quaking body. Only then did she allow Alex to slowly remove himself. In his attempt to avoid hurting her tender flesh, he kicked over an open carton of white rice.

"Well, not too bad," he said, referring to the rice spread over the floor.

"Not bad at all," Julia agreed, referring instead to his lovemaking. She raised up, allowing Alex a first-hand view of her naked, well-loved body before turning to begin cleaning the mess on her floor.

"Stop that," he commanded as she righted another carton that had fallen and spilled. "Let me look at you."

With new womanly satisfaction, Julia smiled as Alex drank in her appearance. She, in turn, did the same, finally running a finger across his chest. *I love you,* she thought quietly to herself. *Tonight, our lovemaking is worth the hurt I know I'm going to suffer later when I have to leave. But I'll always have the memory. No more fantasies for me. I'll always have the reality of your lovemaking. I'll always know that once I had perfection, that it was briefly mine.*

Alex reached down and cradled her to his chest. "Come home with me tonight." Julia looked at him uncertainly. "Julia, please. Get some clothes. It'll be safe. Lydia never set foot in my bedroom, and tonight I want a big proper bed. I want to make love to you again, and do it right."

"Right?" Julia queried with a raised eyebrow. "It felt pretty right to me."

"That wasn't what I meant. I want to go slow, to drive you crazy, to make you truly feel." He grinned, but then his smile faded as Alex turned totally serious. "Julia."

Julia turned to face him. "You really were..." he began.

"Yes." She nodded, and with her fingertips she traced feather-light strokes over his firm shoulder blade. She knew Alex was asking about her virginity. "I was."

"I didn't mean to," Alex started to say, but Julia silenced him by putting her right forefinger to his lower lip and caressing it.

"I wanted you to," she said simply. She closed her eyes. "I'll remember my first time forever. It was perfect. It was everything I wanted it to be, and more. I'm glad it was you." *I've waited my whole life for it to be you,* she didn't add.

"You're unlike any woman I've ever known." Alex kissed her finger, sucking it into his mouth and teasing the end. His blue eyes darkened. "Come home with me, Julia. I want to make love to you again, in a proper bed. Not that poor excuse for a futon." His lips teased her and his voice huskily pleaded with her. "Unless you don't want me to make love to you again."

Julia stretched lazily, her chest rising and falling suggestively. A thrill of anticipation ran through her when Alex could do nothing but stare.

"Oh, yes, Alex. There's no question that I want you to make love to me again."

"Then I will." Alex gave her an unconstrained smile. "First, however, I see a little bit of rice that got stuck right here." Alex leaned his mouth down to catch a grain that had attached itself to Julia's stomach.

"Oh," was all Julia could say as the desire built again.

"There's one here, as well." Alex leaned down to capture a grain that had stuck to her lower breast. His tongue licked it off and he gave her a wicked grin.

Two hours later they gave up leaving Julia's apartment, and sent the chauffeur home. Alex cradled Julia in his arms, brushed the hair from her face with his fingers, and with deep, contented sighs, they both finally fell asleep on Julia's very mussed futon.

ALEX BUTTONED UP HIS CUFFS while he stared down at Julia's sleeping figure. Blond hair fanned out around her face, and the result was almost angelic. He hated leaving her. He could easily wake up to a face like that every morning. The thought shook him. Waking up every morning to Julia. He stared at her and remembered Chelsea's cryptic words. Had he found his soul mate? Had he found the woman he would have children with, the woman to grow old with?

It was an alien thought, commitment between a man and a woman, and he wasn't sure how to go about it. If only he could have had a legitimate reason to claim her, a reason to make her stay.

Her long eyelashes fluttered open. "Alex?"

"Right here, sweetheart." He leaned down to kiss her on the tip of her delightful nose. "It's morning and even though I'm the boss, I've got to go in today as much as I want to play hooky with you."

"Oh." Julia blinked.

Alex sat down on the futon beside her, his weight rolling her toward him. She was naked, and it would be so easy to slide back into bed and love her all over again. He groaned. "I'm going to go home and shower and I'll see you at the office in a few hours, hmm?"

"How should I act?" Julia pulled up the covers to her chin and Alex smiled. She was precious, an innocent delight. No, not so innocent anymore. He allowed himself a delighted smile. Their night of passion had sealed that. Never had lovemaking been so good, felt so right. Alex knew that being with Julia wasn't just lust. It was more. Much more. He reached out to run a forefinger down her cheek. "Just act normal at the office, except plan the two of us going out to lunch. We're not through discussing this yet."

"This?"

"Us." As Alex watched Julia's eyes widen, he felt a strange emotion—panic.

"But I'm leaving in a week. I'm only staying until

next Saturday. Then I can move to New York. My apartment will be ready.''

A bit of a fear gripped him, but Alex managed to nod. He needed her to believe there was an *us*. ''I know, but New York isn't far.'' He didn't think Julia needed to know that if all went according to his new plan she never would make it to New York. ''We'll work it out, Julia. We'll discuss it at lunch. Get some sleep, sweetheart, and I'll see you at the office in a few hours.''

''Okay.'' Julia yawned. Alex could tell she was still tired. He was tired himself. They had made love most of the night, the last time only two hours ago.

''I'll show myself out.'' He kissed her lips lightly, not allowing himself to explore them more. If he did he would never leave. Humming a tune to himself, he let himself out, making sure the door locked tightly behind him. It was going to be a great day.

Chapter Twelve

Julia had hardly arrived when Tessa stood over Julia's desk. The look on her face was demanding. "Well?"

"Huh?" Julia looked up and blinked. The lights of the office seemed unusually harsh today.

"You look like you didn't get any sleep last night," Tessa accused. Her eyes narrowed. "What happened?"

"I gave him the message," Julia replied, deliberately being evasive. She ignored Tessa's raised eyebrow indicating her disbelief. There was no way she was telling Tessa anything.

"And?" Tessa's tone revealed she wasn't about to give up easily.

"And as I'm sure you already know, he called Chelsea to tell her she won. Alex dumped Lydia." Julia stifled another yawn. Once Alex had left her apartment she had rolled over and caught only an hour of sleep before getting up and struggling into the shower.

"Okay, I can tell you need some motivation. How about you explain this?" Tessa placed the tabloid down on Julia's desk with a flourish. Spread across the bottom of the front page was the picture of Alex kissing Julia. The headline boldly proclaimed Out With The Old, In With The New.

"Ooh, that's tacky," Julia said, her eyes reading the caption. Interesting though. Even Julia could see the passion in the kiss Alex was giving her. And he looked so good, too. Of course the paper had spelled her last name wrong, but the paper had gotten her first name correct. She'd put it in her scrapbook anyway.

"Care to explain?"

"Not really." Julia blinked and rubbed her temples in order to focus. "Is there Mountain Dew in the soda machine? I need caffeine. I think I had too much champagne at the party last night."

"You had a little more than that. Come on, spill the beans."

"Look, Tessa, nothing happened." Julia lied with a practiced ease.

The ding of the elevator saved her from continuing to defend herself. Julia's apprehension gave way to relief as Alex strode easily across the gray carpet.

"Oh, I see you have our fine photo," he said as a way of greeting. "Thanks for helping me make sure Lydia got the message that I was serious."

"No problem," Julia replied. "I've set the mail on your desk already."

"You've gotten quite efficient in three weeks, haven't you?" Alex smiled. "Good morning, Tessa. Don't you have work to do? Like calling my sister and gloating or something? I'm sure she's dying to hear from you."

Tessa looked a little taken back. Julia smiled to herself. Her legs hidden by the desk, she instinctively crossed them. Despite her beating him into the office, he looked as if he had had coffee. Unlike bleary-eyed Julia, Alex was crisp and professional. His Armani suit was crisply pressed, and even the Bruno Magali loafers he wore were polished.

"Julia?" Alex waved a hand in front of her face. "Julia?"

"Oh! Yes, Mr. Ravenwood." Julia coughed and sat up straight in the chair.

"Late night?"

"Yes, Mr. Ravenwood. A Harrison Ford movie was on cable. I had to stay up and watch it. I figured since it was my last day, well, you wouldn't mind."

"I mind. Come to my office pronto. I need you to take a memo." Alex turned. "Tessa, are you still here?"

"Going," Tessa replied with an indignant huff.

Julia stood up and obediently followed Alex into his office, where he shut and locked the double doors behind them.

He turned to her with a grin. "I didn't expect you to be here so early. Come here."

"Why?" Julia teased back, her body already responding to his unspoken desire.

"Because we just lied to poor old Tessa. Because I'm starting to ruin my reputation for always being honest. Because I want to kiss you, and I've thought of nothing else all morning."

Julia simply smiled as he pulled her to his chest and lowered his mouth to hers. The kiss tasted of coffee and cream, and paradise. Despite her dislike of java, Julia would drink this heavenly elixir of Alex's anytime.

"That was nice," Julia said, opening her eyes as Alex broke off the kiss.

"It gets better," Alex said. He led her by the hand to his couch.

"What does?"

"This does. My office," he whispered.

Julia's eyes widened. "We can't!"

"We can," Alex said, lowering his mouth to kiss her again. "I'm the boss, and you follow my orders. Remember? Besides, I don't think I can wait until lunch. I didn't want to leave you, and now that I've seen you…" Alex's words faded away as he deepened the kiss.

"Mmm." Lost in the joy of being connected again with the man she loved, Julia could only murmur as Alex's tongue began to send her spiraling into the abyss of passion once again.

LYDIA OLSON DIDN'T SHOW UP in the office until noon. By that time Alex and Julia had held one long staff meeting on his office sofa and another in his executive bathroom shower.

Tessa had discreetly held all calls and avoided looking Julia directly in the eye when she emerged from Alex's office with flushed cheeks. It was as if Tessa knew both Julia and Alex were only going to lie.

Julia smiled to herself and absently twirled her hand in the spiral phone cord. Alex was taking her to lunch in a half hour, and then they were taking the afternoon off. He had told her that between leaving her apartment and coming into the office he realized he didn't want to leave Julia, and that work could wait. And with the few adjustments he was making now to his schedule, work would wait.

The buzzing of the telephone intercom jolted Julia from her reverie. She picked up the phone. "Incoming," the main-floor security guard forewarned. "One pissed-off ex-girlfriend has entered the elevator."

"Thanks." Julia disconnected the guard and buzzed Alex. "She's here."

"Then you need to get in here," Alex's terse voice answered.

"Too late."

Julia set the receiver down as the elevator doors at the end of the hall opened. Julia could hear Lydia's shriek long before she saw her.

"Alex! Alex Ravenwood, I know you're here! You cowardly bastard, you get out here and face me like a…you!" Lydia's malicious gaze lighted on Julia. Julia froze as the black-haired devil herself came storming across the carpet.

Daggers of hostility and hate shot from Lydia's eyes as she rounded Julia's desk. "You!" she shouted again. "This is all your fault! How dare you? I warned you not to mess with me!"

The sound of the slap resounded off the walls and instantly Julia put her hand up to her cheek.

"Lydia!" Alex's voice boomed through the outer office area as he strode out of his office and over to Julia. "Don't you touch her again."

Alex ran a finger over Julia's cheek and she shuddered. "Julia, are you okay?"

"I'll be fine," Julia managed to say. The slap hadn't really hurt, it was more shock that she was reeling from. Julia bit back the tears. There was no way she was letting Lydia see her pain. She wouldn't let Lydia win. She wouldn't let her last memories of Alex's office be of this ugliness.

Alex turned his attention back to an enraged Lydia. "I think you need to leave."

"Not until you listen to what I have to say," Lydia screeched. "This little scheming tramp has been lying to you, Alex, and all the time making moves on you herself. She's deliberately done this to me.''

Alex looked slightly confused. ''Done what?''

''Driven you away from me!'' Lydia screamed hysterically. ''Ever since she's arrived at the office, you haven't returned any of my faxes, or any of my messages. I doubt you even got them. I left two on your answering machine the night I left for Hawaii, and I sent at least a dozen faxes. Ask her where they are. Ask her!''

''Mr. Ravenwood, please, I need to go look at my face. It stings.'' Julia gave Alex a way to remove her from the scene. Alex looked at her, his blue eyes seeing her but not seeing her, and Julia knew that until he dismissed her she had to remain rooted to her spot. Tension built in her as Alex turned his attention back to Lydia.

''Lydia, look, it doesn't matter what she did or didn't do,'' Alex stated flatly. ''I've done a lot of soul-searching these past three weeks. With or without Julia, I was going to end our relationship. We're not right for each other.''

''Not right for each other? We are right for each other, Alex. Not her! I keep showing up places to find you. First the art gallery! Then last night! I called to tell you I was going to be late! Instead, when I arrive everyone's buzzing about your public displays with that, that hussy! No matter how much money you spend to make her presentable, she's not going to be accepted into your pristine world!'' Lydia spit the words out at Alex.

''You were at the art gallery?''

Julia cringed as she saw the look of disbelief in Alex's eyes. Like Julia, he had thought Lydia had canceled. At that moment Julia realized the extent of Tessa's manipulations. She had rearranged Lydia's message to suit her own purpose.

"Yes!" Lydia shrieked. Her face had contorted into that of a hysterical madwoman. "I flew in just for the night, and flew out again the next morning. I wouldn't have missed your birthday, Alex. I was going to tell you, but Chelsea had her baby and your secretary won't connect me! Anyway, can you imagine my humiliation when the women at the gallery told me you ran off with Morticia! Then last night at the cocktail party, Tom the human leech tells me you kissed her! In public! And it's in the papers!"

Lydia dissolved into tears and Julia watched Alex's face. He seemed distant, almost impassive, and Julia felt a wave of fear wash over her. Alex knew he had been set up, but Julia knew that until now he hadn't realized the extent of the deception Tessa and Chelsea had pulled.

"Well, I got messages that said otherwise." Alex shielded Julia and pressed the intercom button. "Tessa, I want to see you right now."

Tessa must have been waiting around the corner, for she appeared instantly. Alex turned to her, his face still a mask. "Tessa, what messages did Lydia leave yesterday?"

Tessa drew herself up and looked directly at Alex. "Two, Mr. Ravenwood," Tessa said without blinking. She sniffed with disdain and looked over at Lydia. "The first said she wasn't going to arrive until seventhirty. The next, not at all."

"I never spoke to you a second time," Lydia shrieked.

"Are you telling me I'm lying?" Tessa's eyes narrowed and she crossed her arms in front of her. "For weeks I've had to deal with your childish behavior. My job does not revolve around you or your hysterics. I will not tolerate insults from anyone, especially you. Mr. Ravenwood, if I'm finished here?"

"Yes." Alex's dismissal told everyone whom he believed. "Tessa, help Julia into my bathroom, okay? She may need some first aid for her face." Alex waited a moment as Tessa and Julia disappeared inside his office.

"Alex, please, they're against me," Lydia pleaded. "Can't you see a setup when you see one? Are you that blind?"

"Yes." Alex's tone was odd. "I must be, Lydia. I should have seen your true colors when Chelsea first warned me. You can rest assured I'll deal with her later. I know my sister's been behind this whole thing, and I know Tessa's lied. But, it really doesn't matter. I'd rather love a beggar than have a society wife I don't love, and I'm sorry, Lydia, but I don't love you. You aren't my soul mate. In fact, I never really noticed until today how nasty and vicious you are. If I had seen it, we never would have dated this long."

Lydia shook as she tried to control her rage. "I hate you, Alex Ravenwood. I hate you!"

Alex shrugged. He knew she was venting, that when she calmed down she would realize she missed the idea of being Mrs. Alex Ravenwood more than Alex himself. "Whatever, Lydia. Really, I'm sorry it went down this way, but it's over. You should be going. I need to see what you did to Julia's face. She could press assault charges if she chooses, but if you go quietly I'm sure she'll consider the matter closed."

"You're a fool, Alex Ravenwood! You'll see that your precious Julia isn't what she seems to be. Mark my words. You'll see. And don't think you can come crying to me when you do." With that, Lydia turned on her heel and strode to the elevator.

Alex stood quietly for a moment and watched, as if waiting for Lydia to storm back and begin venting again. He lifted his shoulder blades and inhaled a deep breath of air. Exhaling, he lowered his shoulders to their normal position and forced himself to relax by slowly unclenching his fists. Poor Julia. But it was over. Ugly, but over. Now he could concentrate on the woman who did mean something to him. Satisfied that Lydia wasn't coming back, he headed to his bathroom to see how Julia was doing.

"THERE." TESSA PRESSED a wet towel to Julia's cheek. The cool moistness helped ease the pain. "You're lucky. No marks."

Julia rubbed her cheek after Tessa moved away to rewet the towel. "I think I'm as glad as you and Chelsea to see her go."

"Oh, we're beyond glad." Tessa came back and replaced the towel. The coolness felt good against Julia's cheek. "We couldn't have done it without you. You did the right thing by accepting Chelsea's offer."

"What other choice did I have?" Julia sighed and worked her jaw for a moment. "When his theater run ended, Kyle tricked me out of all my money and ran off with the coat-check girl. I always warned Chelsea about men who take advantage of women, but since I wasn't rich I didn't think it would happen to me."

"Well, now that Operation Free Alex is over, we'll both get nice fat checks from Chelsea." Tessa smiled. She saw the look of horror cross Julia's face. "Oh Julia, surely by now you know Chelsea and I planned this whole thing from the very beginning, right down to my pretending not to know a thing. By fooling you about my involvement, you never questioned anything I did, or anything I asked you to do.''

''This is too much to comprehend. I really believed Lydia sent those messages. I didn't know you faked them. I can't believe Chelsea was behind all this.'' Julia shook her head. ''I thought I knew her.''

''You do. But you don't know me.'' Tessa grinned and stepped back to rewet the washcloth again. ''It was imperative that you remained as innocent as possible in this. We had it all on index cards, right down to getting you an apartment near where Alex lives rather than closer to the office.''

''I can't believe it.'' As the enormity of the entire scheme hit her, Julia felt somehow empty. Even the best of intentions didn't diminish the fact that her best friend had used her as a pawn in a game to get what she wanted from her brother. Julia's voice sounded resigned when she next spoke.

''So did you plan on me sleeping with him, too?''

''Not at first.'' Tessa replaced the cloth. ''But Chelsea said Alex had a thing for you, so when I saw that he couldn't keep his hands off Julia Brown, well I kept throwing you together. I didn't think you'd mind. I mean, who wouldn't jump at the chance to explore the body of a man like Alex? Anyway, Chelsea told me you'd had a crush on him since you were in college together. She said you always used to disappear every time Alex came to town and it was a dead giveaway. But I'll admit, she wasn't keen on you getting involved with him, and in fact tried to warn him off.''

''I've sold my soul,'' Julia mumbled, rising to her feet and moving away from Tessa. Julia placed her hands on the marble countertop and looked at herself in the mirror. Her eyes seemed hollow, and her face was ghostly pale except for the residual pink now fading across her cheek. How could she face Alex? She'd lied, cheated, and been just a pawn in a greater scheme. He wasn't going to understand the extent to which she'd been duped. She should have told him the truth last night. She should have told him about the money, and that she didn't want it, she wanted him. But she had been afraid. She had wanted him to make love to her. She wanted him to love her.

He had trusted her not to trap him, but wasn't that exactly in a sense what she had done by not telling him the truth?

"Oh, for someone so young you're so antiquated, Julia. I'd stop worrying about it. It's not like he'll know." Tessa scolded as she tossed the washcloth in the sink. "I'm taking my payoff and buying a fur coat. You take your money and go get your fresh start in New York. Tomorrow you can walk away from it all. But hey, if you change your mind and decide to stay and have a go at Alex, what of it? You're both adults."

I wish I felt like one, Julia thought, closing her eyes. Her head pounded, and she felt the migraine begin behind her right temple. Julia shifted her weight and brought her hands up to her temple. She massaged her fingers in a circular motion, but it did little to help. Giving up, Julia slowly opened her eyes.

"Alex!"

ALEX WATCHED JULIA WHIRL around to face him, all the color draining out of her face. If she had been a turtle, he knew she would have tried to crawl back inside.

"Julia." Alex's voice sounded deadly calm to his own ears. He saw the fear cross Julia's face. His own blood had chilled, and in the mirror Alex saw that his eyes were the palest blue he had ever seen, and that his face was an unreadable mask.

Julia glanced at Tessa, and Alex noted that the other woman's face was pale, as well.

"So if I overheard this right, your temp pay isn't all the money you're getting." Alex practically spit the words out. He had been so certain she had just been a pawn, and now to find out she was a willing conspirator, it was offensive. "So tell me, Julia, exactly how much additional is my sister paying you?"

"Alex, I can explain," Julia began, but at his angry stare she stopped helplessly. He watched as her gaze sought Tessa for some backup assistance, but the older woman had already slinked out of the bathroom and left Julia to fend off his rage all by herself. Alex grimaced. Had he just this morning been considering a future with her? That stung. She had been planning on leaving him high and dry all along, only using him for cash on the way through. And to think he had planned to convince her to stay. He felt like a fool for even thinking she was worthy of commitment.

"Oh, Julia, cut the lies." Alex ran a hand through his hair, disgust evident. How had he read the situation so wrong? "Lydia's gone. You did your job. You've earned your money. I just wanted to know what the going rate is for sleeping with Alex Ravenwood."

Julia had never experienced pure, sheer panic before, and suddenly she understood what Kyle had called stage fright. Her whole body seemed rooted to the gray tile. By the look of disgust on Alex's face and the way his baby-blue eyes had now darkened to angry midnight pools, Julia knew nothing she could say could correct the situation. So she simply told him the truth.

"Ten thousand dollars," Julia heard herself whisper, and winced when she saw the look that quickly crossed Alex's face. Without him actually saying it, she knew her words had cut worse than a knife.

"I see." Alex's voice had become calmer, even more controlled. His voice was soft as he slowly pronounced each word, and Julia's heart broke. There was no way he would forgive her. In his eyes she was now just as much a liar and a cheat as his sister and Tessa. Only she was worse than either of them. She'd played him for a fool. She'd used him.

"Well, I guess you got what you wanted. Money and the valuable service I provided to your love life."

Julia could see the hurt, visualize the open wound her lies had caused. If only she had told him about the money earlier! "Alex, no! Last night was special! Last night was…"

"Last night was a lie. Everything was a lie."

The muscle in Alex's cheek quivered as he controlled his temper. "Go, Julia. Get out of my office, get out of my sight. Your job's done, and I'm sure my sister's dying to know all about it and hand you your blood money. When you see her, tell her she can give it to you in good conscience. I'm through with Lydia, and after today, I'd say I'm through with women for quite a while. Seems they're all lying schemers."

"Alex, I'm sorry. Tessa and Chelsea conspired against me. I honestly thought Lydia sent the messages."

Alex cut her off again with a bitter laugh. "Don't talk to me about honesty, Rachel Juliana Grayson. You have no idea what the word means. Just do me a favor, just keep your college pattern of avoiding me. Make sure I'm not around when you visit my sister. It'll be better that way.''

"Oh, Alex!" Julia cried in anguish. Her hands flew to her face and tears flowed down her cheeks. Alex remained unmoved at the sight of her cascading tears. His face was so cold. With a start Julia ran past Alex and out of his bathroom. Unlike her heart, there were only a few pieces in her desk to collect. These she threw into her purse in under a minute.

"Julia?" Tessa's voice called from around the corner, but Julia ignored her and headed to the elevator. Blinded by tears, she frantically pressed the down button.

"Julia! Wait!" Tessa's voice sounded closer and Julia quickly stepped into the elevator as the doors opened. Through her haze she could see Tessa approaching, still calling Julia's name. Julia jabbed the lobby button and the door close button. She slumped back against the elevator wall as the express elevator doors closed on her past. *Goodbye, Alex. I'm sorry.* Tears rained down her cheeks as she began her descent into the hell that she knew would begin the rest of her life.

Chapter Thirteen

"She didn't take the money and you're a stupid fool."

"I don't believe you." Alex banged his fist against the wooden mantel over the fireplace of Chelsea's Chevy Chase home. Never had he felt so out of control of his life.

"That's why you're a stupid fool." Chelsea shrugged and readjusted her nursing daughter. "She wasn't involved to the extent Tessa and I were. So, are you going to keep berating me or have you seen the light yet?"

Alex let out a long sigh. He wasn't sure why he was back at Chelsea's, but before work he had found himself in his Corvette, driving around the District like a maniac, until he had unconsciously found himself turning into his sister's driveway.

It was Friday, exactly a week since Julia left. Rita had returned, the Florida business crisis was over, and his life should be back to normal. But it wasn't. If anything, it was worse. Much worse.

There was a hole in his life. His office seemed empty without Julia's presence. He missed her smile, the smell of her perfume, her fresh perspective.

"Just admit to yourself you miss her," Chelsea said,

her voice cutting into his thoughts. "Maybe you can get on with your life then."

"I don't miss her!" Alex shouted, again trying to convince himself of the lie he told. He had been trying for a week, but nothing had worked. How long would it take for his life to become less of a nightmare? When would the pain stop? That was what knifed the most, that one of the beautiful moments in his life had been nothing but an illusion, nothing more than a fraud.

Chelsea rolled her eyes. "Of course you don't miss Julia. You've just moped around so much that Tessa's still afraid to go to the office, fur coat or no fur coat."

"You paid her to sleep with me," Alex accused angrily, slamming his fist down on the mantel again. The candlestick on the edge wobbled a bit but didn't fall.

"I did not!" Chelsea drummed the fingers of her free hand on the end table beside her chintz sofa. "I paid her to break you and Lydia up, and sleeping with you wasn't part of the equation. My God, Alex, I made her ugly so you wouldn't hit on her! She's my best friend, at least I hope she is after she forgives me. She still refuses to answer my calls. Do you think I would deliberately hurt her? If you do, then you're a bigger fool than I thought."

"Maybe I am," Alex said in resignation. "Maybe I am."

"Oh, Alex, please," Chelsea snapped. For once her fury was clearly evident. "Get a clue, would you? If she's had this much of an effect on you, then you need to do something about it. It's not as if she doesn't love you. I mean she's always loved you! She used to stare at your picture when she thought I wasn't looking. When you danced with her at my reception I thought she was going to faint, she was so delirious."

Alex stared at Chelsea. His sister had told him almost the same thing earlier in the week, minus the part about Julia's loving him. Suddenly Julia's words the night they made love, her words about wanting him for the longest time, made sense. A flicker of hope lit inside him.

"Go on," he said flatly. "Convince me."

As if sensing his capitulation, Chelsea nodded. "She didn't really want a part of this, but she wouldn't take my offer to set her up in business or give her a loan of any kind. No handouts, she said. I'm still living in fear that she'll find out I got Viscountie to check her out. I knew she just needed a break. She's one of the proudest people I know."

"You're digressing," Alex said impatiently.

"So sue me," Chelsea retorted. "This is my story, I can tell it the way I want. Anyway, she trusted Kyle. He told her he loved her. When he left town he took her money. She was almost broke, but she wouldn't take my money without earning it. So I convinced her to play secretary and break you up. But she didn't take any money. Payroll called me today and asked me what they should do with her last check. She returned it."

Alex ran his finger through his hair and began to pace the room. He came over to stand beside Tara's bassinet as Chelsea lowered her daughter onto the soft blanket.

"She's beautiful," he said, gazing at his sleeping niece.

"She needs cousins." Chelsea leaned back against the sofa and gazed up at her brother. "You're a mule, Alex Ravenwood. I've learned long ago not to tell you what to do. I'm just going to say that I think you're a fool. Remember, I've grown up with you and I've lived with her for four years. I know each of you pretty well.

Julia's the real thing, and I, of all people, should know. If I had told her the extent of everything, she wouldn't have done it. In fact, when she left here she was angry at herself for not having told you everything earlier. She wanted to, but I think she wanted you to love her and was afraid you wouldn't.''

Alex stared at his niece and then looked up at Chelsea. Could he forgive her? It struck him as odd that he had somehow already subconsciously forgiven his sister.

But Julia's deception ran deeper. Or maybe it didn't. She had nothing to give him except herself, and what she had given had been pure and untouched. No man had ever made love to her except for him, and no woman had ever made him feel the way she had. Even at Chelsea's wedding the chemistry had been there. Alex had felt it, and it had frightened him. The flame could burn with passion, or hurt like hell.

And she had taken nothing. No money, no chance of a fresh start. All she had left were his bitter words as he threw her out of his life. Now, after talking with Chelsea and thinking rationally about the situation, he knew Julia had been in the dark about the messages. She'd been guilty only of not telling him the whole story. Guilty only of loving him.

"She loves you," Chelsea repeated again quietly. Alex looked at his sister. Chelsea's face was kind and quiet. His sister radiated the wisdom only a woman who was a mother possessed.

"She's always loved you, Alex." Chelsea gave her brother a wry, sad smile. "Why do you think there never was anyone else who got under her skin like you? Even Kyle never held her heart. He took her pride, but not her heart. You took that. You've always had it.''

Alex felt the pain stab full force inside his chest. "I need to go." He walked quickly to the mantel and grabbed his sunglasses.

"She's not there." Chelsea said, as if knowing where he was going, what he was thinking. Alex turned, his eyes narrowing.

"What?"

"I said she's not there," Chelsea repeated.

"I heard you. What do you mean?" Alex rubbed the back of his neck, his agitation growing.

"I mean she flew back to St. Louis."

"St. Louis?" Alex couldn't believe it and he stared at Chelsea.

"St. Louis."

"Will you stop repeating me and explain?" Alex's agitation had reached a crescendo.

"After she left your office she came here, like I told you. After yelling at me, which I deserved, she went to the apartment, packed her bags, and flew out on the first flight. She's been settled for a week."

"Where?" Alex's voice was sharp.

"At her parent's house. She doesn't leave for New York until Sunday."

"Why didn't you tell me this earlier?"

"Because I'm not going to let you hurt her again." Chelsea raised her chin stubbornly and got to her feet. "Kyle did a number on her, and then you. I'm not going to see her shattered all over again. She's my best friend and I care about what happens to her."

"So why are you telling me this now?" Alex watched as his sister moved over to a Victorian secretary and opened the top drawer.

Chelsea didn't respond immediately. Instead Alex

heard some shuffling and then Chelsea turned back to him. In her hand was a small black box.

"I had Scott get this out of the safe-deposit box the day I got home from the hospital. I figured you'd be needing it, one way or another." Chelsea walked over to him and pressed the box into his hand.

Alex opened the lid of the gold-rimmed box, almost knowing what was inside. The two-carat solitaire that had adorned his mother's finger glittered as the light hit it.

"Mother wanted her ring passed on to your bride. I think it's time you used it, don't you?"

Alex closed the box with a snap and saw Chelsea smiling at him. A feeling of amused trepidation came over him. "I know that look, Chelsea."

"As well you should, Alex. It means I have a plan on how you can win her back. And you, for once, are going to listen to me and follow it. We've got very little time. Understand?"

Alex gave her a wry smile and gave in. "Yes, ma'am."

ON A HOT DAY THE BALL FIELD at Busch Stadium could heat up to 120 degrees. Julia waved the scorecard in front of her face in an attempt to keep cool. Why she had chosen to go to a ball game was beyond her, but her older brother Liam had insisted. He had an extra ticket to the rare double-header and vowed it would get her out of her late summer doldrums.

The St. Louis Cardinals had won the first game against the Chicago Cubs in twelve long innings. People were milling about, long stuffed on nachos, hot dogs and beer, as they waited for the second game to begin at 7:05 p.m. Julia reached over and grabbed her brother's arm and glanced at his watch. Only six-thirty. There still was a long way to go before sunset and the concrete stadium began to release the built-up heat.

"Having fun?" Liam grinned at her.

"Loads," Julia lied. She smiled wistfully, wishing she had put a higher SPF suntan lotion on her legs. Even through her sunglasses she could tell the tops of her legs were an ominous shade of pink.

"Forgive me for trying to get your mind off him," Liam said, turning to talk to his friend on his right. Julia turned her attention back to the electronic monitor above the right field bleachers. It was playing a Cardinal baseball highlight video.

Julia sighed. She couldn't fault Liam for trying. They had great seats in the dugout boxes about one hundred feet past third base. Still, even truly awesome front-row seats and a sold-out stadium crowd didn't make Julia feel better. She had been emotionally empty for about a week, and after four innings the guy on her left had finally turned his attention elsewhere.

She had skipped the wave, skipped the seventh-inning stretch and skipped the beer. Even listening to the endless shouting rivalry between the left-field and right-field bleachers didn't interest her anymore. Nothing did, and there was still another game to sit through.

Idly she filled in the diamonds she had drawn on the scorecard, having given up on keeping an accurate record after the second inning.

"Julia. Julia."

Julia jerked her head up and the pencil slipped from her fingers and fell to the concrete. She glanced around, looking left to right to hear the faint words that seemed to be coming from…the left-field bleachers?

"Julia! Julia!"

"Hey, they're calling your name." Liam poked her in the ribs.

"I don't think so." Julia pushed her brother's hand away and stared across the field. All she saw was an endless sea of anonymous, indistinct faces. The shouting continued.

"Well, maybe not," Liam said, looking through his binoculars. "Although there's some guy standing in the aisle. Take a look."

Julia took the black binoculars from her brother, and glanced through the lenses and zeroed in on the left-field bleachers. She went past the figure waving in the aisle between section 591 and 593, and then brought her binoculars back to him before they dropped with a clatter from her fingers.

"Hey!" Liam shouted as he reached to retrieve them. "Those are expensive!"

"That's Alex!" Julia's lip quivered. "In left field!"

Liam trained his binoculars on the left-field bleachers. Across the stadium came another faint round of "Julia. Julia."

"Cool!" Liam got his friends' attention. "Hey, guys! They're yelling for Julia. Yell back! Say Alex!"

"No!" Julia shouted, but it was too late as Liam's fifteen friends began the chant.

"Get to your feet, Julia," Liam commanded. "Wave! You're on."

"On what?" Julia stood like a newborn colt and looked down at her brother.

"The screen!" Liam pointed toward right field.

"No!" Julia covered her face with her hands as the video screen beamed her image to all fifty-five thousand people in stadium. She felt Liam jerk on her arm and she turned and gave a shaky wave before sitting back down in her seat.

"Now what are they saying?" Liam leaned forward and looked toward the bleachers. "Sounds like…."

"Marry me," one of the guys next to Liam said.

"Moon me," another proposed.

"Maybe it's meet me," someone else threw out helpfully.

"Hey, look on the screen!" Liam pointed. There, on the screen was Alex, standing in the aisle holding up a poster.

"'Julia, Meet Me Now, Stan The Man.'" Someone near her read the poster aloud. "I was right."

"What's that mean?" someone else asked.

The chorus came from left field again, and Julia threw up her hands and looked at Liam.

"I think you're supposed to meet him outside at the statue of Stan Musial." Liam smiled at her.

"Now?"

"Now," Liam said gently. "Go, Julia."

"You knew!" Julia accused, still not believing Alex was in the ballpark making a fool of himself.

"I did. Chelsea called me. She planned this with Alex. She told me to give you a message. She said you'd know what 'an average Joe' means."

"I do." For the first time in a week Julia felt hope flow through her. The black cloud that was her life lifted.

Liam put his hand on hers. "Go, Julia."

Julia rose to her feet. Alex, the man she loved, had come all this way and found her at a ball game. The idea was incredulous, ludicrous even. But there, across the field, was the man she loved still waving a stupid, undignified poster. "I'm going!"

A cheer rose from her section and Julia waved at the crowd as they began to shout yes. "He's going," Liam announced as Julia grabbed her purse and began to climb over seats on her way out of the stadium.

How Alex made it to the bronze St. Louis landmark before she did Julia would never know, but she saw him immediately. Whereas she was wearing a sleeveless Cardinal red polo shirt and blue-jean shorts, Alex wore a white linen camp shirt and khaki shorts. He looked impeccably handsome. In his hand he held a bouquet of flowers that Julia recognized as coming from one of the street vendors working around the ballpark.

Her pace quickened, almost to a run, as she approached him. Only pride kept her from throwing herself into his arms.

"Alex," she said, as calmly as she could for one who'd raced out of the stadium.

"Julia." Alex smiled a thousand-watt smile that made his blue eyes twinkle. Julia felt her heart flip. "I'm kidnapping you."

"Kidnapping me?" Julia tilted her head in bewilderment.

"Thank my sister later." Alex reached forward to place the flowers in her hand, and ushered her to a waiting limo. Within moments they were leaving downtown behind.

"Where are we going?"

"Shh." Alex put a finger on her lips. "It's a surprise. I promise to explain it all to you." He handed her a bottle of water.

Julia leaned against the seat, watching the driver turn off Highway 40 at Forest Park Parkway. Within minutes they were in Clayton, pulling up the driveway to the Ritz Carlton.

"Why are we here? I'm not dressed to eat here," Julia said. Alex placed a hand on her elbow and helped her from the limo. "I've never even been inside."

Alex gave her a smile, guided her inside and up to the penthouse suite. The room was beautiful, and sunlight filtered in from the room's western exposure. Julia noticed that there were vases of roses everywhere.

"I didn't want to talk to you in the ballpark, but I did want to get your attention," Alex began.

"You got it." Julia nodded. She clutched her now-empty water bottle like a shield. "Your doing something silly convinced me to talk to you."

"Chelsea said it would. She said I had to do something dramatic. But I only followed her advice to a certain extent." Alex thrust his hands into his pockets. "I guess we could sit down."

Julia saw his nervousness and sat down on the sofa. Alex came to sit beside her. Her heart was bursting. Somehow she knew whatever was going to happen was good. "I'm listening, Alex."

"I've made a terrible mistake."

Julia knew how hard the words were for Alex, and she put her hand out onto his. Immediately fire burned between them.

"It seems I've misjudged you, hurt you, and basically botched things up. I want to apologize, but more than that, I want things to go back to how they were. No, I want them better. Julia, I've missed you. I've had this whole week to think, to see things clearly, to realize that I held my happiness in my hands and that I let it slip through because of my foolish, stubborn pride."

Hope filled Julia at Alex's words. "It's okay, Alex."

"No, it isn't, Julia. I reacted badly. I didn't let you explain. I didn't listen to Chelsea. I just told you to go.

Even though I was hurting, I shouldn't have treated you that way.''

"Alex, I deserved it. I'd lied. I wanted to tell you about the money, but it never seemed like a good time. I didn't take it.'' Julia tightened her grip on his hand. Even though she could feel his tension, it was loosening, which was a good sign. She loved this man, and she didn't want to lose him again.

"I know you didn't take it. That's what showed me how much of a fool I was.'' Alex slid his hand out from hers and reversed the grip so he was now holding hers. "We had just made love, one of the most wonderful experiences of my life, and over lunch I was planning on convincing you to stay in D.C. I wanted us to explore our relationship. Then I heard Tessa gloating about the money, and my pride got in the way. I felt used. Cheap.''

"Alex.'' Julia's heart overflowed with love. "I'm so sorry. I never would have made love for money, I only did it…'' She paused, deciding how to put it into words. She decided on the truth. "I made love to you because I love you. Not for any payment.''

Alex spread her fingers out and laced his hands between hers. His blue eyes twinkled, making Julia feel warm. "I know. And I love you for it, just the way I love you.''

They were the words Julia had waited her whole life to hear. Her mouth dropped open in shock, but she wasn't sure if it was his admission of love, or if it was the fact he was now down on his knee in front of her. "I need you to do something else for me, Julia. Say yes that you'll wear this, Julia Grayson, and say yes that you'll marry me.''

Julia's hands flew to her open mouth as she stared in

astonishment at the ring glittering against the black velvet.

"This was my mother's, Julia, and I've never shown it to anyone. With it, I offer you my heart. Will you let me love you until we're old and gray? Will you say yes? Will you be my wife?"

"You love me." Her tone was a mixture of incredible joy and stunned disbelief.

"Enough that I let Chelsea concoct this scheme where I'd look foolish waving a sign as a symbol that I've changed. I love you, Julia, and I can't imagine my life without you. I've been a fool. I miss you, my love. I need you in my life. You're my soul mate, my other half." Alex paused, and reached forward and took Julia's left hand in his own. Heat instantly sizzled between them, and the ring felt wonderfully cool as it slid perfectly onto her finger. "I love you. Say yes."

Julia looked at her adorned finger, and then back at Alex. Mirrored in his baby blues was all the love and more that she had ever hoped to see. A tear of happiness slid down her cheek.

"Yes," she whispered. Finding her voice, she tilted her chin upward to him. "Yes!" Her voice was louder, and Alex swooped his mouth down to kiss her.

Alex's kiss sent shivers along Julia's spine, and she clung to him, feeling her whole body quiver as it came home. Alex leaned forward to give Julia a kiss on her neck. Julia moved her neck so his lips traveled up toward her ear. Chills went through her as Alex's lips worked their magic.

"There's a nice big bed in the other room," Alex said between kisses. "We've needed a proper bed, don't you think? And after all, Chelsea's buying. She owes us ten thousand dollars."

"Mmm, that she does." Julia turned her face so Alex could find her lips.

He kissed her gently. Then he pulled his lips away and spoke in a teasing tone. "So, you're sure my kidnapping you was okay? That you don't mind missing the home run derby at the ballpark?"

Julia reached up her fingers and brought Alex's lips back down to hers. This was the man she loved, her soul mate, her fiancé. And he loved her just as much. "The only home I want to be in is found in your arms, Alex." She gloried in the love she saw shining in his eyes. She sighed. "By the way, now that I no longer work for you, can I give the orders?"

Alex raised an eyebrow at her as he traced her neck with his forefinger. "My love, your wish is my command."

"Good. Carry me to that bed, and make love to me."

Alex grinned, love radiating from every pore. "Yes, ma'am." And he did exactly that.

Your Romantic Books—find them at

www.eHarlequin.com

Visit the *Author's Alcove*

➤ Find the most complete information anywhere on your favorite author.

➤ Try your hand in the Writing Round Robin— contribute a chapter to an online book in the making.

Enter the *Reading Room*

➤ Experience an interactive novel—help determine the fate of a story being created now by one of your favorite authors.

➤ Join one of our reading groups and discuss your favorite book.

Drop into *Shop eHarlequin*

➤ Find the latest releases—read an excerpt or write a review for this month's Harlequin top sellers.

➤ Try out our amazing search feature—tell us your favorite theme, setting or time period and we'll find a book that's perfect for you.

All this and more available at

www.eHarlequin.com
on Women.com Networks

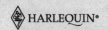

This Christmas, experience
the love, warmth and magic that
only Harlequin can provide with

Mistletoe Magic

a charming collection from

BETTY NEELS
MARGARET WAY REBECCA WINTERS

Available November 2000

HARLEQUIN®
Makes any time special ™

Visit us at www.eHarlequin.com

PHMAGIC

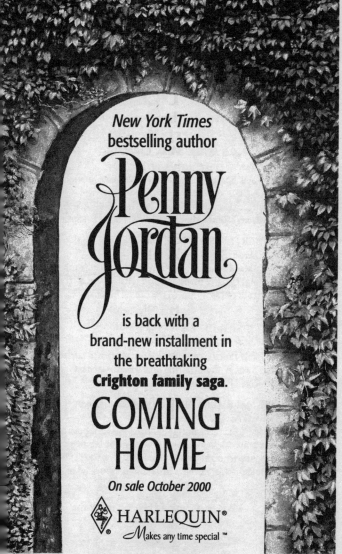

HARLEQUIN®

A M E R I C A N ✦ R O M A N C E ®

COMING NEXT MONTH

#849 SECRET BABY SPENCER by Jule McBride
Return to Tyler
Businessman Seth Spencer was surprised to see Jenna Robinson in Tyler,
Wisconsin, especially once he discovered she was pregnant—with his
baby! Though she claimed she planned to marry another, Seth was not
about to let Jenna's secret baby carry any other name but Spencer.

#850 FATHER FEVER by Muriel Jensen
Who's the Daddy?
Was he the father of Athena Ames's baby? Was the enigmatic beauty even
really expecting? Carefree bachelor David Hartford was determined to
uncover the truth and see if Athena was behind his sudden case of father
fever!

#851 CATCHING HIS EYE by Jo Leigh
The Girlfriends' Guide to...
Plain Jane Emily Proctor knew her chance had come to catch the eye of
her lifelong crush. With a little help from friends—and one great big
makeover—could Emily finally win her heart's desire?

#852 THE MARRIAGE PORTRAIT by Pamela Bauer
Happily Wedded After
When Cassandra Carrigan accepted Michael McFerrin's marriage of
convenience proposal, she'd thought it was a sound business deal. But
spending night after night with her "husband" soon had her hoping
Michael would consider mixing a little business with a lot of pleasure....

Visit us at www.eHarlequin.com